By Andrew Grant

FALSE
WITNESS

FALSE WITNESS

A NOVEL

Andrew Grant

BALLANTINE BOOKS

NEW YORK

Published in the United States by Ballantine Books, an imprint of Random House, a division of Penguin Random House LLC, New York.

BALLANTINE and the HOUSE colophon are registered trademarks of Penguin Random House LLC.

LIBRARY OF CONGRESS CATALOGING-IN-PUBLICATION DATA
Names: Grant, Andrew, author.
Title: False witness : a novel / Andrew Grant.
Description: First edition. | New York : Ballantine Books, [2018] |
Series: Detective Cooper Devereaux ; 3
Identifiers: LCCN 2017041944 | ISBN 9780399594335 (hardcover) |
ISBN 9780399594342 (ebook)
Subjects: LCSH: Police—Alabama—Birmingham—Fiction. | Serial murder investigation—Fiction. | BISAC: FICTION / Suspense. | FICTION / Action & Adventure. | FICTION / Crime. | GSAFD: Suspense fiction. | Mystery fiction.
Classification: LCC PR6107.R366 F36 2018 | DDC 823/.92—dc23
LC record available at https://lccn.loc.gov/2017041944

Printed in the United States of America on acid-free paper

randomhousebooks.com

1 2 3 4 5 6 7 8 9

First Edition

Book design by Caroline Cunningham

For my father, Captain John Grant (1924–2016),

who taught me never to bear false witness—

and so much more besides.

Between falsehood and useless truth there is little difference.

As gold which he cannot spend will make no man rich,

so knowledge which he cannot apply will make no man wise.

DR. SAMUEL JOHNSON,
The Idler No. 84, November 24, 1759

FALSE
WITNESS

One year ago.

LAST SEPTEMBER, LUCAS PALTROW SAVED DEBORAH HOLT'S LIFE.

More accurately, he fixed her car. But to Deborah that amounted to the same thing. Because when her faded green Chevy Nova ground to a dead stop near Paltrow's workshop late on that stifling Monday afternoon, she was well on her way to making the biggest mistake of her short, misguided life. It would have been a fatal mistake, she was certain, when she looked back. But by the time Paltrow had coaxed some life into the ancient, half-seized motor, Deborah was set on a new path. She turned the car around. Swallowed her pride. And for the first time in almost two years, she completed the journey home.

Deborah had woken up in bed alone that day, which was nothing new. It had been that way most days for the last couple of months. Usually the apartment was empty by the time she staggered to the bathroom, but that morning was different. Her stomach was calmer. It wasn't the urge to vomit that had finally forced her to open her eyes. It was the sound of the front door scraping shut. She checked her phone. It was 6:18 am. Normally she slept until around 11:00, when she heard Thor—her boyfriend—getting ready to go meet his buddies. Then she'd doze for another hour or so. Or for as long as the nausea would allow.

What was Thor doing up so early? No one else from the music business would be awake at that time, and with his kind of artistic sensibility it was impossible for him to work a regular job. Could he have changed his mind about that? Their money troubles *were* getting out of hand. She'd been fired from two local bodegas because she couldn't handle the mornings, and none of the other neighborhood stores would hire her once she'd become known as unreliable. The band was on hiatus, with her unable to perform. Thor wouldn't let her risk going onstage, given how rowdy the clubs could get. He wouldn't let her do bar work, either, for the same reason. Which was sweet in a way, but still—a few extra dollars would be very welcome. Figuring she would ask him about it later, Deborah settled back down on her pillows.

The bedroom door inched open. Thor was silhouetted for a moment before he switched out the hallway light. He was barefoot. His T-shirt—the expensive one she'd bought him for his birthday—was screwed up in his hand like an old rag. His long blond hair was sticking out from his head at all kinds of crazy angles. His jeans were unzipped. They were slipping down his thighs. He didn't have on any underwear . . .

"Asshole!" Deborah opened both eyes wide and hoisted herself up onto her elbows. "You scared me. I thought you were leaving. Where the hell have you been?"

"Sorry, babe." Thor hitched up his jeans and took two uncertain steps toward the bed. "I was trying to be quiet. I didn't want to wake you."

"Well, you did." Deborah grabbed a pillow from Thor's side of the bed, flung it at him left-handed, but missed. "So tell me. Where have you been?"

"I had to meet someone." Thor fastened his zipper. "An A&R guy. From a major label. Out of New York. He's leaving town this morning. First thing."

"Really?" Deborah flopped back down. "That sounds like total bullshit. Why am I only hearing about it now? Why didn't you mention it last night? You said you'd come to bed as soon as the game was over. Honey? Are you lying to me?"

"Of course I'm not lying!" Thor grinned, his whole face lighting up the way he knew she couldn't resist. "I only heard about the guy after you were already asleep. I got a text from Rudy. And I figured, I had to try. It could have been the breakthrough, babe. After all this time."

"Could have been?" Deborah lifted her head.

"Things didn't go too great." Thor looked at the floor. "The guy said he'd be in touch, but . . ."

"That's too bad." Deborah sat up. "But at least you tried. Now come kiss me before I run to the bathroom. Then we can sleep."

Thor moved a little closer, leaned down, and pecked her on the forehead. It was the briefest of contacts and he was only within range for a moment, but it was enough. Deborah could smell the whiskey on his breath. The dope smoke in his hair. And another woman's perfume on his chest.

"Goodbye, Oliver," she said under her breath as she closed the bathroom door. It was the first time she'd spoken his real name out loud since she'd followed him from Birmingham to Nashville, and she suddenly realized she didn't care where he was pretending to have been. It was time to face facts. She was two days shy of her twentieth birthday. Pregnant. Broke. With no prospect of work. And her boyfriend was a liar and a cheat.

In other words, it was time to cut and run.

———

Deborah had never liked living in Birmingham. She'd been born in Wetumpka, a small friendly town ninety miles to the southeast that was famous for its meteorite crater, and she'd never forgiven her mother for making them move after her father had abandoned them when she was fourteen. She'd spent the next four years dreaming of ways to get out. Her teachers at Ramsay High had talked up the merits of good grades and college, but she had other ideas. Her voice. Thor's guitar. A recording contract. Fame. Fortune. And glory. It was her destiny. All she needed to make it happen was transport, so throughout high school she worked a minimum of two jobs at a time at the jumble of bars and clubs around Five Points South, not far from her mother's new house. She was too young for many of those jobs to be legal, but she quickly learned that if she made her skirt short enough and her top tight enough, her male bosses would happily pay cash and keep her off the books. She also learned that with the right kind of outfit and an open mind, there were other ways to earn cash from the male customers . . .

When she finally put the Magic City in her rearview mirror, two weeks after she turned eighteen, she never planned to return. I-65 was slick with water after an unexpected, short-lived rainstorm and the low fall sun was glinting off the surface as if it was plated with rose gold. Deborah could feel it drawing her northward, promising a fabulous new life of glamour and independence.

Deborah's dream died the morning she realized that Thor had betrayed her. She finally had to accept that the promise of a rock star lifestyle was an empty one. It took her another couple of hours to organize herself, after Thor fell asleep. And even then she didn't consciously plan to head back south. But after she'd driven for two and a half hours, the tall buildings of downtown Birmingham loomed large through her windshield and she saw that the sky was again obscured by clouds. This time, though, the road surface was dry. It was pitted and dull. Like quicksand, she thought. Innocuous-looking, but sucking her relentlessly down. All the way back to her miserable old world.

Deborah's eyes filled with tears, making it hard to negotiate the elevated left-hand curve onto 20/59 and blurring the unwelcomely familiar images of the park and courthouse and art museum below and to the side. The chimneys of Sloss Furnaces rose ahead of her like the charred trunks of ruined trees in some post-apocalyptic nightmare, prompting her to make the habitual right onto Stephens. She glanced out of her side window, across the flat roofs of the wide, lower buildings, and toward the City Federal in the heart of downtown. As she looked, the bold neon sign on its roof blinked into life. It was red. Red was for danger. What was she doing?

Deborah shook away the thought and forced her attention back to the road ahead. She cruised past the brick fortress of St. Vincent's hospital, as she'd done hundreds of times before. She fought the feeling of being boxed in as the raised section of road came to an end and the trees and shrubs on both sides grew taller and closer, their leaves already turning orange and gold. But when she approached the off-ramp to 21st Avenue—a stone's throw from her mother's house—she found she couldn't reach for the blinker. She couldn't turn the wheel. Some invisible force was making her keep going straight. And press harder on the gas.

OK, then, she thought. *New plan. Stay on this road till I hit 459. Take that to 20. And keep going southwest till I get to Mexico . . .*

Deborah stayed on track for almost seven more miles, but as she cut under I-65 she felt the car suddenly lose power. Was she out of gas? No. So what else can go wrong with cars? She had no idea. Fearfully she gripped the wheel and willed the faithful old Chevy to keep going. The engine seemed to recover and Deborah gained a little speed as she passed the on-ramp to 65 South and the entrance to a small strip mall. She saw an auto shop offering tires and oil changes and considered stopping, but what would she tell them? The car seemed OK again. Maybe it was just a hiccup?

Deborah covered another mile without incident and was beginning to breathe more easily when all the dashboard lights came on at once. The engine cut out. Her speed plummeted. A woman in a blue SUV almost plowed into the back of her, just managing to swerve in time, honking furiously. Rattled, Deborah fought with the steering, which had suddenly become unbelievably heavy. She tugged desperately on the wheel, turning it just enough for the last of her momentum to carry her into the mouth of Deo Dara Drive. The Chevy rolled a little farther until its front wheel met the curb. It rocked back slightly on its aging springs and Deborah stamped frantically on the parking brake, scared that she'd bounce all the way back into the busy traffic. When she was sure the car was stationary, Deborah switched off the ignition. She counted to three, then cautiously turned the key back the opposite way. There was no response. She tried again, twisting harder, almost bending the slender strip of metal. Still nothing happened. She gave it one more futile attempt then climbed out and slammed the door with all her strength.

Fine, she thought. *So my car's betrayed me now, too, just like everything else in my life. Well, so what? I'm not giving up. I'm not going back. I'll just hitch a ride to the border . . .*

Deborah popped the trunk, and as she leaned in to retrieve her two bags she felt someone watching her. She straightened up, looked around, and saw a guy staring at her from the far side of the street. He looked like he was in his mid-thirties. He was around six feet tall. Slim, but clearly muscular. She could tell that from the way he held himself, despite his blue, loose-fitting mechanic's coveralls. His cheeks and chin were covered with a couple of days' stubble, and his thick dark hair was artfully mussed up, like he'd just walked out of a salon. Deborah thought he looked good. But more than that. Familiar. And so did the building he was standing in front of. It was a single story high with a shallow pitched roof, white walls, and blue wood trim. Like a low-rent industrial version of a Swiss chalet she'd once seen on TV, Deborah thought. But where did she know the place from? And who was the guy?

She fussed with her luggage for a couple more minutes until she remembered. The guy had been a regular at one of the bars she'd worked at before leaving town. The Horny Toad. He'd hit on her a couple of times in a cranky, impatient kind of way, but had always left with different girls. And he was always handing out business cards with a picture of his workplace on them. He was named Lucas Paltrow, she recalled, and he did something with cars. Auto electronics, maybe? Meaning he wasn't a regular mechanic, which was unfortunate. But hey, what did she know? She was no expert. Maybe her car just had a dead battery or something. It wouldn't hurt to ask him, before abandoning it and trying to hitchhike a thousand miles.

Paltrow didn't take much persuading to look under the hood. He told Deborah to steer while he pushed the Chevy onto the forecourt in front of his workshop. Then he showed her to the waiting area, gave her a glass of water, and disappeared back outside. Deborah flicked through the stack of magazines on the low table in the center of the room, rejected them all, and moved to the window to watch Paltrow work. He had the hood open as well as both front doors, and seemed to spend most of his time fiddling with something up high behind the dashboard near the glove box. After twenty minutes he slid across to the driver's side, turned the key, and Deborah punched the air with delight as the engine sluggishly turned over and reluctantly fired.

"I've got it running." Paltrow shouldered open the waiting room door and peeled off his work gloves. "But it won't get you far. It's in terrible shape. Needs a complete overhaul. I could see six other things wrong with it, right off the bat. And to tell the truth, a car that age, it's probably not worth the money. Where are you heading?"

Deborah picked up her purse. "Mexico."

"Not a chance." Paltrow shook his head. "You won't make it half-way."

"That's no good." Deborah clutched the purse tight. "I have to make it!"

"Why?" Paltrow glanced at Deborah's abdomen. "Is that where the baby's father's at?"

"The father?" Deborah took a step back. She hadn't realized that her condition was so obvious. "He's not in the picture anymore. Like that's any of your business."

"How old are you, anyway?" Paltrow took stock of Deborah's face, her chest, her legs. "I remember you. I haven't seen you around these last couple years, but I always figured you were underage, working those bars. So what does that make you now? Eighteen? Nineteen?"

"I'm twenty." Deborah tried to inject some confidence into her voice. "In two days."

"So you're nineteen." Paltrow crossed his arms and leaned back against the doorframe. "You're knocked up. You're traveling alone. Your car's a wreck. How much money have you got? Have you even got enough for gas? Mexico's a good couple days' drive from here."

Deborah shrugged. "I know that. I've got enough to get by."

"And how about when the baby comes?" Paltrow frowned. "You're on your own, and babies are expensive. They need clothes. Food. A decent place to live. How are you going to afford all that?"

"I'll get a job." Deborah stuck out her chin.

"A job." Paltrow shook his head. "Doing what? And who's going to hire you? To them, you'll be an illegal immigrant with a newborn baby in tow."

"There are ways . . ." As hard as she tried, Deborah couldn't keep her voice from cracking. "Things I can do. Things people pay for, baby or no baby."

"Things people pay for." Paltrow levered himself upright. "You mean, things men pay for? You really want to go there? Pregnant? Nursing? With a toddler? What kind of life would that be?"

"I don't know." Deborah blinked hard, desperate to stop her earlier tears from returning. "But I can make it work. If I have to."

"Time will tell, I guess." Paltrow took a step toward her. "But all that aside, I'm glad you've got some money now. Because you owe me for the work I did. A new ESC module, plus labor. Call it two hundred dollars even. Want me to make out an invoice?"

"No need." Deborah rummaged through her purse, but it was just for show. She knew she didn't have that kind of cash.

"Well?" Paltrow put his hands on his hips. "What are you going to do? I don't work for free."

Deborah paused for a moment then sighed, sank to her knees, dropped her purse, and reached for the buttons at the front of Paltrow's coverall. *Oh God,* she thought. *This again. Please make it quick . . .*

"No." Paltrow held up both hands and stepped back. "I've got another idea. You used to work those bars in town, so I'm guessing you have family somewhere nearby. Your mom and dad, maybe? A sister? An aunt?"

"Just my mom." Deborah's voice could barely be heard above the sound of the traffic outside.

"That's good." Paltrow nodded. "Tell me about her. Was she mean? Did she hit you? Anything like that?"

"God, no." Deborah looked up. "She's my mom. She's lovely. She's kind. She's just . . . boring. And she could never understand me. What I—"

"Screw whether *you think* she understood you." Paltrow took Deborah's hands and pulled her to her feet. "That's adolescent bullshit. This is the reality: You're only nineteen. You'll be twenty when the baby comes. Not even twenty-one yet. You've got your whole life ahead of you, pretty much. So here's the deal. Don't pay me. Do this instead: Go home. Go back to your mom. Make your peace with her. And give your baby a chance. Do that, and we're even."

"Really?" Deborah scuttled back and scooped up her purse, trying to figure out what angle she was missing. "You'll forget the two hundred dollars, and all I have to do is go home?"

"Go home." Paltrow stepped aside and opened the door for her. "Give your baby a chance. That's all."

Deborah paused, halfway to her car, and looked back over her shoulder. "I don't get it. Why are you doing this? What's in it for you?"

"Doesn't matter." Paltrow gestured for her to keep moving. "You wouldn't understand, anyway. Just do what I say. And if you ever need help, with anything at all, you know where to find me."

Chapter **One**

One year later.

ON FRIDAY MORNING, EDDIE STANDEN FOUND DEBORAH HOLT'S BODY.

More accurately, he found a parcel about five foot six long by eighteen inches wide, neatly wrapped in a white bedsheet. A second sheet had been rolled up like a ribbon and tied around it, like the finishing flourish on a birthday present. Eddie had no reason to think it had been left for him. There was no label. No note. He could have ignored it and gone about his business. He wished he had, later, when he looked back. But he'd been intrigued. What could be inside the sheets? And why had it been left at the gates of the cemetery where he worked?

Cooper Devereaux was woken by the phone. He'd been in bed alone, in his apartment, which was a fairly new and unwelcome development. He'd spent almost every night at Alexandra Cunningham's house, over the mountain, ever since they'd got back together a few months ago. Alexandra was his girlfriend, for want of a better word. She was also the mother of his daughter, Nicole. They'd been separated for eight years until a recent kidnapping case had unexpectedly brought them back in contact. Things had been going pretty well since then. What had started as small tentative steps had become strong confident strides in the course of rebuilding their relationship. Until certain facts about Devereaux's background had come to Alexandra's attention. She hadn't taken them well. And as a result she'd been holding him at arm's length the last couple of days, using ominous words like *needing time to think*.

Devereaux hoped it was Alexandra on the line, calling to reconcile.

It wasn't.

"Cooper." Lieutenant Hale's voice was loud in his ear. "Get up. Right now. I need you at the Hoover cemetery. Go to the main gate. Tommy will meet you there. We've got a suspected homicide. It's a weird one . . ."

Hoover cemetery had been designed in the Egyptian Revival style. The entrance, which also housed the facility's office and storerooms, was set at the end of a winding, single-track road off Grove Boulevard. It was built to look like a ceremonial arch, and it spanned a small tributary from the nearby Black Creek. The idea was to symbolize the passage of the dead across the River Styx. That was fine in theory—assuming any grief-stricken mourners were in a state to pick up on the reference as they followed their loved ones on their final journey—but the reality was a nightmare for the maintenance guys. The foundations hadn't been dug deep enough, so the walls of the building were constantly cracking and crumbling as the whole structure shifted and sank in the gritty, unstable earth. The site had been earmarked for closure half a dozen times in the last decade, but on each occasion a group of history-conscious local citizens had campaigned successfully for it to be spared.

A line of blue-and-white Birmingham Police Department sawhorses had been set up to block the road thirty yards from the arch. Devereaux pulled up behind a dusty black Dodge Charger, which he knew was issued to his longtime partner, Tommy Garretty. In front of that was a plain white panel van, which Devereaux guessed would belong to the crime scene unit. The case must be a weird one indeed, he thought, for those guys to have rolled on it so quickly. The vehicle at the front of the line was a BPD patrol car, parked sideways. A uniformed officer was leaning on its trunk with a clipboard in his hand. His job was to keep the scene secure and maintain a record of any essential personnel who were allowed to enter. Devereaux had hated that duty when he'd been in uniform. It had always seemed like torture, to be so close to the action but not to be allowed to take part. The guy working the fence that day didn't seem too frustrated, though. He nodded to Devereaux as he approached. Handed the clipboard to him. Checked his entry for legibility. Asked politely to see his shield, to verify his badge number. Pointed out the designated entry and exit route to the left-hand side of the road. And then went back to enjoying the warm morning sun.

Devereaux made his way carefully between the parallel strips of crime scene tape until he reached Garretty and a pair of crime scene technicians who were standing near the entrance arch. On the ground in front of them, laid out on a white sheet, was the body of a young woman. She was naked. Her eyes were closed. Her long red hair was neatly arranged. Her right arm was stretched across her breasts, and her left hand was delicately covering the area between her thighs.

"So." Devereaux looked across at the technicians. "Aside from the obvious, what have we got?"

The taller of the pair—a guy named Isringhausen, who Devereaux recognized from a couple of crime scenes they'd worked together in the past—eased down his mask. "Well, she's a Caucasian female, as you can see. Age, late teens to early twenties. I'd say she was killed yesterday afternoon, maybe early yesterday evening, but the ME will put a better time frame on it. The cause of death looks like manual strangulation. See the thumbprints around her larynx? How clear and distinct the bruises are? Whoever killed her grabbed hold and didn't let go till she was dead. Usually you see some blurring or a bunch of smaller marks where the killer had to adjust his grip or shift position. But not this guy. This was done by a strong, angry son of a bitch."

"Was she sexually assaulted?"

"It looks that way." Isringhausen sighed. "There are signs, but the ME will have to confirm."

"Did you find any clothes? Or personal effects?"

"No. Nothing."

"So we have no idea who she was?"

"None. I scanned her prints and sent them to the lab. We'll hear back soon if she's in the system. But I wouldn't hold your breath. She was clearly healthy and well fed. There are no signs of drug use, so she probably wasn't hooking. And look at her skin. Her hair. Her nails. That's the result of some serious spa time, right there. So I'd say she wasn't hurting for cash."

"Was she killed here?"

"I doubt it. There are no signs of a struggle, and the soles of her feet are clean. So are her knees and elbows. Everything is, apart from the back of her right heel. No. I'd say she was killed somewhere else, brought here, and dumped."

"It's a good place for a dump site." Devereaux looked around. "It's secluded. There's no chance of being seen from anywhere. You'd get good warning if anyone showed up. There aren't any security cameras, I'm guessing?"

"There are, but they only point into the cemetery. They were put in three years ago, after there were some problems with graves being vandalized. Remember that Satanist cult thing? Turns out it was here."

"Any indication where she might have been killed, assuming it wasn't here?"

"Nothing so far. We'll bag her hands and feet so the ME can get samples of anything microscopic that's caught under her nails. I was hoping the sheets would be some kind of fancy brand that's easy to identify, or that they'd have hotel logos on them or something, but no luck. They're too ordinary to tell us anything on their own. We'll take them to the lab anyway, though. See if there's any trace evidence stuck to them, or soaked into them."

"So if she was moved, how did she get here?"

"Someone drove her." The second technician—a short, stocky guy named Ryan—pointed to the ground to their left. "Look over here. This soil isn't the best for holding impressions. It's too gritty. But you can see where a car or a small van stopped fairly recently. Then we've got three sets of footprints leading from that spot to where the body was found, and back. All the prints are the same size and pattern, so I'm guessing they were made by one guy, who made three trips. The first would be to set out the first sheet. The second, slightly deeper, to carry the body—if you look right there you can see an elongated oval impression, like maybe one of her legs slipped out of his grip, which could be when her heel hit the ground. And then the guy finished up with a final trip to tie up the package with the second sheet."

"What was tied up? What second sheet?"

"You didn't hear how she was left?" Garretty called up a photograph on his phone and passed it to Devereaux. "The guy who found her said the sheets were a lot neater, originally. He undid them a little bit to see what was inside. Once he found out, he tried to put them back like they were, but he didn't do a great job. He was freaking out apparently. Seems strange, a guy who works at a cemetery being so upset by the sight of a dead body, but there you go."

Devereaux studied the image then handed the phone back to Garretty. "Bizarre. I've seen plenty of bodies over the years, but none wrapped up like a birthday present. So, the guy who found her. Where is he?"

"In the office. A uniform's keeping an eye on him. I didn't want to talk to him till you got here."

The cemetery office was dark and cramped. It smelled musty. And it didn't have any of the things Devereaux normally associated with admin work. There were no desks. No computers. No filing cabinets. Just a pair of battered leather armchairs, a low wooden table, a coffee machine next to a stack of half-gallon water containers, and an old-fashioned fridge. A uniformed officer had been perched on the arm of one of the chairs, but she got up and excused herself as soon as Devereaux and Garretty arrived. That left just a guy in his mid-fifties, sitting on the deep windowsill on the far side of the room. He had on faded blue coveralls and heavy black work boots with traces of red mud around the soles and he was leaning forward with his head almost between his knees, breathing deeply.

"Mr. Standen?" Devereaux took a step toward the center of the room. "I'm Detective Devereaux with the Birmingham PD. This is my partner, Detective Garretty. Do you mind if we sit?"

Standen waved toward the armchairs without looking up, so Devereaux and Garretty made themselves comfortable.

"Do you mind if we call you Eddie?" Devereaux took out his notebook.

Standen grunted.

"So, Eddie, I'm sorry to hear you had a traumatic experience this morning. I'm sure you'd rather not revisit the details right now, but it would really help us if you could answer a few questions. Would that be OK? We'll be as quick as we can."

Standen straightened himself up, shuffled back on the windowsill, and ran both hands through his thick, curly graying hair. "Sure. If it'll help. I guess."

"Excellent." Devereaux opened his book. "Now, let's start with a little background. How long have you worked here, Eddie?"

"Thirty-seven years, this coming November." There was a note of pride in Standen's voice.

"That's a long time." Devereaux nodded appreciatively. "What is it that you do?"

"I'm a senior groundsman." Standen pretended to slam his palm into his forehead. "Sorry, groundskeeper. I must learn to be more PC."

"Mustn't we all." Devereaux flashed a reassuring smile. "So, you're a senior groundskeeper. What does that involve?"

"What it sounds like, mainly." Standen shrugged. "Keeping the grounds nice. If someone's due to get planted—I mean, if there's an interment coming up—I make sure the area around the new grave's in good shape. And I tidy up afterward. You wouldn't believe the mess people leave behind. I clear up the floral tributes people leave on graves, once they're past their best. And then there's the general up-keep of the whole graveyard. I prune the trees when they need it. I repair any headstones that fall over, and that happens a lot, specially with the older ones. That kind of thing."

"What about *office* work? Do you spend a lot of time in here?"

"Not really." Standen glanced sheepishly at the detectives. "This isn't really an office, to tell the truth. It used to be, years ago, when the cemetery first opened. It was one of the first cemeteries not at-tached to a church in the whole state of Alabama. Did you know that? Because of the industrial revolution. The churchyards were overflowing with bodies, so they had to figure out something else to do with them. Anyway, these days we just use the place to get out of the sun when we need to. Grab a drink. Cool down. You know."

"I get it." Devereaux glanced at his watch. "I hear you were at work early this morning. Was there a special reason for that?"

"No." Standen shook his head. "I always start early. What can I tell you? I'm an early riser. Always have been."

"So you arrived at your regular time. Then what?"

"I parked up—"

"Where? I didn't see any cars outside."

"In my regular spot." Standen gestured vaguely toward the door. "It's up the hill to the right a little way. By those two old cottonwoods. There's good shade there. Keeps the cab nice and cool."

"Good thinking. What do you drive?"

"An F-150. I always buy Ford. Or GM. No foreign garbage for me."

"I can respect that." Devereaux guessed a full-size truck was bigger than the vehicle that had left the tire marks out front, but made a mental note to check with Ryan anyway. "Then what?"

"I walked back toward the gate, to unlock it like I always do. That's when I saw her. It. The . . . sheets. You know. It's like I said when I called 911."

"The girl whose body you found. Did you know her?"

"No. I'd never seen her before." The last of the color drained from Standen's face. "Look, if I'd known there was a body in that sheet I'd never have touched it."

"I don't blame you." Devereaux paused. "Now I need you to think real careful for a minute here, Eddie. In the last couple of weeks, did you notice any strangers hanging around outside the cemetery? Anyone taking an unusual interest in the place?"

"No." Standen shook his head. "No one I can think of. But you get kind of immune to it after a while. You wouldn't believe the weirdos we get here. A couple of years ago there were these Satanists who—"

"What about vehicles? Were there any cars parked nearby, that aren't normally there? Or small vans?"

"I don't remember any."

"OK. No problem. Let's get back to the dead girl. We need to identify her. Are you sure you didn't recognize her?"

"Absolutely."

"You'd never talked to her in a bar, or at a store?"

"No. Definitely not. Why do you keep asking me that?"

"Let me tell you a little about murder investigations, Eddie." Garretty leaned forward in his chair. "See, there are two stages. In the first stage, right after the body's found—which is the stage we're in now, by the way—the detectives on the case tend to be sympathetic. If it turns out the victim got killed by accident, or because of something that happened in the heat of the moment, or maybe if the victim— sweet and innocent as she might look, lying dead—had been asking for it in some way, we might be inclined to help. Stress the mitigating factors. Make sure the facts of the case are presented in the most favorable light. That can make a big difference. We're talking years of jail time. Maybe even taking the death penalty off the table. But if the guy who did it's not cooperative, forcing us into the second stage, by which time we've got our bosses yelling at us and the press crawling up our asses, then all bets are off. When we catch the guy—and we always do—we throw the kitchen sink at him. We show no mercy whatsoever."

Standen looked from Garretty to Devereaux and back, his face clouded with confusion. "I don't get it. Why are you telling me this? All I did was find the body."

"OK." Garretty closed his eyes for a second. "Let me tell you something else about murder investigations. When we find a dead woman, the first person we look at is her husband. Why? Because statistics tell us he's the most likely to have killed her. But the girl lying outside, she's not wearing a wedding ring. There's not even an indentation on her finger, which there would be if her ring had been stolen. So we move down the list. And guess who's in the number two spot?"

"I don't know." Deep wrinkles spread across Standen's forehead. "I don't know anything about murder."

"The person who found the body." Garretty spoke slowly, putting extra stress on every word.

"It's nothing personal, Eddie." Devereaux kept his voice soft and low. "But we have to ask you these questions. Can you tell me where you were yesterday afternoon?"

"I was here. Working."

"Was anyone with you?"

"Yes. Two of my coworkers. I can give you their names."

"That would be good. What time did you finish?"

"Around three."

"And what about after that? Where did you go?"

"I had a doctor's appointment. I have bursitis in my elbow, and I needed a shot."

"OK. We'll need your doctor's details."

"No problem. Her name's—"

"Detectives?" Isringhausen appeared in the low doorway. "Sorry to interrupt, but we've got something. A hit on the victim's fingerprints. We have her name and address. But this thing could be messier than we thought. If we're right about the time of death being yesterday, it means she was killed on her twenty-first birthday."

Chapter *Two*

Friday. Morning.

ALEXANDRA MADE SURE THAT NICOLE WAS MAKING AT LEAST A LITTLE progress with her math problems, then quietly moved to the living room. She loved her daughter. She enjoyed homeschooling her—most of the time. But that morning she needed some quiet time alone, to think things through.

She wasn't being reasonable. Alexandra knew that. After all, she was the one who'd asked Devereaux to give her some space. It wasn't as if he just hadn't bothered to come home because he was out getting drunk with his cop buddies, or sneaking off to sleazy strip clubs like a couple of her friends' husbands did. He'd done exactly what she said she needed him to do, and yet she was still pissed with him. What was wrong with her?

Nothing was wrong with her, she decided, after an uncomfortable hour of introspection. It was the circumstances she was in. That they were in. Assuming there was still a *they*. The confusion she was feeling about Devereaux and his past was driving her crazy. It was no longer just a question of who he really was. Or what that meant for their relationship. Or even the implications there may be for their daughter. The uncertainty of the situation was changing who *she* was. Who *was* this indecisive, unstable, whining person she saw when she looked in the mirror? Not her old self. Not the woman who'd breezed through her undergrad at Notre Dame. Who'd crushed the LSAT. Who'd aced every law school assignment that had been thrown at her at Duke. No. Alexandra could feel the difference in herself. And that was completely unacceptable.

Enough of this emotional nonsense, she told herself. *That's not you. Time to put your professional head back on. Approach this problem dispassionately. Distill it to the basic facts and make a rational decision. And how do you do that? It's easy. Just like you were taught. Do the research. And call on the experts.*

Chapter Three

Friday. Morning.

Ask ten cops what they love most about the job and you'll get eleven different answers. But ask them which part they hate the most and there's only one thing you'll hear. Breaking the news that someone's relative is dead. That goes double when the relative was the victim of a brutal murder. And triple when the victim was someone's child.

Devereaux had been introduced to the concept of receiving bad news at an early age. He still had nightmares about the time when a pair of detectives had come to his house, dragged him out of the crawl space where he'd been hiding, and told him that his father was dead. The episode was playing again in his head as he pulled up outside the address that Isringhausen had given him. It was on 21st Avenue, between Arrington and Stephens. One of a row of older houses, set back a modest distance from the street. Tired-looking. A little shabby. Somehow feeling like it was set adrift from a previous era. And a stone's throw from the giant cast-iron statue of Vulcan, god of the forge, standing guard over the city from his column on the side of the Red Mountain. The area around the statue had been Devereaux's safe haven from a succession of foster homes in the years after he was orphaned. Cursing fate's cruel sense of humor, he climbed out of the car and followed Garretty down the path to the front door.

The woman who answered Devereaux's knock appeared exactly like he'd have expected the dead girl from the cemetery to look, if only she'd lived for another thirty years. The red of her hair was a little muted and a web of fine lines embraced each of her eyes, but there was no missing the family resemblance.

"Mrs. Holt?" Devereaux showed her his badge. "Are you Deborah Holt's mother?"

"I am." The color drained from Mrs. Holt's face. "Why? Is my daughter OK? Is she in trouble?"

"Deborah's not in any trouble." Devereaux tried to smile reassuringly. He hated having to mislead someone whose life was about to be shattered, but he'd learned the hard way that if you need to gather information, you better do it before you drop your bombshell. "But we think she may have been involved in an accident. Would it be OK if we come in and ask you a couple of questions? We need to figure out what might have happened."

"What kind of accident?" Fear added a brittle edge to Mrs. Holt's voice as she led the detectives to her living room at the rear of the house. There was a tiled coffee table in the center of the space, surrounded by a pair of love seats and a well-worn armchair. Each piece of furniture was partly covered by a faded plaid blanket, and in the center of each blanket lay a cat. A tabby. A tortoiseshell. And a Manx. All three studiously ignored the detectives as they took in the TV in the far corner, which was small by modern standards. The bookcase to its right, which was filled with religious titles and social histories of Birmingham. And the carved stone mantelpiece, with two birthday cards propped up at the center. "Is it serious? Is Deborah hurt?"

The detectives paused in the doorway.

"Don't mind Magnus and Sparky." Mrs. Holt gestured to the cats, which were jealously guarding the love seats. "Please, sit. Tell me what's happened to my daughter. Is she in the hospital?"

"I'd like to start with some background information, if that's OK?" Devereaux lowered himself into the corner of the seat facing the window, keeping as much distance between his pants leg and the cat as possible. "Could you tell us a little about Deborah? It would help us if we could understand her better as a person."

"Deborah's a good girl." Mrs. Holt perched on the front edge of the armchair's sagging cushion. "Look, Detective, I won't lie to you. She had her wild years, when she was in her teens. That's no secret. After my husband left me and we had to move to the city she had a hard time adjusting. She carried a lot of anger around for a while back then. But she's put all that behind her. She's turned her life around. Ever since she came home, she's made a massive effort. I'm so proud of her."

"That's good to hear," Devereaux said. "What about work. Does she have a job?"

"She's a facilities assistant at Invetrade Inc. At their main office, in the Empire building. But why does that matter? Did something bad happen at her work?"

"How long has she been with them?"

"Just over four months."

"How's that going?" Devereaux took out his notebook. "Has she had any problems with coworkers or anyone else the job brings her in contact with?"

"Problems? No." Mrs. Holt shook her head. "Nothing like that. She's doing really well there. She fits in, she's popular, she really likes it."

"Has she had any arguments with friends, or anyone outside of work?" Garretty asked.

"Not that I know of. She lost contact with most of her high school friends when she moved away. There's only one girlfriend she really talks about. Carrie Medders. She's a nice girl. Deborah sleeps over at her place sometimes, after their girls' nights out."

Devereaux handed Mrs. Holt his notebook. "Could you write down Carrie's details for me?"

Mrs. Holt wrote out the name and address and handed the book back to Devereaux. "You said Deborah had been in an accident. Now you're asking about friends and arguments. I don't understand. Did she get in a fight? Did someone hurt her? Please—just tell me what's going on!"

"I'm getting to that." Devereaux glanced down at the book to check that he could read Mrs. Holt's handwriting. "What about family? Is Deborah close to any relatives?"

"The only family we have is each other." Mrs. Holt started picking at the skin around her thumbnails. "And the cats. My parents have both passed. I'm an only child. She's an only child."

"What about her father?" Devereaux watched Mrs. Holt's expression closely. "Does she have any contact with him?"

"Absolutely not." Mrs. Holt's nose wrinkled as if she'd smelled something bad. "We haven't seen hide nor hair of that man for almost seven years. Not since he walked out and left me with a teenage daughter to raise."

"Is there any chance he might have been in touch with Deborah without you knowing?"

"No. She'd have told me."

"Could she have reached out to him?"

"Definitely not. She hated him."

"OK. This is all really useful, Mrs. Holt. Thanks for helping us. What about the time before Deborah worked at Invetrade? What did she do then?"

"Invetrade's her first real job, aside from a bit of waitressing during high school. She came back home about eight months before she started there, but she needed time to straighten a few things out. She couldn't get a job right away."

"Now I'm sorry to ask you this next question, Mrs. Holt, but it's important. Has Deborah ever had any involvement with drugs?"

Mrs. Holt looked at the floor and took a minute to gather her thoughts. "In her teens? I couldn't put my hand on my heart and swear that she hadn't dabbled with things she shouldn't have. Nothing serious, though, I'm sure. But since she came home? No way. Have you seen her lately? She's in the best shape of her life. She's really been taking care of herself. She goes to the gym four times a week. Watches what she eats. She's even become a vegetarian."

"That's impressive." Devereaux paused. "So, she's been home with you for a year. What was she doing before that?"

"Not much." Mrs. Holt frowned. "She was living up in Nashville. She went there when she was eighteen with her awful boyfriend from high school. They were going to become rock stars."

"How did that work out for them?"

"Surprise, surprise, it didn't. But it was something she was dead set on doing. She burned a lot of bridges getting there, so it took a lot of courage for her to admit she'd made a mistake and come back."

"I'm sure it did. And what about this wannabe rock star boyfriend? Is she still seeing him?"

"Heavens, no. She left him behind in Nashville. Why? Has he come back to Birmingham? Did he do something to Deborah?"

"We don't think so. We just need to be thorough. Can you tell us his name?"

"You might not believe this, but it's Thor."

"Thor?" Devereaux paused before writing anything down. "That was his real name?"

"I don't think so. But Deborah never said either way. Maybe we should ask her? Where is she?"

"Do you have an address for where Deborah and Thor were living in Nashville?"

"Of course. I'll write it down for you. I can't guarantee he'll still be there, though. He was always broke and conveniently unable to work for one reason or another, so he's probably slumming it in some squat without Deborah to support him."

"I wouldn't be surprised." Devereaux paused, trying to gauge how much longer he could keep Mrs. Holt talking. "What about other boyfriends? Is Deborah seeing anyone at the moment?"

"Oh, yes." A hint of a smile crept across Mrs. Holt's face for the first time since the detectives arrived. "A guy named Ben Warren. He's one of the top executives at Invetrade, where she works."

"It sounds like you approve?"

"Well, it's early days. They've only been seeing each other three months. But I've never seen her happier. He's a little older than her. He's doing well at the firm. He's kind to her. Look, I know it's up to Deb to decide who to spend the rest of her life with, but every mother wants her daughter to be happy. And I must confess, if I said I hadn't daydreamed about the two of them walking down the aisle together one day, I'd be lying."

"It was Deborah's birthday yesterday, wasn't it?"

"Yes. Her twenty-first."

"That's quite a milestone. Did she go to work? Or take the day off to celebrate?"

"She took the day off. She was here all morning, then went out to do something with Ben. She left around lunchtime."

"Did he pick her up?"

"No. She went to meet him."

"Do you know where?"

"I don't. Deb was moping around all morning because she hadn't heard from him. She thought he'd forgotten, can you believe? Then the mail came. It was late for some reason. So she opened his card and her whole expression changed on the spot. She literally squealed with joy. Then she ran upstairs, changed, and bolted out of the house."

"Is his card on the mantel?"

"Yes. It's the one on the left."

"Mind if I look?"

"Be my guest."

Devereaux crossed to the fireplace, picked up the grander of the cards, and looked inside.

"It just says Happy Birthday." He set it back down. "There's nothing about meeting anywhere."

"There was a note inside. I saw her take it out and read it. That was when she squealed and rushed upstairs."

"Do you know what she did with the note?"

"She took it with her, I think."

"Did she drive, or take a cab?"

"She drove."

"What kind of car does she have?"

"A Chevy Nova. It's green. A horrible old thing, but she loves it. She bought it after high school with the money she earned waitressing."

"Could you write down the license number for me?"

"Oh my God!" Mrs. Holt got to her feet as if she'd been stung. "Did Deb get in a car wreck? Is she hurt?"

"We're still trying to piece together exactly what happened." Devereaux reclaimed his spot next to the cat and gestured for Mrs. Holt to sit again, too. "After Deborah read the note from Ben and left, did you hear from her again?"

"Yes." Mrs. Holt closed her eyes, willing herself to focus. "Later in the afternoon. She sent me a text. It said something about her phone not connecting—I didn't really understand what she meant—and that she might not be home till tomorrow—which is today—so not to wait up."

"Can I see the message?"

Mrs. Holt produced her phone. Devereaux took a picture of the screen, including Deborah's number and the time stamp, then showed it to Garretty.

"We'll take a look at Deborah's phone records, in case that throws up anything unusual." Devereaux handed the phone back to Mrs. Holt. "In her message, Deborah said she might not come home last night, and I guess she didn't. Was that kind of thing normal for her?"

"That's a very loaded question, Detective." Mrs. Holt crossed her arms, her fear beginning to turn into anger. "I don't like what you're insinuating about my daughter. And you're making me worried. Now please. Stop stringing me along. Tell me what's going on."

"I'll tell you as much as we know, in just a second. But first I have to ask you one more thing. Would it be OK if I took a quick look in Deborah's room?"

"Why?" Mrs. Holt's voice jumped up an octave. "What's happened to her?"

"Mrs. Holt, I'm afraid I have some very bad news for you." Devereaux took a breath. "Sometime yesterday afternoon, or possibly evening, Deborah was assaulted. She was injured. The injury was very severe. By the time she was found, it was too late to do anything to save her. I'm very sorry to have to tell you this, but your daughter didn't survive. We're truly sorry for your loss."

Garretty stayed with Mrs. Holt while Devereaux went upstairs to find Deborah's bedroom. It was at the front of the house, with a view over the street. The bed was neatly made, with a pink gingham comforter cover. A pair of soft toys—a monkey and a pig—were sitting on her pillow. Her clothes were hanging neatly in her wardrobe—dark, sober work outfits on the left; shorter, brighter weekend items on the right. There was a polished wooden jewelry box on the dresser, with a heap of cheap, costume pieces in its top level and a handful of more expensive items tucked away below. The bookcase held more CDs than books, and the few volumes that were there all related to music in some way. The only other item was a dog-eared shoe box in the center of the bottom shelf. Devereaux opened it. He found it was crammed with photographs. They were all of Deborah. At home. At school. In Nashville. Onstage, singing. On vacation. In clubs. Asleep. Drunk. The pictures were all loose and had been bundled together in no particular order. Except for a pair in one envelope Devereaux found tucked away at the bottom of the box.

It held one ultrasound image of a fetus, in utero.

And one hospital portrait of a newborn baby boy.

Mrs. Holt was in the same chair, her feet tucked up underneath her, when Devereaux came back into the room. She was rocking gently back and forth, and there was no sign of the cats. Garretty had brought her a glass of water, but she hadn't touched a drop.

"Mrs. Holt, I know this is an awful time, but there's one more thing I need to ask you about." Devereaux showed her the baby picture. "Is this Deborah's child?"

Mrs. Holt didn't respond.

"Please. I know this is hard. I know what it's like to lose a loved one. But this is important. It might help us catch whoever took your daughter from you."

"Yes." Mrs. Holt made an effort to sit still. "The baby was hers."

"Was Deborah pregnant when she came back from Nashville?"

Mrs. Holt nodded.

"Where's the baby now?"

"I don't know." Mrs. Holt rubbed her eyes. "She gave him up for adoption. It wasn't my idea. I promised to help her look after him, but she refused. She said she wanted a normal life. To get a job. To date. To go out at night. She couldn't do all that with a baby, she thought. And she said there are all kinds of other women out there, desperate for babies, who can't have their own. She convinced herself that everyone would win."

"Who was the baby's father?"

"I don't know. She never said. I didn't press her."

"Could it be this guy Thor, from Nashville?"

"Maybe." Mrs. Holt shrugged. "I figured it probably was, but Deborah never said."

"Do you know which agency handled the adoption? We'll need to make sure the baby's all right, just in case it's the father who's behind all this."

"Alabama Unified. I remember the caseworker. Mrs. Forrest. She was really lovely. Her kindness made the whole thing as painless as it could be."

"OK, then, Mrs. Holt. You've been a huge help. We won't take up any more of your time. But before we go, is there anyone you'd like us to call? Could someone come and stay with you a while? A relative? Someone from your church, maybe?"

"No." Mrs. Holt's voice sounded small and distant. "I don't have any family left, and I'm not a churchgoer. Anyway, it's OK. I'd rather be on my own. I can't . . . I keep thinking I'll hear that crappy car of hers pull up outside. I feel so awful. I was always on her case about that car. I was embarrassed, if I'm honest. Because of the neighbors . . . Now I'd give anything to hear that stupid car again. What happened to it? Did you find it?"

"Not yet. But we will. The whole of the police department will be looking for it."

"Oh my God! This is my fault! I should never have let her stay out all night. I should have made her come home. If only I had—"

"Mrs. Holt—no." Devereaux's voice was firm. "This is not your fault. It's the fault of the person who took your beautiful daughter away. Whoever that is, however far he runs, wherever he hides, we're going to find him. And we're going to see that he pays. You have my word on that."

Chapter *Four*

Friday. Late morning.

"Is this about Debbie?" Ben Warren was on his feet behind his shiny, riveted aluminum desk before Devereaux and Garretty were fully through his office door.

"That's an interesting question." Devereaux gestured toward a pair of chrome-and-leather visitors' chairs. "Do you mind?"

The detectives sat down without waiting for an answer.

"I'm worried about her." Warren moved around to the front of his desk and leaned against the edge. "She didn't come into work today, and she's not answering her cell. Has something happened?"

"We'll get to that. First, though, tell us about yesterday."

"What about it?"

"It was Deborah's birthday. Her twenty-first. You met up at lunchtime. What did you do next?"

"I'm sorry?"

"It's not a hard question. But if it'll help, I'll back up a step. Where did you meet Deborah yesterday?"

"Where are you getting your information from? I didn't meet Debbie yesterday. I couldn't. I was in New York."

"It was your girlfriend's twenty-first birthday, and instead of celebrating with her, you went to the Big Apple?"

"I didn't want to. I had to. It was work. A commitment I made months ago, before I even met Debbie. I couldn't get out of it."

"What time did you get back to Birmingham?"

"About an hour ago."

"You were in New York overnight?"

"Yes. I had meetings all day, then a dinner. Why?"

"Can anyone verify that?"

"Of course. But why would they need to?"

"Because we need to trace Deborah's movements yesterday, and we have a witness who says she left her house around lunchtime in order to meet you."

"That's ridiculous. I *wish* I could have met her for lunch. But like I told you, I was in New York. Anyone who says otherwise is lying."

Garretty leaned forward in his chair.

"OK." Devereaux glanced sideways at his partner. "Let's all just calm down. There's obviously a misunderstanding here, and we need to figure out where it's come from. We were just at her house. Her mother told us that Deborah opened the card you sent her, was very excited about something inside it, and rushed out of the house. Right around lunchtime."

Warren blinked rapidly, several times. "Right. Yes. That makes sense. Mostly. Her mom must have *assumed* Debbie was coming to meet me. Actually, she'd have been going to collect her present. But why did she leave it till lunchtime? I thought she'd have been more excited."

"The mail was late, apparently. Her mom said Deborah left the moment she opened the card. To collect her present?"

"Right. I was upset when I realized I was going to miss Debbie's twenty-first—she was really understanding about it, though, it's not like she was pissed or guilted me into anything—so I decided to do something special. As the day grew closer, I didn't say anything. I acted like I'd forgotten. I didn't call her from New York that morning, or anything. But what I did, I made this crazy gift certificate and put it in her card. I thought it would be a fun surprise, finding out that way and then going to get it."

"I guess it was. Her mom said she squealed. But what was the present?"

"Her mom didn't know? Debbie didn't go home? Wait—where is she?"

"The present, Mr. Warren. What was it?"

"Oh. A car."

"Seriously?"

"Sure. Why not. I can afford it. And you should have seen the piece of crap she was driving around in. Not the kind of ride that was fit for my future wife."

"You guys are engaged?"

"Well, no. Not technically. Not yet. But we've talked a lot about building a future together, and I'm going home this weekend to tell my folks. My mom always said that when I found the right girl, she'd let me have my grandmother's ring to give her."

"That's nice. But isn't it a bit quick? How long have you guys been together? Three months?"

"Sure. It's quick. But so what? When you know, you know. I'm not one to let the grass grow. Swift and decisive, Detective. That's me. Always has been. You don't achieve what I have before you turn thirty, otherwise."

"I'm sure." Devereaux fought to keep the sarcasm out of his voice. "And it all sounds very romantic. But are you certain there isn't another reason for acting so fast?"

"You mean, is she pregnant?"

"Call me cynical, but when two people suddenly ramp up their wedding schedule, that's usually the reason."

"I never said we're getting married any time soon. Just engaged. We have plans. Debbie wants to tie the knot at the top of the Eiffel

Tower. And I don't mean the one in Vegas. That takes time to arrange. I just love her, and I want everyone to know it. As for kids, we talked about it, and neither of us want them."

"OK." Devereaux nodded. "That sounds good. But let's go back to the car for a second. What kind of thing are we talking about here?"

"Nothing too crazy. An SLK. A Mercedes."

"That's not crazy, for a twenty-one-year-old? OK. Is it new? Or used?"

"New, of course."

"From the main dealer in Birmingham?"

"Right."

"Who's your contact there?"

"A guy named Bill Bolitho. Why do you need to know?"

"I'll get to that. One other thing, first. You said neither of you wants kids. I guess for her that would be *more* kids, right?"

"No. She doesn't have any kids. Neither of us do."

"I'm talking about the baby she gave up for adoption. You knew about that, right?"

Warren went back to the other side of his desk, sat down, and pressed the palms of his hands briefly against his eyes.

"I guess there's a conversation Debbie and I need to have. No. She hadn't told me. I don't know why not. Maybe she was ashamed. Maybe she was afraid about how I'd react. But whatever the reason, it doesn't make any difference. I'm still going to make her my wife. Now. Again. These questions. What's going on? What aren't you telling me?"

Devereaux paused. He took a breath before continuing.

"Mr. Warren, I'm sorry, but I have some very bad news for you. Yesterday, most likely in the afternoon, Deborah became the victim of an assault. She sustained a very severe injury. By the time someone found her, it was too late to do anything. Deborah didn't survive. Detective Garretty and I, we're truly sorry for your loss."

Warren flopped forward onto his desk, sending his coffee mug fly-ing onto the floor where it sheared into two identical pieces. Then he wrapped his arms around his head and moaned like a wounded ani-mal. "No." He suddenly sat straight up. "This can't be true. I don't believe it. It's some kind of trick. You're making it up."

"I'm sorry, Mr. Warren. We're not."

"This can't be happening." Warren pressed his hands on either side of his head. "It's too much. You know what? Yesterday, when she didn't call to thank me, I was pissed with her. It was her last day on this earth and I was pissed with her. Over some stupid car."

"Is there anyone we can call for you? Or if you want to talk to someone about this, we can give you some numbers."

"No. I just want to be with my family. I already have my plane ticket. Is it OK if I still go?"

"Where does your family live?"

"Laramie, Wyoming."

"That's fine. Go see them. But keep your cellphone on. And don't leave the country. Just in case we have any follow-up questions."

Chapter Five

Friday. Late morning.

THE HARDER YOU WORK, THE LUCKIER YOU BECOME.

Alexandra couldn't remember who said that, but she'd always believed it was true. And here was a perfect example. She'd given Nicole another set of math problems to work on and then, true to her new mission, begun to look for articles online about genetic inheritance. She started with half a dozen that she thought looked promising, opening each one in a different tab on her laptop in her usual way. The first two didn't hold her interest, but when she switched to the third, the author's name immediately grabbed her attention. Actually, the fact that his biography said he was another Notre Dame alum was what initially hooked her. It took her another minute before she remembered the guy himself. Timothy Jensen. He was Dr. Jensen now, of course. But she still thought of him as Tadpole Tim—a nickname he'd acquired in his freshman year after an off-the-books experiment he was running about amphibian mating cycles went awry and famously flooded one of the newly refurbished bio labs. Anyway, not only was Dr. Jensen now one of the leading lights in the field she was newly interested in, but according to his

LinkedIn profile he was carrying out a research project about identical twins at the UAB hospital. Right there in Birmingham. Ten minutes' drive from Alexandra's house.

Alexandra switched to her mail program and began to compose a message explaining what she was trying to find out. She felt she should include some background, rather than just hit the guy with a series of questions after not having had any contact for a couple of decades. But, as often happened, her lawyer's brain started to trip her up. She didn't want to reveal her true motivation, preferring to keep her dirty laundry private, but neither did she want to lie too egregiously. The words kept piling up and the verbal acrobatics grew more and more convoluted until finally she hit the delete key. She switched back to her browser. And googled the hospital's switchboard number.

Chapter Six

Friday. Early afternoon.

THE DETECTIVES DIDN'T WANT TO TAKE TWO CARS BACK OUT TO Hoover, where the Mercedes dealer was, so Garretty tossed a coin. And won. Devereaux wasn't surprised. That's the way it goes with Garretty, he thought. It had grated on him when they'd first become partners, the way that everything always broke in Garretty's favor. He could somehow instinctively pick the fastest route, wherever they were going. The winning ticket in a department raffle. Who'd be named MVP in the Iron Bowl, even before the first down was made. But over the years Devereaux had become used to it. He'd found that sometimes it could even be useful.

Devereaux's apartment was in the City Federal, a diagonal block from the Empire building as the crow flies, so it made sense for him to move his Porsche into its underground garage rather than leave it on the street. Garretty picked him up outside the entrance on Second Avenue and looped around to jump on Stephens for the quick blast south. It wasn't the route Devereaux would have picked, but he'd learned years ago not to worry about his partner's navigational skills.

The road had changed its name twice by the time they cut under I-65, and Garretty was about to make a joke about that when he had to slam on his brakes, killing the detectives' conversation for a moment. A silver Toyota Camry from the early '90s had started to make the turn into a strip mall, then suddenly swerved back out in front of them almost at stalling speed. It kept going for another mile, ten miles an hour below the limit, finally making a right into Deo Dara Drive.

"Don't you sometimes wish you were back on Patrol?" Garretty sped up to ten over the limit. "So you could pull assholes like that over? People ought to learn how to drive."

"He was probably just lost." Devereaux looked back over his shoulder. "There was a car service place back by that mall, and he just pulled up outside an auto electrician's shop. Probably had something wrong with his car."

"All right, then. Maybe I'll give him a break." Garretty pointed straight ahead. "Anyway, forget him. Here we are."

Bill Bolitho was waiting for the detectives at the main entrance. He shook their hands, then led them through a cluster of gleaming silver sedans and SUVs to a meeting room at the rear of the showroom.

"First of all, I want to assure you gentlemen that everything was absolutely legal and aboveboard." Bolitho slid a manila folder across the table. "Here's all the paperwork you'll need. The original order, showing the full specification. The receipt for the deposit, which was made on Mr. Warren's Amex card. The receipt for the balance, made by electronic transfer. A screenshot of our bank account, showing that the payment cleared. And a copy of the invoice we got from the manufacturer, showing that we sold the car at a fair market price. If you want anything else, just say the word."

Devereaux pushed the folder away without opening it. "We're not here about money laundering, Mr. Bolitho. We're happy that there's nothing untoward about the purchase of the car. No. We're looking into something else altogether. You see, Ms. Holt was the victim of a crime sometime after she left your dealership. We need to reconstruct her movements throughout the day, so we need you to talk us through what happened when she came in to collect the car. In as much detail as you can. Even the smallest, most trivial thing might turn out to be important."

"That's terrible." Deep lines appeared in Bolitho's forehead. "She seemed like such a nice girl. Is she OK?"

"I'm afraid not. Ms. Holt was murdered."

Bolitho closed his eyes for a moment. "Please tell me it wasn't a carjacking. I had a customer two years ago, he got shot when he wouldn't give up the keys to an SLS AMG I'd sold him. You know the one, with the crazy gull wing doors? I felt just horrible. Like I was responsible somehow. I starting telling all my customers, if anything like that happens, let them take the car! It's only metal. It's insured. Or it should be. But my boss made me stop. She said it was hurting sales."

"We don't know for sure," Devereaux said, "but given the circumstances I'd be very surprised if this had anything to do with car theft. Anyway, take a moment. Get a drink of water if you need one. Then please, tell us what happened while Ms. Holt was here."

"Right." Bolitho closed his eyes for a moment and took a deep breath. "Of course. OK, well, really, everything was totally normal. There was only one thing that stood out."

"What was that?"

"We thought she wasn't going to turn up. Mr. Warren told us to expect her first thing, so we got the handover bay all ready the night before. I don't know if you guys have experienced this kind of thing before." Bolitho glanced out the window at the dusty department-issue Charger that Garretty had left blocking one of the service spaces. "But what we do here, we have a special area, and we cover each new car with a red silk sheet ready for when the customer arrives. Then, once the expectation level has built up good and high, we do a big unveiling. People love it. The problem was, we had three other customers due in that morning. When Ms. Holt didn't show, we had to move her car out of the way. And when she rushed in after lunch, we weren't ready. We had to have our service manager distract her with paperwork while we brought it back in."

"Aside from showing up late, how did she seem?"

"Out of her mind with excitement. I mean, she was a twenty-one-year-old kid and her boyfriend had just bought her a sports car. How else could she be?"

"So you stalled her with the paperwork, did the unveiling, then what?"

"The normal things. Walked her round the outside of the car, to confirm it was in perfect shape. Talked her through its features and controls. Tried to interest her in a monthly service plan, which she refused. Then told her to call me if she had any questions."

"Did she call about anything?"

"No. I didn't hear from her after she drove away."

"She drove here, didn't she? So what happened to her old car?"

"It's still here. She was supposed to be coming back for it. I offered to dispose of it for her. Have you seen it? There's no chance we could sell it, but I told her we could probably get a few dollars in scrap value. She wasn't interested, though. Said she didn't care what it was worth, she wanted to keep it."

"Can we see it?"

Bolitho led the detectives around the back to where the Nova was hidden from sight. He'd had her leave the keys so they could move it. Devereaux looked inside but couldn't see anything interesting.

"Don't let anyone near it. We'll have it taken to the lab. Maybe there's a reason she was so anxious to hold on to it."

"Sentimental value, I'd guess. Probably her first car. Is there anything else I can help you with, Detectives?"

"Just one other question. When she left, which way did she go?"

"Sorry. I didn't notice."

"What about your security cameras. Do they cover the exit?"

"I'm not sure. But our security manager will know. Do you want to talk to him?"

Bolitho led the detectives to the security office, which was more like a closet with no windows. A metal table had been squeezed in crossways against the rear wall, and two split-screen monitors, a keyboard, and a mouse were perched on it. The security manager used them to call up the relevant footage. It showed Deborah pause on the forecourt for a couple of minutes, fiddling with some controls in the center of the dashboard. She took her phone out of her purse and pressed various keys on it for another couple of minutes. Then she approached the exit. She signaled right. But almost immediately changed her mind and went left, toward central Birmingham.

"What was she doing?" Devereaux turned to Bolitho.

"It's hard to tell. I couldn't see too well. From the area she was concentrating on, I'd guess she was either setting up the navigation, or the entertainment system. If she wanted the Sirius radio, for example, she'd have to have called in with a promo code to activate it. Or she could have been streaming music from her phone."

"What about pairing her phone, for Bluetooth? I'm assuming the car has hands-free."

"Of course. It could have been that, I guess."

"That would make sense." Devereaux turned to Garretty. "Remember Deborah's mom said she texted something about her phone not connecting?"

"Right." Garretty nodded. "And about not coming home that night. The question is, who was she planning to spend it with, given that Ben Warren was out of town? And was that where she was headed when she left here?"

Chapter **Seven**

Friday. Afternoon.

When Tim Jensen said he had a free slot in his schedule in an hour, Alexandra thought she could easily make it to the hospital in time. But she'd not counted on how long it would take to print out the French vocab flash cards she planned on using to keep Nicole occupied. How slow moving Nicole could be, when she was unenthusiastic about going somewhere. Or how hard it would be to find a parking space near the entrance she needed to use. She'd been tempted to copy what she'd seen Devereaux do countless times and just dump her Range Rover in a no-parking zone, but resisted the urge. After all, if she could pick up his bad habits without even being related to him, it would render her whole research trip pretty pointless.

Alexandra followed the directions Dr. Jensen had given her through a maze of color-coded corridors until she reached the waiting area outside the office suite he was using. There was a toy hamper in one corner, a drawing board on an easel with a selection of colored chalks on a shelf beneath it, a rug decorated with bright pictures of jungle animals, and sitting on a couch opposite the window, their feet not touching the ground, was a pair of twin girls, maybe six or seven years old. They were shrieking and kicking at each other while tugging at a rag doll, and then only quieted down marginally when they saw Alexandra approaching.

A character in Alexandra's favorite historical mystery series frequently asserts that men don't become interesting until they're over forty. She could have been talking about Tim Jensen, Alexandra thought when she saw him emerge from his office. Gone was the painfully thin, geeky undergrad she remembered from Notre Dame. The new Tim was rugged and tanned, and looked like he'd be equally at home conquering peaks in the Himalayas as conducting experiments in a laboratory.

"Alex, you made it!" Jensen leaned in for a hug. "And this must be your daughter. Nicole? She's beautiful! The spitting image of you."

"Thank you."

"You know, I didn't realize you were married."

"I'm not."

"All right, then. Well, let me just take my foot out of my mouth. Then why don't we get Nicole situated, and we can get started. I've got another pair of twins on their way in about forty-five minutes. These guys here were with me earlier, and we're just waiting for their mom to come and pick them up. I'm sure she won't be much longer."

Chapter *Eight*

Friday. Afternoon.

CARRIE MEDDERS WAS AN IT MAJOR AT UAB, BUT ON SATURDAYS AND two evenings a week she worked at a store on First Avenue named Pocket Pooches. Devereaux had walked past the place many times and had always scratched his head at the collection of tiny, dog-shaped Crimson Tide jerseys and Auburn hats they had on display in the window. He wasn't any more impressed with the tiny canine faces he could see peeking out from the stack of little cages at the back of the store. If you want a dog, he thought, get a *dog*. Something that can run for miles in the woods. Catch other animals. Defend your home from intruders. Not something you'd be constantly worried about losing down the back of the sofa, or stepping on. And he certainly hadn't developed a better appreciation for the place after one of the residents in his building had bought a miniature Affenpinscher there, and a neighbor the guy was having a dispute with called Pest Control, claiming to have seen a rat in his apartment.

Devereaux and Garretty arrived at the store before Carrie's shift started, so they waited in the car out front—in a no-parking zone—

until they saw a twenty-something approaching, wearing a uniform-style blouse decorated with cutesy prints of cartoon dogs and bones.

"Carrie Medders?" Devereaux climbed out of the car.

"Yes." Medders put her hands on her hips. "How did you know?"

"It says so on your pet store name badge."

"Oh. OK. Well, who are you?"

"I'm Detective Devereaux." He showed her his badge. "My partner's Detective Garretty. You're not in any trouble, but we were hoping you'd spare us a minute to answer a couple of questions. It's about your friend Deborah Holt."

"Debs? Oh no. What's she done?"

"A little privacy might be good." Devereaux opened the rear door of the car. "We just need a minute of your time."

Medders climbed into the car. "Has something happened to her? You're freaking me out a little bit here."

Devereaux got back in the passenger seat and swiveled around to get a clearer view into the rear. "Ms. Medders, I'm very sorry to tell you this, but yesterday Deborah was the victim of an assault. A fatal assault, I'm afraid. She didn't survive."

"No!" Medders bit her lower lip and turned her face to the window. "I knew something was wrong when she didn't show up. I should have done something. Told someone. This is terrible."

"You had plans to meet Deborah yesterday?"

"Not plans, exactly. She texted me after lunch, said she had an amazing surprise to show me, from Ben. Her boyfriend. She said maybe we could grab a quick glass of something afterward. Which is Debs-speak for let's stay up all night and get completely off our faces."

"So you didn't have an exact time or place lined up?"

"No. Debs didn't like being tied down to routines or schedules. She just had a habit of appearing when it suited her."

"And when she didn't appear, what did you think?"

"Look, Detective. I don't want to speak ill of the dead. But Deborah wasn't the most dependable of girls. If she said she'd meet you, it was fifty-fifty at best. She was like that with everyone, apart from Ben. When she didn't show up, I figured he'd maybe come back from New York early, as another surprise. He loves to surprise her. Oh God, this is so awful. It was her birthday . . ."

"What's Ben like?"

"Ben? He's the sweetest guy. Kind. Generous. Good-looking. They were perfect together. I know it hadn't been long, but I couldn't ever see them splitting up."

"Did you ever see him lose his temper?"

"No. Can't say I did."

"What about if something surprised him? If he found out about something he didn't like?"

Medders shook her head. "Like I say, Detective, he was very level-headed. He seemed to take everything in stride. Debs said she'd told him about all her skeletons, on like their second date. You've got to understand, she'd done some crazy shit when she was younger. She said she didn't want to be always worrying about what he might find out."

"OK. What about other people in her life? Can you think of anyone who might have wanted to hurt her? Had she argued with anyone recently? Or mentioned if any strangers were hanging around her work, or her home?"

"No. Nothing like that. I mean, if you'd told me this had happened a year ago, I wouldn't have been surprised. Or for a few years before that, to be honest. But not now. She was amazing. She'd totally turned her life around. Apart from being a little flaky, organization-wise, she was a model citizen. Ever since she came back from Nashville. She was, like, a different girl. We've been best friends since we were fourteen, so I know. Believe me. Some of the nonsense she pulled before she left town? Let's just say you wouldn't want your daughter doing a tenth of it, if you know what I mean."

"Do you know why she came back from Nashville?"

"She finally figured out she wasn't the next Madonna. And she could no longer hide from the fact that her boyfriend was cheating on her."

"Her boyfriend being this guitar legend Thor?"

"Ha. Yes. That hopeless loser."

"Was Thor the father of her baby?"

Medders paused for a moment. "You know about that. Yes. He was the father. Lucky for the poor kid he'll never know him."

"How did he feel about Deborah giving his kid up for adoption? Was he pissed?"

"Oliver? I doubt it. He was probably relieved. He only cared about things that would make his life easier. Or more exciting. I doubt diaper changing and midnight feeds are on that list."

"His real name's Oliver?"

"Yeah. Oliver Casey. A twenty-four-carat scumbag. Everyone could see it, apart from Debs. Until he become so blatant about not being able to keep it in his pants, and the penny finally dropped."

"Did he ever show up in Birmingham after she came back?"

"Not that I know of. He already had some other skank on the side, and Debs wasn't working or earning money, so why would he bother?"

"Did she ever get back in touch with him?"

"No. I don't think she would have done that anyway, but specially not after the thing that happened on her way home. She said there was no way she was going back to her old habits after that."

"What thing?"

"It sounds so lame, but it really made an impact on her. So, she finally grew the stones to leave Oliver and started driving, kind of at random. Before she knew it she was back in Birmingham. Heading for her mom's house. But she couldn't go there. She just freaked out and came up with this crazy, spur-of-the-moment plan to drive to Mexico. She was pregnant. She was broke. It was crazy, right? But she'd have done it. She was that kind of girl. But before she was out of the city her car broke down, and some guy fixed it for her. Some mechanic type, with tools and spare parts and all that. And here's the thing. She had no money to pay him so she was about to blow him for it—I told you she did that sort of thing, when she had to—but he refused. He told her all the payment he wanted was for her to go back to her mom's. Give herself a second chance at life. And that's exactly what she did."

Chapter *Nine*

Friday. Afternoon.

"DON'T LOOK SO ALARMED!" JENSEN SCOOPED UP A HANDFUL OF CARDS which were covered with strange ink-blob shapes from the couch in front of his desk and gestured for Alexandra to sit. "They're based on the Rorschach test. Want to give it a try? Just look at this one, don't think about it, and tell me what you see."

"Are you a psychiatrist now, Tim, as well as a researcher?"

"Not at all. I'm only interested in these from a statistical point of view." Jensen retreated to the other side of the desk and held up one of the cards. "Take this one, as an example. Ninety-five percent of children under eight say it looks like a giraffe. Four percent say it's a dinosaur. The others—weird things. This is only part of my study, but what I'm trying to do is determine whether, where you have one twin who falls into the four percent or even the one percent, is the other one more likely than statistically normal to do the same."

"I see." Alexandra didn't think the shape looked like either a giraffe or a dinosaur, but wasn't sure she should admit that. "And what will that prove?"

"Who knows?" Jensen smiled disarmingly. "But I'll think of

something. Anyway, enough of my work. What is it that I can do to help you?"

"Well, I'm not so interested in shared characteristics in siblings. What I have is . . . let's say, a person of interest. Call him Person A. Let's assume that Person A's father displayed some seriously anti-social characteristics. Criminally anti-social. What I need to know is, how likely are those characteristics to be inherited by Person A?"

"Hmm. Intriguing. Is this for a defense you're working on? A variation on an insanity plea? Or diminished responsibility, at least?"

"Something along those lines. I'd rather not be too specific at this point. I just need to know whether I'm totally barking up the wrong tree. If there's nothing to suggest that person A's behavior is likely to be affected by traits inherited from his father, that's no problem. In some ways it would be a relief, in fact. Because there's another direction I could quite happily go."

"OK. Let's think this thing through. How severe are the crimes that this Person A's father committed?"

"Extremely severe. We're talking about multiple murders. Brutal ones."

"OK. And did these happen recently? Or at a distance in the past?"

"In the 1970s."

"Has there been much contact between Person A and his father in the meantime? I'm trying to gauge the role of environmental factors here."

"There's been no contact. His father died a long time ago. It's been forty-odd years."

"No prospect of comparative testing, then." Jensen couldn't keep the disappointment out of his voice. "You know, I'm going to have to think about this one. It doesn't fall squarely into my field, and there are lots of things to consider. There's some recent research I was just reading about, for example. Epigenetics. There's evidence emerging that suggests gene function can be altered without changes to the base sequence." He noticed the blank look creeping across Alexandra's face. "It means that it may be possible for acquired traits to be passed on to future generations, as well as purely genetic ones. I need to talk to a couple of people. Read up a little bit. How about we get together again later and I'll let you know what I've come up with then?"

"That would be great." Alexandra checked herself. "If it's not too much trouble."

"Of course not. Although my schedule is pretty crazy next week. How about this for an idea—let's meet tomorrow. I'll buy you dinner. What do you say?"

As they emerged from the office, Alexandra was still trying to recover from the surprise of having said yes. That hadn't been part of her plan, and it didn't leave her enough mental bandwidth to register that the twins were still sitting on the couch. That they were no longer making a ruckus. That one had a fresh bruise above her eye. Or that the rag doll they'd been fighting over was now tucked in next to Nicole, in the chair she'd chosen on the other side of the room.

Chapter Ten

Friday. Late afternoon.

"TELL ME YOU'RE CLOSE TO MAKING AN ARREST." LIEUTENANT HALE pushed three empty coffee mugs aside on her desk and drained the final drops from a fourth. "Imagine what the press'll do to us if this guy's still on the loose come Sunday, with all those feature column inches to fill."

"I can't make any promises." Devereaux locked his fingers and stretched his arms out in front of him, coming dangerously close to dislodging a stack of papers that was teetering on the edge of Hale's desk. "The crime scene didn't give us much. There was no weapon, obviously, since the victim was strangled. There were no witnesses. The body was probably dumped out of a car or small van, but we're nowhere with the make or model. We don't even know where the woman was killed."

"The lab guys are processing the sheets the vic was wrapped in," Garretty added. "They're also all over her old car. We have an APB out on the one she just collected, so that might give us something if it turns up."

"We got nothing off her phone records," Devereaux said. "Just the texts we already knew about, to her girlfriend and her mom. The phone itself is switched off, so we can't trace it."

"No one's tried to use her credit cards," Garretty said.

"Suspects are thin on the ground, too," Devereaux said. "We ruled out the guy who found the body. There's no indication of the vic having had a beef with anyone. She'd apparently kept her nose clean this last year, ever since an encounter with some mysterious mechanic Good Samaritan on her way back from Nashville. The boyfriend looked like a good bet for a little while, but it turned out we were backing a loser there."

"Are you sure?" Hale spun her cup around. "Could he be worth another look?"

"Maybe." Devereaux shrugged. "I really don't like him for it, though. His reaction seemed genuine when I told him Deborah was dead. He said he'd been getting ready to propose to her. He was flying out west to collect some family heirloom ring. And he's got a rock-solid alibi for the time of the murder."

"He could have used the New York trip as cover and paid for a hit," Hale suggested. "You said he was rich, right? What if he found out about the baby she gave away and didn't want to lose face with the family by dumping her?"

"It's too big a stretch, Lieu." Devereaux shook his head. "Couples break up all the time. The family would have understood. And I sprang the baby thing on him. He seemed genuinely surprised."

"All right," Hale said. "I trust your judgment. What else is there? How about her old running buddies? Could one of them have resurfaced? Someone with an old grudge? Or who wanted her to go back to her old ways and took it badly when she refused?"

"The only possible candidate so far is her old boyfriend." Devereaux smiled. "Thor, aka Oliver Casey. The father of her baby—as far as anyone knows. He's a long shot, though. He knew Deborah was pregnant when she left him and made no attempt to see her or the baby. And the baby's fine—we checked via the adoption agency. If this was a scenario where he just found out about the adoption and went ballistic, you'd expect him to have gone after the kid, too. But just in case, we reached out to Nashville PD. They've put a BOLO out on him. If they scoop him up and he can't account for himself yesterday, we'll head up there and have a conversation."

"It's thin, but it's the best we've got." Hale scribbled a note on a scrap of paper. "A friend of mine's a lieutenant up there. I'll give him a call. See if we can get some extra weight behind it."

Chapter **Eleven**

Friday. Early evening.

DEVEREAUX COULD HAVE ASKED GARRETTY FOR A LIFT FROM POLICE headquarters to the City Federal, but he preferred to walk. The leisurely eight-minute stroll would give him time to think. About the case. And about Alexandra. He hadn't heard from her all day. Should he call her? Text her, maybe? Head over to her place and try to talk, face-to-face? Or give her space, like she'd asked him to?

He was still wrestling with the dilemma when he crossed 20th Street. He ruled out the phone. That was too impersonal. So it was either head down into the garage and collect his car. Or up to his apartment. And spend another evening alone.

The apartment won.

Devereaux came out of the elevator on the twenty-fifth floor, turned right, and stopped dead. He wasn't alone. A guy was sitting on the ground with his back against Devereaux's apartment door. Devereaux recognized him. His name was Tim Kendrick. And at that moment, Kendrick was the second to last person on earth that Devereaux wanted to see. The last would be Kendrick's grandfather, Chris Lambert. Because Lambert—an ex-instructor who Devereaux had hated ever since their days at the Police Academy—was now in bad health, and that had obliged him to rope his grandson into helping with the blackmail scheme that had led to Alexandra's discovery about Devereaux's past.

"You shouldn't have left the hospital like that last night." Kendrick got to his feet. "My grandfather doesn't have much time left."

Devereaux shrugged. Lambert was in the geriatric special care unit, which was a place Devereaux hated more every time he was obliged to visit it. He couldn't stand its cloying, oxygen-rich, antiseptic smell, and the impersonal bleakness of the tomb-like basement rooms gave him the creeps. The thought of ending his days in one of them was his idea of a nightmare. So the moment Lambert had finished making his play the previous night—a promise to provide information that would exonerate Devereaux's father in return for half a million dollars—Devereaux headed for the door. He didn't even stay long enough to wish his aging nemesis a speedy journey to Hell.

"I'm serious!" Kendrick shoved his hands in the back pockets of his jeans and momentarily arched his spine. "You're going to miss your chance. Now listen carefully. You won't be able to see my grandfather again for a while. He took some kind of a turn, immediately after you left. A bad one. His heart rate flat-lined. All the monitor alarms went off. A nurse came racing in—right away, luckily—with the crash cart. She got him stabilized. But they had to sedate him. He's still sedated now. No one knows how long they'll have to keep him under. So this is what I suggest. Get the money together. We know you can afford it. Then keep it close to hand. That way, the moment Granddad's ready to talk, we can put this thing to bed."

"Have you got a twin brother?" Devereaux was having a hard time fighting the urge to punch Kendrick in the face.

"A twin?" Kendrick scowled. "Why?"

"Because there was a guy in your granddad's room last night who looked just like you." Devereaux crossed his arms, disguising the way his hands had involuntarily balled themselves into fists. "If you don't have a twin, it must have been you. But if it was you, you'd have heard me invite your granddad to bite me. I don't pay blackmailers. Or more accurately, rip-off merchants who turn out to have nothing to interest me."

An angry pink rash spread rapidly from Kendrick's neck to his cheeks. "That was me in the room last night. I heard you insult my grandfather. But you're wrong. On so many levels. Granddad's not trying to rip you off. He has something to sell you. Information. Extremely valuable information that you can't get from anyone else."

"Maybe family loyalty's turned your head." Devereaux forced his hands to relax. "Or maybe you're a moron. I don't know. But it should be obvious what your grandfather's doing. It's the oldest trick in the book. He's trying to pull a bait-and-switch. The information he parceled out about my father to get my attention? That was genuine. I'm not denying it, bad as it made me look. But this conspiracy theory he wants five hundred grand to tell me about? This magic bullet that'll instantly rehabilitate my poor dead dad? Give it up, Tim. It doesn't exist. It's complete crap."

"You're wrong." Kendrick shook his head. "This is new information. And it's for real."

"Is it?" Devereaux looked Kendrick in the eye. "OK, then. Give me a sample. Something tangible. A gesture of good faith."

Kendrick held up his hands. "I don't have a sample."

"Why not?" Devereaux took a half step closer. "You had plenty of dirt to dish out in those envelopes you left on my girlfriend's doorstep. Old documents. Photographs that hadn't seen the light of day for decades. So how come you can't show me any of this new stuff? It should be much easier to put your hands on."

"My grandfather memorized it all. That's why." Kendrick pointed to his temple. "It's all in his head."

"Convenient." Devereaux slowly nodded and pulled an exaggerated frown, as if struggling with a complex equation. "But what did he memorize? Where did he get the information from?"

"Pay him and he'll tell you." Kendrick crossed his arms. "We both know you can easily put your hands on the cash."

"Maybe I can." Devereaux shrugged. "Maybe I can't. But affordability isn't the issue here. Proof is the issue. Because if there's no proof, there'll be no cash. Tell that to your grandfather, assuming he ever wakes up."

"He said you were a stubborn jackass, but this is ridiculous. He's trying to help you!" Kendrick thrust his hands back in his pockets and brushed past Devereaux, heading toward the elevator. "But all right. I'll talk to him. And I'll be in touch. This is for real, Devereaux. You'll see."

"Maybe." Devereaux took out his keys and waited for Kendrick to disappear into the elevator car before unlocking his door. "But I won't hold my breath."

Chapter **Twelve**

Saturday. Early morning.

JIM DEFOE WAS NOT THE KIND OF GUY TO BE PUT OFF BY GOSSIP. HE knew that people talked behind his back about his job at the crematorium. He heard the jokes—some of them, anyway—like the ones his buddies liked to whisper when they went out for pizza at the place on Second Avenue South with the real wood oven. But he didn't care because the work was easy. He earned good money. And there was always plenty of overtime to be had. Which was fortunate, because he needed to save up for a ring for his long-term girlfriend. They'd been together since high school, and recently the hints she'd been dropping about how all her friends were married or at least engaged had become impossible to ignore. He'd honestly have preferred to be at his favorite fishing spot, where he usually spent his Saturday mornings, but in the circumstances he figured it would be wiser to pile up a few more dollars and put them toward the jewelry store down payment.

Defoe parked his dark red Toyota Tundra in his usual spot at the far corner of the rectangular parking lot and made his way toward the entrance of the building. It was built of pale brick and shaped like a capital *T*, with a rectangular chamber much like the nave of a modern church making up the central section. That's where the ceremonies were held, and when they're done the mourners leave to the left, to the garden of remembrance. The coffins leave to the right, to be converted into ashes. Defoe hadn't been involved in the design, but he appreciated the efficiency of the setup and took pride in playing a part in keeping things running smoothly.

The entrance to the main chamber was covered with a deep, verdigris-coated copper overhang to provide some shelter from the sun for pallbearers as they unloaded the hearses. The fall sun was bright that morning but low, casting a long shadow, so Defoe didn't notice the parcel until he was almost on top of it. He stopped dead in his tracks, then took a cautious step forward. It was something long—five foot eight, maybe five nine. About a foot across at its widest part. And wrapped up in a pale blue sheet, with another folded into a narrow strip and tied around it in an intricate bow.

The detectives and the crime scene techs stood in a shallow horseshoe, six feet from the body, and for a good few minutes none of them spoke.

"So." Isringhausen eventually broke the silence, his voice flat and depressed. "It's the same basic deal as yesterday. She looks a little taller. A little older, maybe. Brown hair, not red. Not quite as glam. But she was wrapped up the same way. She was strangled. Look at her throat—there's the same distinct, confident marks. Her breasts and genitals are covered. And there are the same signs of sexual assault. God damn it, I was hoping Deborah Holt was a one-off."

"We all were." Devereaux sighed. "Anything on an ID?"

"I've sent her prints to the lab." Isringhausen shrugged. "We'll hear back soon. Who knows, maybe we'll get lucky again."

"Are we assuming this is another dump job?"

"It's impossible to be sure." Ryan scratched the side of his nose.

"It's been dry the last week and the area's paved, so there's nothing to record any tire marks. Or footprints. Or signs of struggle. However, given all the other similarities with yesterday's case, I'd say it's a virtual certainty."

"This might be a stupid question." Garretty hesitated for a moment. "But what about the sheets? They're a different color. Yesterday's were white. These are blue. Could that be significant?"

"Who knows?" Devereaux shrugged. "It could be the key to this thing. Or it could be that the guy just grabs the next set out of the closet. It's not a stupid question, though. It would be worth talking to Linda Irvin, from the Bureau. I'd like her take on why the guy left both the bodies at funeral sites—"

Devereaux was interrupted by the sound of an approaching helicopter, swooping low.

"It was only a matter of time before the press got wind of this, I guess." Devereaux scowled. "At least we're under cover here. When it's time to move the body, though, make sure your truck pulls right up close. Whoever our vic was, she probably has family. The last thing they need is to see her like this on the ten o'clock news. Meantime, Tommy and I'll talk to the kid who found her."

"Why did I touch it?" Jim Defoe was sitting in the center of the first row of seats in the main chamber, hunched over with his head in his hands. A uniformed officer had been sitting next to him, trying to offer some comfort. She stood up when she saw Devereaux and Garretty approaching, shook her head, made a gesture that said *I tried,* and then made her way outside. "Why did I do that? I must be crazy. What an idiot."

"You're not an idiot, Mr. Defoe." Devereaux took the seat that the other officer had vacated. "A parcel's like a puzzle. It's designed to make you curious. Don't feel bad about it. Anyone would have done the same."

"How can I not feel bad?" Defoe sat up straight. "Did you see what was inside?"

"We did."

"I thought someone was playing a trick on me. One of my fishing buddies. And then, oh God, her face! I close my eyes, I can still see it. Will it ever go away?"

"You've had a terrible shock, Mr. Defoe. No one can deny that. But you know the best way to move past it? Work with us. Help us to find whoever did this."

"OK. But how? What do you want me to do?"

"Just answer a few questions. Then leave the rest to us."

Garretty climbed into the Porsche next to Devereaux while they called Lieutenant Hale on speakerphone to bring her up to speed.

"We've got nothing. No prints. No tire tracks. No weapon. No witnesses. The crime scene's a total bust, unless the ME or the lab guys can pull something out of a hat. And worse, we've got no idea who the vic is this time. Her prints came up empty. The guy who found her didn't recognize her. Plus he doesn't usually work Saturdays, and he hadn't noticed any strange people or vehicles hanging around the area when he was here."

"That doesn't surprise me," Hale said. "And I'm not too worried about it. The fact that we have a carbon copy of yesterday's scene means we have to look in a different direction. We need to figure out what connects these victims. And then how the killer came in contact with them. And we need to do it fast, before there's a third nasty parcel on someone's doorstep."

"Unless—it's a little out there, but let's not dismiss Ben Warren yet." Garretty frowned. "The guy just seemed too perfect to me. And with his resources, if he had Deborah killed while he has an alibi out of town, he could have had this second girl killed as a cover. Again, while he's out of town."

"That's not impossible," Hale said. "Not completely. But let's keep it on the back burner for now. Our priority has to be to ID the victim, then find the connections. I've got someone checking missing persons, just in case. We're reaching out to Nashville PD again, in case they crossed paths there. Now, Deborah Holt worked in an office, downtown. It's probably closed today, so find out who their HR chief is. See if he or she recognizes today's vic. If not, try other businesses in the area. Coffee shops. Lunch places. And don't forget— wait, hang on one second, I'm getting another call. This might be something. I'll call you back."

"What about the Mercedes dealer?" Devereaux suggested after Hale hung up. "We should give Bill Bolitho another call. See if this vic just bought a car there, too."

"That's worth a shot." Garretty nodded. "And we could—"

Devereaux's phone rang. It was Lieutenant Hale.

"Gentlemen, this might be our lucky day. I've just been told that yesterday afternoon, 911 took a call from a citizen. She saw a man and a woman arguing in the street. The fight ended when the pair got in a vehicle and drove away. But the caller said she felt like the woman didn't get in the car voluntarily. She had the impression she was forced against her will. The woman matches the description of our victim. And get this. The caller knows this woman. She can give us a name."

Chapter **Thirteen**

Saturday. Morning.

EVERYTHING IN BETTY GOODMAN'S APARTMENT WAS BLACK AND white. The stark leather furniture. The bleached wood floors. The immaculately painted walls. The dozens of photographs in thin metal frames, all the same size, precisely lined up. The only splash of color the detectives could see when the door opened was the red emergency button that Mrs. Goodman wore around her neck.

"I don't need it." Mrs. Goodman caught Garretty staring at the device. "My daughter makes me wear it. She says she worries about me."

"That's nice." Devereaux showed her his shield. "Thanks for seeing us, Mrs. Goodman. We were hoping you could let us know a little more about the incident you called 911 about yesterday."

"Very well." Mrs. Goodman stepped back and led the way to the sitting area in the center of the large, open-plan space. "What do you want to know about it?"

"Everything." Devereaux spread his hands wide. "Please start at the beginning, and don't leave anything out. Any detail, however small, might be very important to us."

"I was right then?" Mrs. Goodman took the seat nearest to the window. "That man was up to no good?"

"We're not sure yet. That's why we need to know exactly what you saw."

"Then I'll try my best to be thorough. The altercation I called your people about occurred at just after half past five. I'm sure of the time because I was paying extra attention on account of the hideous Vulgarian that was—"

"The what?"

"I'm sorry." Mrs. Goodman paused for a moment. "A Sports Utility Vehicle, I suppose I should say. Or a Stupid Ugly Vulgarian, as my husband used to call them. He was very particular about cars, you see. The name stuck, and we eventually shortened it to just Vulgarian."

"You were suspicious of this SUV?"

"Yes. I was. Because it parked outside Siobhan O'Keefe's house at five o'clock—I noticed because its engine was so appallingly loud—but no one got out. This is a residential street, Detective. Why would someone park here and not get out? It's not as if they could be waiting for a meeting to convene. Or for a doctor's appointment. Or for a class to begin. No. It struck me as very odd."

"Could you see the driver?"

"No. That wasn't possible. The vehicle was facing in the other direction, and the side and rear windows were almost completely blacked out."

"Did you recognize the brand of vehicle?"

"Yes. It was a Cadillac."

"Are you sure?"

"I'm certain. Cadillac was the only brand of car my husband would drive. The Rolls-Royce of automobiles, he used to call them."

Devereaux didn't immediately know how to respond, and Garretty wasn't any help.

"It was a joke, Detectives." Mrs. Goodman sighed. "It wasn't his own. He stole it from someone on television. Jay Leno, I think. Anyway, we only had respectable sedans, of course, I might add. Nothing vulgar like that overgrown station wagon from yesterday."

"Did you happen to get a look at the Cadillac's license plate?"

"Yes. I could see it clearly. It was one of those tasteless vanity plates. 34 TIDE."

"Are you absolutely sure?" Devereaux hesitated before making a note in his book.

"Of course." Mrs. Goodman's tone turned cold. "I was a professor of Fine Art Photography at UAB for more than two decades, Detective. If there's one thing I notice, it's detail."

"Of course. I'm sorry. What happened next?"

"Siobhan arrived home. That's her car there—the silver Volkswagen. She got out, and that's when the man I called about emerged from the SUV. He seemed to call out to her, and she stopped and began to talk to him. He showed her something—a kind of leather folder, a little larger than the one your police badge is in, Detective—and her body language changed. She seemed worried, to start off with. Then angry. Then the man gestured toward the SUV. This is where I began to get seriously concerned. It was clear from her posture that she was reluctant. But he was relentless. He didn't actually grab her, or push her, but I could tell Siobhan was under duress. She eventually did get in, and they drove away. The whole thing just seemed off to me. But I didn't want to seem like a mad old lady. So I let the recollection percolate for ten minutes. And in that time, the impression only grew stronger. I was sure that what I saw wasn't right. That's why I called 911."

"Can you describe the man who forced Ms. O'Keefe into the Cadillac, Mrs. Goodman?"

"Of course. I'd say he was between thirty-five and forty years old. He was reasonably tall, perhaps between six feet and six feet two. In good shape. Strong-looking. But lean, like a runner, not a weight lifter. He had dark hair. A little stubble, but not a beard. And his hair was rather a mess."

"And what about Ms. O'Keefe? You told the 911 operator that she's five foot eight with long brown hair?"

"Yes. That's right. Is it significant?"

"Mrs. Goodman, I need to show you a photograph now. I want you to tell me if the person in the photograph is Siobhan. But first I must warn you. The person in the photograph is dead."

"Don't worry, Detective. When you reach my age, you've seen your share of dead people. And I don't shock easily."

Devereaux handed Mrs. Goodman the photograph, facedown. She turned it over and took a moment before she spoke again.

"Oh yes." She dabbed a tear from the corner of her eye. "That's Siobhan. The poor girl."

"Would you excuse me for a moment?" Devereaux stood up and stepped away. "I have to call my lieutenant. She needs to know that you confirmed Siobhan's identity, and she can start the process of tracing the license plate you noted."

"Did the man I saw kill Siobhan?" Mrs. Goodman turned to Garretty.

"We don't know yet." Garretty placed his hand on Mrs. Goodman's forearm. "But we will find out, and your help has been invaluable. Is there anything else you can tell me about her?"

"I don't think she was very happy, I'm afraid." Mrs. Goodman gently shook her head. "She wasn't married. Her boyfriend left her last year. And her parents don't seem to have anything to do with her. The poor thing."

"That's very useful background." Garretty removed his hand and started to stand up.

"Detective?" Mrs. Goodman took hold of Garretty's hand. "Before you go, tell me one thing. And be truthful. Am I in any danger as a result of calling you?"

"That's a good question." Garretty squeezed Mrs. Goodman's hand. "Let's figure it out. Did you go outside at all while the SUV was here?"

"No." Mrs. Goodman shook her head.

"Were your lights on?"

"No."

"Did you tell anyone else that you called 911?"

"Absolutely not. I kept that strictly to myself."

"Then there's no reason to think you could be in harm's way. As always, though, it makes sense to exercise good safety precautions, such as not opening your door if you're not one hundred percent sure who's there. And if you're still worried, maybe think about going to your daughter's place for a while?"

"Certainly not!" Mrs. Goodman snatched her hand back. "I'd rather take my chances with a street full of murderers than spend a night under my daughter's husband's roof."

"Well, OK." Garretty got to his feet. "And you can always call me if you're worried. Or if you see that Vulgarian again."

"All right, Detective. I will." Mrs. Goodman smiled.

Mrs. Goodman started to lead the way to the door, but Devereaux ended his call and came back over to join them.

"One last thing, Mrs. Goodman." Devereaux took out another photograph. "Would you mind if I show you one more picture? I'm afraid it's also of a dead woman. I need to know if you've ever seen her with Siobhan, or even anywhere else."

Mrs. Goodman studied the image carefully. "No. I've never seen her."

Devereaux's phone rang again before the detectives had left the building. It was Lieutenant Hale.

"Will you hug that old lady for me?" Hale sounded excited. "She's a gold mine. Thanks to her, we have two new pieces of information. Yesterday was Siobhan O'Keefe's birthday. She was killed the day she turned twenty-one, just like Deborah Holt. And we have an ID on the owner of the Cadillac. You won't believe who it is. We'll have to handle this one very carefully . . ."

Chapter *Fourteen*

Saturday. Late morning.

LAWTON VETCH HAD BEEN MAKING HEADLINES IN BIRMINGHAM FOR more than two decades. First as a high school football prodigy. Then as a record-breaking running back for Alabama. He gave countless interviews leading up to the NFL draft. He was at the center of interminable speculation, when an injury delayed his debut. He became the subject of sympathy when his knee blew out on his second start for the Bears. The focus of a docudrama detailing his many surgeries, rehab attempts, and failed comebacks. Then there was surprise, when he reinvented himself as an actor in a succession of low-budget TV shows. Shock, when he became established as a solid, mid-level star. First in a historical series about union busters in Birmingham's industrial revolution–era iron foundries. And more recently as a maverick detective in *Magic City Blues*.

Devereaux wasn't a fan of the show.

"Remember, take it easy." Lieutenant Hale took hold of Devereaux's elbow as they approached the giant house that Vetch had built in Mountain Brook. "When we take him in, the press will be all over us. We'll be under the microscope like never before. Plus the kind of money this guy's got, he'll have an army of lawyers on hand in no time. The last thing we want is for him to walk on a technicality. Or worse, hit us with a countersuit if he suffered any kind of unfortunate accident."

A housekeeper opened the double-width front door and led them through the marble-floored hallway and fern-filled sunroom, before reaching the exit to a dual-level deck. Vetch was luxuriating in a hot tub set into the sloping hillside just beyond the rustic hand-milled railings around the lower level.

"Mr. Vetch, I'm Lieutenant Hale with the Birmingham PD." Hale flashed her shield and held up a sheaf of paperwork. "We have here a warrant to search your house and a Cadillac Escalade that is registered in your name. I hope you'll ask your staff to cooperate with us. I'd also like you to come with us to the precinct and answer a few questions. We'll be as brief as we can, and the whole thing shouldn't take up too much of your time."

"Awesome!" Vetch stood up and clapped his hands. The waist-high water swirled around him, bubbling vigorously, but it was still apparent that he wasn't wearing a bathing suit. "You're the best yet. Totally believable. If it wasn't for those idiots Tony sent around last week for that children's hospice telethon thing, I'd totally have fallen for it. What's the cause this time? And how much do you want? How about this—leave the details with Claire, my assistant, and I'll have a check biked over to the event. Or if it's something I'm really into, maybe I'll bring it over myself, personally. Give your ratings a bit of a bump."

"We're not from some lame TV show, jackass." Hale unclipped her handcuffs from the holster at the back of her belt. "We're here to take you to jail. So you can put on clothes. Or not. It's all the same to me. But if it's ratings you're thinking about, I'd recommend you cover up."

Devereaux thought about the headlines that would follow if they marched Vetch to headquarters, cuffed, in his birthday suit. He thought about the charges that would inevitably follow. And he couldn't help but smile.

Hale chose to lead the interrogation herself, with Devereaux relegated to the second chair.

"Let's start with something straightforward." Hale's tone was brisk and businesslike. "The black Cadillac Escalade, license plate 34 TIDE, that we found in your garage. Can you tell me who it belongs to?"

"It's mine." Vetch sounded bored. "I got it three weeks ago."

"All right." Hale made a note at the top of a fresh legal pad. "And can you tell me where you were yesterday, between five and five-thirty pm?"

"Yesterday afternoon?" Vetch took a moment to think. "I was at home."

"Can anyone confirm that?"

"No. I don't think so. I was on my own till about eight. Then I had dinner with a couple of buddies from the TV show."

"Oh dear." Hale shook her head theatrically. "That didn't last long. And yet you started out so promisingly. Just like your football career, I guess. How ironic. Anyway, let's try again. Where were you? Yesterday? Between five and five-thirty? The truth, this time."

"What's up, Lieutenant?" Vetch grinned. "Are you pissed that I've had two successful careers, while you're still stuck in the first job you took out of college? Or because I make ten times what you do? Look, jerk my chain all you like. I get it. But whatever you do, you can't change two facts. Everyone loves me. And they think the real police are douches. If it's irony you're concerned about, it must really suck to be you."

"How much do you think people will love you when we charge you with two murders?"

"When you do what now?" Vetch's voice grew louder, with a

harder edge. "Wait a minute. Enough of this bullshit. I want to speak to my lawyer."

"No problem." Devereaux intervened, taking the reins from his boss. "You're not under arrest. You can speak to whoever you want."

"I can go?" Vetch looked from Devereaux to Hale and back.

"You can." Devereaux nodded. "But if you try to go before we've got this thing cleared up, then we *will* arrest you. And if you ask for your lawyer, we'll get him for you. That might be a smart move for you. I don't know. I don't know your lawyer. Maybe he's got your best interests at heart. Or maybe he'd sniff a big payday. A chance to get a few minutes in the spotlight himself. So he might start trying to build a case against the big bad BPD. But here's the thing. It won't be him in the holding cells. It won't be him in county, when the judge denies bail because all your money and resources make you a flight risk. So why not help yourself instead? Get out ahead of this thing, before it gets out of control. If you really didn't do it, help us to understand. Let me give you an example. We've got a witness who saw you driving your Escalade at five yesterday afternoon. Tell me why she's wrong."

"I don't know." Vetch had his voice under better control now. "I *was* at home. I have no idea why someone would say they saw me somewhere else. Maybe she's crazy? You have no idea how many weirdos you have to deal with, when you're in the public eye."

"I've spoken to her." Devereaux was firm. "She's not crazy."

"Then she's lying."

"I believed her. So would a jury."

"Then she must have seriously messed-up eyesight." Vetch sneered. "Was she wearing glasses? How thick were they? Did you test her vision? Because let's face it. I must be the most recognizable guy in Birmingham. If she saw someone she thought was me, there must be something wrong with her eyes."

"She identified your car. She got the make. The model. The color. Every tiny detail, right down to your fancy license plate."

"Wait—she thinks she saw my car? Yesterday?" Vetch sounded

triumphant. "Then she's definitely mistaken. Because my car was in the shop. It was there all week. I was having the sound system upgraded. It only got returned this morning."

"Which shop was it in?" Devereaux felt a shift in the balance of power in the room. "Who was doing this upgrade?"

"It was at Crest." Vetch smiled. "On Montgomery. The place I bought it from."

"We're going to talk to them." Devereaux closed his notebook. "You better hope they confirm what you say. I've been patient with you up to now. But if you're wasting my time, I'm going to introduce you to a kind of trouble you don't feature on your little TV show."

Dear Mom,

I hate my girlfriend! I'm sorry to have to tell you this, but it's true. Hayley's impossible to live with. Her behavior's intolerable. Let me give you an example. Occasionally—very, very occasionally—I might stay out late. I don't go anywhere she should be worried about. Just to Lucas's. Just to hang out with him. And to help him with things. You know he's not that good with computers, as one example, so sometimes there are things he wants me to do online for him. And when I get home, not even that late, she's there, lurking in the dark, lying in wait for me. With her questions. All her goddamn questions. Her _whats_? And _wheres_? And _whos_? And _whys_? And _how longs_? And get this: As well as the inquisition, she's started to check up on me. How do I know? I've seen her. One time she sneaked out to her car to check the mileage, after I parked it in her spot in the garage. Another time she even tried to check my computer—my email, my browser history—as if I'd ever leave anything she could find on it. That's one thing I do know how to do! It's just awful. Intolerable. Honestly, the way she treats me, it makes me want to kill her. She makes me crazy. I sometimes think I should take a leaf out of Lucas's book. He knows what he's doing. After he got rid of his ex-wife, he's never had a problem with a woman. Not for long, anyway. He never keeps them around long enough to get on his nerves.

Chapter **Fifteen**

Saturday. Early afternoon.

DEVEREAUX AND GARRETTY DIDN'T HANG AROUND HEADQUARTERS A moment longer than necessary. Lieutenant Hale was pissed, and that made her a bad person to be around. She was clearly annoyed with herself after their encounter with Vetch. It was obvious the interview hadn't gone the way she would have wanted, but Devereaux suspected there was more to the situation than frustration with a ring-rusty performance. Hale wasn't one to grandstand. She wouldn't butt into an investigation just because the suspect was a celebrity. But someone else in the department would. Captain Emrich. Devereaux could sense his presence lurking in the shadows. He guessed that Hale was trying to hold him at bay, fearing a repeat of a case that had gone sour three years ago. An MLB star had come to town to visit his brother who was a freshman at UAB. Allegations of misconduct with underage girls emerged. Devereaux caught the case and started to dig. Pressure was exerted from above to let things slide. That only made Devereaux dig deeper, causing the player to miss two games in the run-up to the postseason, and the department to end up saddled with the blame for his team missing out on the pennant. Devereaux couldn't find enough evidence to make an arrest stick, so the guy ended up walking anyway, sending Emrich apoplectic in the face of a media frenzy. Devereaux did uncover an illegal betting operation as a consequence, however, eventually sending half a dozen people to jail. But by the time all the loose ends were tied up and the arrests were made, the media spotlight had long since moved away. This time, whether Emrich was looking to avoid the bad press or steal the good, Devereaux wasn't sure.

Even without the need to avoid Lieutenant Hale's temporary ire, Devereaux would have been happy to get out of headquarters. In his experience, there's no substitute for getting out and talking to people. The crime scene guys have their role. So do the profilers and the technical analysts. But for every case that was closed due to science, ten were solved by sniffing out lies and inconsistencies in the stories people told them. A rich guy like Vetch, who isn't a moron, using his own distinctive car complete with vanity plates to commit a preplanned crime? That had never passed the smell test anyway. It was just a step on the path that would lead them to the guilty party, as long as they read the signs correctly.

Crest Cadillac was a half-hour drive from police headquarters, allowing for the heavier than usual traffic. It was less than two miles from the Mercedes dealer they'd visited the day before, on the same street, but Devereaux didn't mind the sense of retracing his steps. He was actually glad to. He had no scientific basis for it, but often felt that cases seemed to center around a particular location. It was as if some kind of gravity was in play, creating a critical mass of clues, so Devereaux was feeling optimistic as they rolled past Golden Rule Bar-B-Q on Montgomery. He even smiled as they went by the Hyundai dealer because someone had rolled their stock of used cars farther down the steep grassy slope between the showroom and the street in the last twenty-four hours, creating the impression of a herd of unruly animals trying to flee a corral.

"What's with all the car dealers on this street?" Garretty pointed to the line of Chevy Silverados lined up on the opposite side, each with its giant hood standing open. "And look at those. That's not a good sign. It's like they've broken down already, before anyone's even bought them."

Next up was Chrysler, its neat white showroom surrounded by tubs of bright plants and a selection of Jeeps perched on steep ramps. Then Nissan, with a horde of smaller SUVs and crossovers crammed in the space in front of a grim, gray building. Then the Honda showroom, painted cheerfully in blue and white with a circular, deco-style central section and a wavy canopy like a mid-century European beach pavilion Devereaux had once seen on a postcard. And finally, before the long gap to Mercedes, they reached Crest Cadillac.

Crest's premises were set back a little from the street, surrounded by neatly manicured lawns. Only six vehicles were visible, neatly arranged in color-coordinated pairs. There were two buildings on the site—a plain, rectangular one, heavy and substantial, and another that was tall and light with an extravagantly curving roof like a hangar at an airport from the days when flying was glamorous.

The service department was housed in the airport-style building, so Devereaux parked the Porsche by the main entrance and followed Garretty inside.

"We need to talk to your service manager." Garretty showed his badge to the guy behind the reception counter. "Right away."

"No problem, sir." The guy lifted his telephone handset. "Normally she wouldn't be here this time on a Saturday, but she's working late today. I'll ask her to come right down."

"No need." Garretty took the receiver from the guy's hand, reached across the counter, and replaced it in its cradle. "Just tell us where she is. We'll find her."

———

Devereaux and Garretty could hear voices before they were halfway up the ornate flight of cast-iron spiral stairs that the reception guy had pointed them to.

"So, what are you going to do about it?" It was a woman's voice, loud and angry but under control. "The work you did was totally unsatisfactory. You kept my car three days longer than you promised. There's still an annoying squeak coming from somewhere in the center console. And what's worse, there's a scratch on the driver's door. Right where I'll see it every single time I get in. And it definitely wasn't there when your guy collected the car, so don't you dare try and pass the blame back onto me."

The detectives paused outside a door marked *Boardroom* at the end of the upstairs corridor, where the sound was coming from.

"Well?" The woman's voice grew louder. "I'm waiting. What are you going to do? I want a replacement vehicle. I want it without delay. I want compensation for all the time you've wasted. I want—"

"You know what?" A man spoke for the first time. "Forget it. I'm out of here."

The door opened and a short, balding guy in a shiny gray suit rushed out, avoiding eye contact with the detectives and practically running for the stairs.

"Who are you?" Inside the room, a woman was sitting on the far side of a wide, pale wood table. She was leaning forward, peering over the top of her turquoise-framed glasses. Her face would place her in her mid-thirties, but that was at odds with the mane of bright silver hair that flowed way past her shoulders and contrasted sharply with her slim-cut charcoal suit coat. "You're not on my list. And why have you both come at once?"

Devereaux introduced himself and showed her his badge.

"Oh." The woman got to her feet and gestured for them to come in and sit. "Sorry for the misunderstanding. My name's Alison Jacques. I'm in charge of service here. We're short-staffed right now—two of my guys just defected to Jaguar—so I'm interviewing for replacements. I thought you must be late applicants."

"No problem." Devereaux took a seat near the door. "How's the recruitment process going?"

"Honestly?" Jacques frowned. "It's slow. I don't know what kind of cars you're accustomed to, Detectives, but we have a very demanding customer base here. Cadillac drivers are very particular about every detail so I like to make sure that if my front-line staff are going to crack under pressure, they do it up here with me rather than downstairs with the people who pay the—"

Jacques was interrupted by a tinny, disembodied voice from the dealership's PA system. "Would the owner of a blue Porsche, license plate DVRX, please make themselves known to service reception. Calling the owner of a blue Porsche . . ."

"Yours?" A hint of pink spread across Jacques's face. "Sorry. And don't worry—you can move it later. Why don't you tell me how I can help. I don't imagine you're here to talk about my HR issues."

"No, we're not." Devereaux shook his head. "We're here to ask you about a vehicle you recently did some work on. An Escalade, belonging to a customer named Lawton Vetch. We need a list of everyone who could have had access to it while it was in your possession."

Jacques slammed her right hand down on the table, palm first. "That asshole. What's he said? What's he claiming's wrong? And frankly, Detective, this is outrageous. My mother—eighty-two years old, never hurt a soul her whole life—called 911 when she saw a couple of kids trashing the zinnias she grows in the front yard, and the police wouldn't do anything about it. Now this guy snaps his fingers and just because he's rich and he's a celebrity, you come running over here? I mean, has he got the chief of police on speed dial? That car was only returned this morning, and you're here already?"

"Mr. Lawton hasn't complained." Devereaux looked around to check the door was properly closed. "We believe his car was involved in a crime. An extremely serious crime. Possibly more than one, while it was in your possession. That's why we need the list."

"Oh." Jacques closed her eyes and sighed. "Sorry, again. I get a little overprotective where my mother's concerned. Wait here. I'll get you the list right away."

Jacques returned five minutes later and handed Devereaux a single sheet of paper. "That was easier than I thought. I've included his home address and contact details. But this is freaking me out a little, Detectives. Do you really think my guy could have been involved in criminal activities? That's creepy. And annoying, if it means I'm going to have another vacancy to fill."

"This only covers one day." Devereaux checked the date at the top of the page. "The day you collected Vetch's car. And there's only one name. We need the details for the whole time you had it. And everyone who could have had access. Mechanics. Salespeople. Receptionists. Managers. Cleaners. Everyone."

"This guy is everyone." Jacques paused. "Let me explain. Vetch called us to do the work because we supplied the vehicle and we like to portray ourselves as a one-stop shop for the full spectrum of our customers' automotive needs. But the things Vetch wanted done were non-standard, so we subbed the work out to one of our specialist contractors. Our guy just collected the car from Vetch's house and took it straight to the contractor's site. That was the sum total of our involvement."

"Except for sending the bill." Garretty couldn't keep the disdain out of his voice. He'd had his own run-ins with car dealers over the years. "Presumably with a healthy markup."

Jacques smiled. "Of course. We're not a charity, Detective. And we didn't force Mr. Vetch to arrange the work through us. He could have gone to the contractor directly, but I guess he values convenience more than saving a few bucks."

"So the Escalade wasn't here on Thursday?" Devereaux folded the piece of paper and slid it into his pocket. "Or Friday? Are you certain?"

"One hundred percent." Jacques nodded decisively. "It wasn't here at all. It never set one wheel on our premises."

"What about after the work was done?" Garretty asked.

"The contractor returned it himself." Jacques shrugged. "Or one of his guys did. This morning. Either way, it didn't come here and none of my people touched it again."

"All right." Devereaux sighed. "In that case, we'll need your contractor's details."

"Really? You could have said so before." Jacques got to her feet. "Come on. Why don't I get them for you on the way out."

"Let's do that." Devereaux opened the door. "And you can give me your mother's details at the same time. I'll make sure that someone takes care of her problem."

Chapter **Sixteen**

Saturday. Afternoon.

THE ADDRESS THAT ALISON JACQUES GAVE THE DETECTIVES FOR THE subcontractor who'd worked on Lawton Vetch's car was at Montgomery and Deo Dara Drive. It was a scant half mile from the Cadillac dealership, as the crow flies. But the main street is divided at that point, so Devereaux looped around in a reverse D shape via Old Columbiana Road to avoid having to overshoot the place and then double back on himself.

Approaching from the west, Devereaux pulled up onto an immaculately swept, weed-free forecourt in front of a blue and white chalet-style building that was set back from both the streets it bordered. A small enameled sign next to the wide roll-up door at the right-hand side of the structure said *Paltrow Auto Electrics,* but there was nothing else to welcome prospective customers. The sound of an old Oasis song from the '90s was just audible from inside so Devereaux glanced across at Garretty, pounded on one of the metal door panels, and stepped back to wait for a response.

"We're closed." The music stopped and a man's gruff voice echoed from somewhere inside.

Devereaux pounded harder.

The door whirled open amid a clatter of chains and pulleys and a man appeared at the far side. Devereaux pegged him as being in his late thirties. The guy was well built, around six feet tall with a jumble of black hair, and was wearing freshly laundered coveralls with shiny black work boots. Behind him was an old Triumph TR6 in signal red. Its bodywork and interior looked immaculate, but the hood was open and the clump of disconnected, multicolored wires protruding from the area near the firewall told another story.

"I told you we're . . ." The guy spotted Devereaux's Porsche and his demeanor instantly became a thousand times friendlier. ". . . happy to stay open a little longer. What do you need? Radar detection? Audio upgrade? Enhanced security? There's a new GPS tracker module just come out, it's so small there's no way any thief will ever find it. Not if it's installed by someone who knows what they're doing. And me—I know what I'm doing. Trust me."

"Are you Lucas Paltrow?" Devereaux took out his badge.

The guy nodded. "I am. What's this about?"

"We need to talk." Devereaux surveyed the area. "It's a little delicate. Is there somewhere private around here?"

"Sure." Paltrow turned and stepped back toward the car he'd been working on. "We can use my office. Follow me. It's through here."

Paltrow's office was at the back of the building. It was small, but exceptionally tidy. There was only one visitor's chair, so both detectives remained on their feet.

"Sorry." Paltrow looked up at Devereaux. "I don't get many visitors. How can I help you gentlemen? I still say you should let me have a look at the security system on that 911. You're asking to have it stolen if you don't upgrade, and it doesn't have to be expensive."

"We'll get to that later." Devereaux paused. "Maybe. First, we need to know where you were at five pm yesterday."

"That's easy." A relieved smile spread across Paltrow's face. "I was at the movies. Summit Sixteen."

"What time did you leave the theater?"

"I don't know, exactly. But let's figure it out. The lights went down at four-oh-five. Give it, say, half an hour for trailers and commercials. Two hours for the movie itself. Then I hit the bathroom on the way out. I'd have been in the car by sevenish. And back here by seven-twenty. Seven-thirty at the very latest."

"You came back to work?"

"No. I live here. In the other half of the building."

"Seems like a strange place to live."

"Not really. It suits me. It used to be a law office before I bought it. Did you see the accident repair center, across the street? All the dealerships used to have them, back before the insurance companies took it all in-house to cut costs. The guy who owned the place before me would literally sit outside in his car, watch the tow trucks go by, then follow them and try to sign up the owners for personal injury suits. Anyway, I lost my house in my divorce. My old partner died, and rather than buy his kids out of his half of the business I sold it and bought this place to work and live in. Two birds, one stone. It's a perfect setup for me."

"OK." Devereaux shrugged. "Whatever floats your boat, I guess. Now, back to the movie. What did you see?"

"*Rush.*"

"There's a movie about the band?"

"Probably. But this one's about motor racing. Formula One. In Europe. In the seventies. There was this battle between a Brit and an Austrian for the world championship. It was legendary. The Austrian dude almost got killed. He got horribly burned. His face was all messed up. It still is, to this day. His lungs—"

"I haven't heard of it. When did it come out?"

"A few years ago. It's not new. The theater does this thing one Friday a month called *The Last Chance Saloon*. They show an older movie, probably for the last time."

"Sounds like a good idea. Can anyone confirm you were there?"

"Sure. My buddy, Dean Sullivan. He came with me. Ask him. He'll tell you. I'll give you his number, if you want it. Or you can wait. He's on his way over. He'll be here soon. But what's this all about? Why do you want to know where I was?"

"How come you and your buddy Dean were free to go to the movies yesterday afternoon? Why weren't you both working?"

"I'm self-employed. I can work when I want. I'd finished the last job I had for the week so I knocked off early. And Dean? His health isn't so good. He's on disability. He doesn't have a job right now."

"Lucas, let me tell you about a case I worked, years ago." Garretty sat on the edge of Paltrow's desk. "It wasn't long after I got my shield. My partner at the time and I, we were trying to alibi a guy out of something, after some allegations had been made. Some serious allegations. Now, this guy claimed he'd been with a buddy at the time in question. The trouble was, his buddy had a better sense of self-preservation. The buddy figured, a situation like that, two detectives sniffing around, maybe there's a deal to be made? And there was. But only one. And guess what? The buddy got it. He walked. The original guy, he should still be in Donaldson. I say *should be* because he got shanked in the exercise yard, halfway through his second week."

"You think we're . . . OK. Never mind." Paltrow eased his chair back a few inches, pulled his phone out of his pocket, and fiddled with the screen for a moment. "Here. Take a look. Two tickets for *Rush,* bought and paid for in advance on the movie theater app. So you can see, Detective. I'm not making it up. Now, your turn. Come on. Tell me what this is about."

"We're getting to it. Tell me this, first. The job you had this week. The one you'd already finished. Was it on a black Escalade, sent to you by Crest?"

"Right. It belonged to some TV dude. I finished it Monday lunchtime, actually. It was a real simple job, but I'll be honest with you: I kept it all week so it would look like there was a lot more to it. See, guys who pay the big bucks for these premium-type cars, they like to feel they're getting their money's worth."

Devereaux made a mental note to have a word with the dealer he'd bought his Porsche from. He'd needed a replacement rear speaker recently, and they'd hung on to his car for weeks . . .

"So you finished the work Monday. Where was the Escalade the rest of the week?"

"Here. I kept it around back in case the dude drove by in another vehicle and saw it. He thought Crest was doing the work, remember. I like it that way, because then they have to deal with the complaints afterward. Believe me, some of these rich guys, they're such whiners."

"Who else had access to it?"

"No one."

"Someone must have. Think harder."

"Oh." A series of parallel lines creased Paltrow's forehead. "Well, there is one guy, I guess. Why is this important?"

"What's this guy's name?"

"Flynn. Billy Flynn. Did someone see him driving the Caddy, or something?"

"Where was he yesterday, around five pm?"

"Here. Minding the shop while I was at the movies. Only he didn't know that's where I was. He thought I was out following up on some business. He's more likely to stay focused that way."

"Was the Escalade here when you got back?"

"Yes. For sure. I remember being annoyed when I saw it, because a woman from Crest had left me a voicemail asking me to return it to the TV dude this morning, and I'd wanted to sleep late. Luckily, Flynn was able to do it."

"So the guy Flynn could have driven the Escalade while you were at the movies, as well, and brought it back here before you arrived?"

"Theoretically. I guess. I can't believe he'd do that, though. He only touches customers' cars when I tell him to. Why would he need to otherwise? He's got his own wheels."

"What kind?"

"A Nissan van. The one the Chevy City Express is based on."

"Where was Flynn on Thursday afternoon?"

"He was here." Paltrow shifted awkwardly in his seat. "Till about three o'clock. He asked to go home early. Said he had something important to do. I didn't ask what that was. Look, Detective, Billy's a good kid. But he's not the sharpest tack in the box. Give him a job to do and he'll do it. As long as it's not too complicated. He doesn't tend to think too much for himself. So why does it matter if he drove the Cadillac, anyway? As long as he didn't damage it. Or if he went home early, without much of an excuse?"

"You're not painting him as employee of the month material, Lucas. Why did you hire him if he's so dumb? Why leave him to watch your place?"

"Look, Detective, not everyone can be Einstein. And it's not like he's a flake. He tries hard, and he does what you ask him to do. Here's the thing. I met him maybe eighteen months ago. He was working in a bar I go to sometimes, bussing tables. He was a little slow. A little clumsy. Some guys started hassling him, giving him shit. He got flustered, and long story short, spilled a half-eaten bowl of chili on a guy's Armani suit. The asshole started raising merry hell, demanding Billy get fired. So I stepped in. Got Billy out of there. Offered him a job at my place. Part-time only, doing simple stuff. I mean, it's not like I can let him loose on car wiring. But it was better than turning a blind eye. Or putting the asshole in the hospital, as I would have done in my younger days."

"How old is Flynn?"

"Thirty-three."

"What does he look like?"

"He's about six feet tall. Keeps himself in shape. Dark hair. Cut short. Doesn't shave very often. But seriously, Detectives, it sounds like you're accusing my employee of something, and I'd really appreciate knowing what it is. Was there damage to the Caddy when it got returned? Because we hear that kind of crap all the time from customers. The TV dude probably reversed into a gate post after Billy delivered it this morning and doesn't want to claim it on his insurance."

Devereaux placed a photograph of Siobhan O'Keefe facedown on Paltrow's desk. "I need you to look at this picture, Lucas. It's of a young woman. I need you to tell me if you know of any way her path might have crossed with Billy Flynn's."

Paltrow turned the picture over and immediately pulled his hand back as if the paper was red hot. "Shit, she's dead?"

"Unfortunately, she is." Devereaux paused. "She was murdered sometime after she was seen being coerced into the TV dude's Escalade. You see the problem we have?"

"Oh." Paltrow covered his face for a moment. "I do see the problem. But it couldn't have been Billy who killed her. He just doesn't have it in him. You're sure it was him that someone saw? How close were they? Are they sure about the ID?"

"I appreciate your loyalty to your friend, Lucas. But I need you to focus. Did you ever see the girl and Billy Flynn together? Or even separately, but in the same location? Did she ever come here, for example? As a customer? Or with a customer, maybe just sitting outside in a car while you talked? Or at the bar where you first met Billy? Or anywhere else?"

Paltrow's eyes narrowed briefly, then he shook his head. "No. I can't think of any way that could have happened. I mean, I've never seen the girl before. So how could I have seen her anywhere Billy was? Your question doesn't make sense."

"OK. So where can we find Billy this afternoon?"

"He's at his other job. He busses tables at a roadhouse. The Double Aught, out on 65. He was supposed to be here all day, but he told me he'd messed up his schedule and had to be there in time for lunch. It pissed me off, to tell you the truth, but I let him do it because he said his boss over there was mad at him after some screwup the week before and would fire him if he didn't show."

"What's Billy's home address?"

"I don't have it. When I need him, I call him on his cell. Do you want me to write his number down?"

"Do that. Now, we're going to head over to the Double Aught and talk to Billy. You're obviously close to him. You might be tempted to get in touch and warn him we're coming. Don't. Am I clear?"

"Don't worry, Detective. I get it. And anyway, there's no way for me to warn him. The owner of the place never answers the phone, and Billy's not allowed to use his cellphone while he's working there. Plus there's no reason for me to. You'll talk to Billy. Clear everything up. And be on to your next suspect in no time. I'm certain of it. But if you could do me one favor, I'd really appreciate it."

"What is it?"

"Well, it's a favor to him, really. When you talk to him, go slow. Use short words. Don't pile on. He'll get flustered if you push him too hard. Maybe do something stupid, like try to run. But if you keep things low-key, I'm sure he'll stay calm and tell you what you need to know."

"I've been doing this a long time, Lucas. You don't have to tell me how to interview a suspect. There is one other thing you can do for me before we head out, though."

"OK." Paltrow's eyes darted around the room, as if looking for a physical trap. "What is it?"

"Take a look at one more photograph. Of another girl. Same question as before."

"Is she dead, too?"

"I'm afraid so."

Paltrow took a deep breath. "All right. Let's get it over with."

Devereaux handed over the picture.

"Shit, no. Really? This totally sucks." Paltrow gazed at the image for half a minute, then blinked hard. "I do recognize this one. Deborah something? She showed up out of the blue, maybe a year ago. She was driving an old Chevy Nova. It had crapped out on her, halfway to Mexico. I got it going again. Never saw her again, though."

"You must be the Good Samaritan."

"What are you talking about?"

"Deborah told her best friend that a mystery guy fixed her car en route to the border, but wouldn't take any payment. Just told her to go home, make peace with her family, and give herself a second chance at life. It was a pivotal moment for her. If you're that guy, you completely changed her life. You did a good thing."

"Not good enough, apparently." Paltrow handed the picture back. "And that's not quite what I said. I told her to give *her baby* a chance at life. She was pregnant when she showed up. The kid must be six months old by now. Poor little guy. I hope his new parents are good to him. I was adopted, myself, when I was not very old. That's what I was hoping to avoid, by sending the girl back to her mom."

Dear Mom,

Lucas is SO MEAN!!!! Honestly, I hate him. I don't
know why I waste so much time on him. Sure, he pays
for dinner sometimes. And he springs for the tickets if
we go to the movies together. Although he always has
to be the one to pick the show. It doesn't matter what I
want to see. And he won't let me get ice cream. Or
popcorn. He won't let me help him work on his stupid
sports car—like he's ever going to get it going. He won't
even let me drive his customers' cars. Even when they're
just sitting around the workshop, not being used. Not
unless it's to deliver one back to its owner, when he
can't be bothered to do it himself. Or if he wants to be
taken somewhere. <u>Then</u> it's all right for me to get
behind the wheel. It would probably be good for those
cars if someone took them for a spin. Keep the engine
turning over, or whatever it is the mechanics say. They
think they're so smart, just because they know how
cars work. Well if Lucas is so smart, how come he
always needs my help with his computer? He calls me
over. Asks me to find something out for him. Gets mad
if I take even one second to check into something on
the side that I find interesting. Or funny, like that
cellphone customer who was named Dick Horney.
Seriously! Or the drilling guy, whose actual name was
David Drille. I'm not making this up! Anyway, the
moment Lucas realized what I was doing he started
yelling at me till I switched back to what he wanted. I
found it for him—of course!—and he said my help was
invaluable. That he couldn't get by without me. Then he

shut me out again. Wouldn't talk to me for hours.
Maybe I should shut HIM out, sometime. See how HE
likes it. Make him do his own dirty work for a change.
Run around the city doing errands. I bet he'd
appreciate me a little bit more then!

Chapter **Seventeen**

Saturday. Afternoon.

THE DOUBLE AUGHT WAS A STRANGE-LOOKING PLACE.

It was built entirely out of rough, smoke-stained wood that had been reclaimed from one of the city's disused factories, but its shape reminded Devereaux of an igloo. The main section was domed. There were no visible windows. And to get in you were supposed to walk through a long tunnel that jutted out along the edge of the small, unkempt parking lot. Devereaux and Garretty climbed out of the Porsche, rounded the end of the tunnel, and when they saw it from the front they realized it was made out of two giant sewer pipes fixed together to look like the barrel of a shotgun. The theme continued inside the building proper. Jars full of cartridge cases were lined up on shelves. Shotguns were hanging from every available inch of wall. All were classic models, exclusively with wooden stocks. Some were old and beat-up. Some looked factory fresh. Some were even cutoffs. If you'd described the place to Devereaux ahead of time, he wouldn't have expected to like it. To him, guns were a tool of his trade, not decorating accessories. But once he was there, he was pleasantly surprised.

Apparently Devereaux was in a minority. Only three other people were visible. One guy, at least eighty years old, was sitting behind a small table in the far corner, playing solitaire. He was using actual cards, which was something Devereaux hadn't seen in a while. Another guy of a similar age was slumped on a stool at the bar, leaning forward with his forehead pressed against the dull, grainy surface, sound asleep. The final guy was standing behind the bar. He was tall with a pronounced gut that was straining the fabric of his faded denim dungarees. His head was completely bald, but his face was almost obscured by an enormous, grizzled, gray beard. He was standing stock-still and hadn't responded in any way to the detectives' arrival. Devereaux could see why Billy Flynn would choose to work there, if Paltrow was right about his slow-paced approach to life. If you set a tortoise to walk across the floor, it would be the fastest moving thing in the place. By a healthy margin.

"We need to talk to Billy Flynn." Devereaux moved closer to the bar and showed his badge. "Get him for us, would you?"

"Can't." The bearded guy slowly reached for a whiskey bottle. "Drink?"

"No. Where's the owner? Maybe he can get Flynn?"

"I am the owner." The guy set three shot glasses down on the bar.

Devereaux made an effort to keep the irritation out of his voice. "Then why can't you get him?"

The guy methodically filled the glasses from the bottle. "He's not here. You should have called. I could have told you that on the phone. Saved you a drive."

Devereaux scowled. "So where is he? We were told he was working here today."

"Nope." The guy picked up a glass and drained it in one. "He's at his other job. In the city. He helps out at an auto electrician's place."

"We were just there. His boss said you'd insisted he come here today, or you'd fire him."

"Nope." The guy spread his arms. "Doesn't look like Billy's services are desperately needed, now does it? Such as they are."

"You're saying his other boss is lying?"

"Nope. Lucas Paltrow's a stand-up guy. If he says something, in my experience, he believes it. Doesn't mean he can't be wrong, though."

"You know Paltrow?"

"Sure. He used to be a customer. Doesn't come in much these days, though. Not after his partner died and he moved to his new place near Hoover. But it's because of him I ended up employing Flynn."

"How so?"

"I kind of owed Lucas. A year ago—maybe a little longer—I got myself a beautiful old Chevy pickup. 1957. Won her in a card game, believe it or not. But when I tried to drive her home from my buddy's place, she wouldn't start. Turned out her wiring was all shot to hell. You get nothing for nothing, right? So I had her towed to Lucas's new shop. He gave me two options. A basic spit and Band-Aid job, which was a little more than I could afford. Or a top of the line, better-than-new rewire, which was *way* more than I could afford. He could see I really wanted the job done right, so he came up with a plan. He'd do the work for free if I threw a few hours at Billy, at the Double Aught, for at least six months."

"That's a strange way to do business."

"Not really." The guy drew himself up a little straighter. "Lucas said he was feeling bad 'cause Billy had lost his job at another bar, but he just didn't have enough for him to do to hire him full-time. This new way, everyone won. Billy kept earning. Lucas didn't have to be always finding make-work for him. And it was like I was paying Lucas back in installments for the truck wiring."

"If that's true, you could have let Billy go six months ago. Why are you still employing him?"

The guy shrugged. "Why not? He's a nice enough kid."

"Nice enough to cover for?"

"No." The guy ran the tip of his finger around the rim of the empty glass.

"My first partner and I, we wanted to talk to a guy who worked in a bar, this one time." Garretty wiped the dusty surface of the nearest stool and lowered himself down. "Right here in Birmingham. The problem was, the guy didn't want to talk to us. He saw us coming and hid himself away in a storage closet. He asked one of the older fellas who worked there to cover for him, by feeding us some bullshit about him being away at another job. The old guy's story wasn't very convincing, but while we were getting to the truth of the matter, the guy we wanted sneaked out the fire escape. Three more young girls were dead before we caught up to him again. And when we did, do you think we forgot about that unhelpful old barkeep? Or do you think some mysterious, never-to-be identified assailants might have given him the beating of his miserable and worthless life, one dark night not long afterward?"

The guy refilled his glass, and as he did so his sides started to heave with the beginning of a long, deep chuckle. "So Billy—Fast Billy Flynn—he's some kind of multiple-murdering, criminal mastermind? That's what you want me to believe?"

"We don't care what you believe," Devereaux said. "We just want you to tell us where he is."

"And I've told you." The guy drained his glass for a second time. "I don't know where he is, if he's not at his other job. He hasn't been here. He wasn't supposed to be here. He's not coming here. Not till Monday, anyway. Monday's payday for him 'cause he doesn't work Fridays. He's bound to show up then."

"How well would you say that Billy interacts with the customers? Has he ever got into any beefs about anything?"

"Billy doesn't interact at all, if he can possibly help it." The guy slammed the empty glass down next to the other ones. "Stays as far away from the customers as possible. Except for one guy. Woody. He used to spend more time outside with Woody, smoking, than he did inside, working."

"Used to?"

"Woody died. The cancer got him, in the end. He always knew it would, but he just didn't want to quit. His choice, I guess."

"The more I hear about him, the more of a screw-up Billy sounds."

"No. That's not fair. I wouldn't say that. He's a nice enough kid, all things considered."

"What's your name, by the way?"

"Albert. Albert Ray."

"Have you got any daughters, Albert?"

"Nope."

"Sisters?"

"Nope. Had one, but she passed away."

"I'm sorry to hear that, Albert. But I want you to imagine something for a minute. Pretend your sister was still alive, and she came home and told you she was dating Billy. Would you be OK with that?"

"Hell, no. I'd fire the son of a bitch." The guy reached under the bar and produced an antique shotgun. "And make sure he knew, if he ever came near Lilly-Ann again, I'd fill his sorry ass full of double aught."

"That's very helpful, Albert. Now I need you to put the gun away." Devereaux waited for the guy to put the shotgun back under the counter, then took a pair of photographs out of his pocket and laid them facedown on the bar. "I need you to look at these pictures. They're of two young women. The pictures aren't pleasant, but I need to know if you recognize either of them. If you've seen them in here. And specially if you've seen them with Billy."

"Billy, with two girls?" The guy shot Devereaux an indulgent look and turned over the pictures. Then the breath caught in his throat and he couldn't tear his eyes away from the twin, morbid images for a good twenty seconds. "They're dead? They're so young." He reached for the glasses he'd poured for the detectives, his hands unsteady, and drained them greedily one after the other. "You think Billy killed them?"

"Do you think he could do a thing like that?"

"No." The guy refilled the glasses and drained the first one. "I mean, I don't think so. But how can you be sure? About anyone? I mean, every time you see some serial killer on TV getting dragged off to jail, his neighbors aren't saying, *I knew it! I could always tell he was a no-good psycho*. No. They're always like, *He was such a nice guy. So quiet. Never caused any trouble. Who would have thought he chopped people up and ate their livers?* Oh God, is that me now? Have I been working with a monster for twelve months? Jesus . . ."

"Take a breath, Albert." Devereaux kept his voice quiet and even. "Get a hold of yourself. We don't know what Billy's done yet. He may have done nothing. That's why we have to talk to him. But it's important we do that quickly. So I need you to think. Have you got any idea where else he could be?"

"Have you tried his home?"

"Do you know the address?"

"Sure. Give me some paper. I'll write it down. He lives with his mom, I think. And his kid brother. I met them once. She came to give Billy a ride home one time when his car was in the shop. It was in there a few days, 'cause it's a diesel and they had to get special parts sent from Japan. Anyway, Billy wasn't ready when his mom showed up and the kid got bored, I remember, and his mom yelled at me when I let him hold a beautiful Westley Richards 10 Gauge. I told her, it's an antique. It doesn't fire anymore. But would she listen?"

Chapter *Eighteen*

Saturday. Early evening.

IT WOULD HAVE TAKEN THE DETECTIVES TEN MINUTES TO DRIVE FROM Lucas Paltrow's workshop to Billy Flynn's house—if they'd gone there directly. As it was, the diversion via the Double Aught had cost them almost two hours. The only positive thing to come out of the detour—other than benefiting from the wisdom of the bar owner's observations—was the opportunity to call Dispatch and request Flynn's full pedigree, now that they'd learned his address.

Billy Flynn, it turned out, had a record. Only it was sealed, because Flynn had been a juvenile when he'd done whatever it was he'd been caught doing. Devereaux banged the steering wheel in frustration when the duty officer called back with the information. As someone with more than his fair share of youthful skeletons to keep buried, Devereaux would normally have been sympathetic to someone who'd strayed from the path as a kid but subsequently straightened out his life. If Flynn *had* indeed straightened out his life. All they knew for sure was that he hadn't been arrested or questioned for any reason as an adult. But that might be because he'd gotten better at planning his crimes. Or controlling his most reckless impulses. It drove Devereaux crazy to know that information, which could help him catch the guy he was hunting was right there in the department's computers, but he wasn't permitted to see it. Especially since he wasn't hunting any ordinary criminal. How many more innocent women's lives would be lost if the killer was allowed to slip through his and Garretty's fingers? Devereaux scowled and pressed harder on the gas, leaving it to Garretty to call Lieutenant Hale and ask her to try to find them a cooperative judge. They had to give it a shot, but experience left neither detective with much hope of getting Flynn's juvie jacket unsealed.

Flynn lived midway down a wide street that was lined on both sides with mature trees. They were planted close enough together for some of their branches to intertwine and they'd grown tall—most were at least twice the height of the rows of single-floor homes they shaded. The pavement between them was cracked, and its surface was bleached almost white after years of baking in the hot Alabama sun.

The horizontal boards of Flynn's house were painted cream, with pale blue trim. The roof shingles had faded to a washed-out gray. The patchy grass surrounding the house was brown and parched, but on either side of a paved path that led to the doorway was a line of dark green shrubs that looked newly planted.

Devereaux pulled up just short of the house to avoid blocking a fire hydrant, still mulling over how best to encourage Flynn to reveal the details of his previous misdemeanor. Garretty was more focused on seeing whether Flynn was even there, so he was out of the car and already on the sidewalk by the time Devereaux had opened his door.

"Look." Garretty pointed at the driveway, where it curved around the side of the house. "Flynn's van's here. We might be in luck."

Devereaux took a step forward to get a better view past the trees, but his attention was instantly diverted by a blinding flash of orange light. It tore across the whole width of Flynn's house, where the wall joined the roof. Sharp tongues of flame ripped through the structure, dancing and rippling in midair for a moment. Devereaux was thumped in the gut by a solid wave of sound—a deep, bass *woomf*—and then he watched openmouthed as the entire surface of the roof lifted off the building. It rose four feet in the air. Eight feet. Ten. It remained perfectly horizontal at first, but a second later the central section continued to climb while the edges flopped back down, folding in on themselves and rapidly disintegrating. Plumes of debris shot up all around the roof's fragmenting remains like flaming confetti. Within seconds burning remnants, large at first but soon decreasing in size, were landing all over the front yard and sidewalk, and clouds of silver-gray smoke were billowing out of the gaps left between the smoldering roof joists.

"Better hope Flynn's not here." Devereaux batted a clump of charred shingles off the hood of his Porsche and turned to Garretty. Or where Garretty had been standing. Now there was no sign of him. "Tommy? Where are you?"

Devereaux rushed around the car and saw Garretty sprawled on his back on the sidewalk next to the twisted remains of a satellite dish. His left cheek was badly gashed and a dark stain was spreading across his white linen shirt, just above his belt line.

"Damn, Cooper." Garretty tried in vain to smile. "Poleaxed by goddamn DIRECTV. Payback for me saying their channel lineup sucks, I guess."

"Don't try to talk." Devereaux shifted his notebook to his pants' pocket then whipped off his jacket, rolled it up, and pressed it hard into his partner's abdomen. "Just tell me if you're hurt anywhere else."

Garretty groaned and tried to wriggle away.

"Hold still." Devereaux ran his free hand over Garretty's torso, neck, and legs, searching for further injuries. He didn't find any, so he pulled out his phone and hit the speed dial key for Dispatch. "Ten zero zero. Repeat, ten zero zero. Officer needs assistance. Get me an ambulance, like yesterday. Notify Lieutenant Hale. And also send the fire department. Put a rush on it. There's been an explosion. A house is on fire. Further casualties are a possibility."

"Don't worry, Tommy." Devereaux slid his phone back into his pocket, took Garretty's hands, and pressed them against the rolled-up jacket. "You're not in such bad shape. Hell, I've seen you worse in Five Points South on many a Friday night. So listen. Just keep the pressure on, right here. A bus is on the way. The medics will have you patched up in no time at all."

"Wait." The pain was evident in Garretty's voice. "Where are you going?"

"Flynn could have been in the house." Devereaux eased his hands free from his partner's grip. "He could be hurt."

"No way." Garretty tried to grab hold of Devereaux's wrist. "It's too dangerous. Wait for the fire crew. Screw Flynn. The odds are he's a murdering asshole."

"Maybe." Devereaux gently disentangled himself and got to his feet. "Maybe not. But either way, we need to know."

Devereaux paused at the end of the path. Every instinct told him to put as much distance between himself and the wreckage of the house as possible. It looked like it was on the verge of complete collapse. Sections of its walls were bent out from the ground at crazy angles like the sides of a broken fruit basket. Inside, the flames were growing brighter and stronger, and crawling their way out along the remaining roof joists. The smoke was becoming thicker and darker. Its taste, more bitter. The windows had all been blown out. The front door had completely disappeared but its frame was still there, unscathed. And so was Flynn's van. It was sitting on the driveway like an obedient dog, ignoring the mayhem swirling incessantly all around it.

Devereaux forced himself forward. He went through the doorway into what would have been a corridor. The heat inside was vicious. He could feel it on his face and hands, searing the exposed skin. The air was so hot it hurt to breathe. The smoke choked him. And it stung his eyes, filling them with tears. He could hardly see. Crouched over, he took another step. And another. He stumbled on until he reached a room at the rear of the house. The kitchen? There seemed to be the warped remains of a modest range and a refrigerator, but he couldn't be sure. He couldn't focus on anything. His ears were filled with the roaring of the flames. Smoldering fragments of wood and paper were being sucked upwards by the heat. Some of them fluttered against his arms. His face. One caught in his hair. He brushed it loose, battling the urge to turn and run out. But which way *was* out? He was suddenly disoriented. His heart was racing. This whole idea was a mistake. Garretty had been right. He was going to die in this house. And for what? To save a guy who'd probably murdered two women? To save him, just so the state could kill him later? And what about Nicole? His daughter? He pictured a pair of officers knocking on Alexandra's door, coming to notify her of his death. Just as he'd been notified of his father's. He still had nightmares about the night he'd been told. Was that what he wanted for his little girl?

Devereaux eased his way back into the corridor, then stopped again and sank to his knees. He was gasping for breath. And another flurry of doubts was crowding into his head. What if Flynn wasn't the killer? What if he was trapped somewhere nearby, defenseless against the flames? What if Devereaux left an innocent man to burn to death? Was that something he could live with? And if Flynn was innocent, they needed to know. Women's lives could depend on it.

There was no option, Devereaux knew. He had to keep on trying. He attempted to call Flynn's name, thinking that might be an easier way to locate him, but his throat was too dry to make much sound. The flames were too loud anyway, he realized, so he crawled forward and poked his head into the next room on his right. It seemed like it had been a bedroom. There was splintered wooden furniture strewn everywhere, some in flames. Heaps of scorched, ragged clothes. A smoldering tangle of wire and fabric near the far wall that might have once been a mattress. But no sign of Flynn.

The temptation to scuttle past the final room and make a break for the outside world was immense, but Devereaux fought it off. He crept through the doorway into what he guessed had been the living room. He could make out the remnants of a couch and a La-Z-Boy-style recliner. Glass from a dozen shattered picture flames was heaped up at the base of the walls, gleaming like shards of amber in the re-flected firelight. A giant set of shelves had collapsed, spilling maybe a hundred DVD cases in jumbled cascades across the floor. And in the center of the wreckage, sticking out from beneath an overturned flat-screen TV, Devereaux spotted a pair of legs.

Devereaux crawled closer and shoved the TV aside. Then he struggled to his feet and heaved the shelves up until they were clear of the body's torso. Devereaux blinked to clear his eyes a little and peered down, trying to get a decent look at the guy's face. It was Flynn, Devereaux decided, based on Lucas Paltrow's description. But despite being freed from the shelves, he didn't move. Devereaux kicked him in the knee, and he still didn't respond. Gasping with the effort and choking on the foul air, Devereaux lowered the shelves back down as gently as he could manage. He looked around the room, his eyes still streaming, until he spotted something he could use. A side table, lying upside down under the window. He righted it, slid it across to the shelves, lifted them high enough to rest their top edge on his bent knee, and shoved the table underneath to take their weight. Then he took hold of Flynn's ankles and desperately slowly, retching from the smoke he'd inhaled and light-headed from the lack of oxygen, he hauled the inert body inch by inch to the center of the room. He reached down. Found the side of Flynn's neck. And felt for a pulse.

He found one. It was weak. It was way too fast. But it was there.

Devereaux staggered back to the window. He leaned out, taking care not to put much weight on the frame for fear of bringing the whole wall down on top of him. He breathed deeply, greedily sucking down great lungfuls of air that was only a little less thick with smoke, but which tasted to Devereaux as pure and sweet as if it had been piped in from a spring meadow. He wiped his eyes and blinked repeatedly, desperate to clear his vision. Then he turned back. Took hold of Flynn's hands. Heaved him up, taking the unconscious man's full weight on his right shoulder. He staggered to the hallway. Turned toward the front door. Safety was within reach, he told himself. He took a step toward it. And another, trying to gain some momentum. Then he heard an eerie, groaning sound, even above the roar of the flames. It grew louder, then *crack*! A flurry of burning joists rained down in front of him. A dense shower of angry red sparks was blasted back up from the ground, twisting and dancing around his face like demented fireflies. A plume of dark smoke enveloped him. And when it cleared a little a few moments later, he realized the exit was barred. Gravity had knitted the fallen joists into an impenetrable, flaming barrier.

He could no longer see out.

He could no longer get out.

He was trapped.

Chapter **Nineteen**

Saturday. Early evening.

ALEXANDRA FELT AS IF HER LIFE HAD BEEN MOVING ON TWO SEPARATE tracks since the previous afternoon.

On the first track—the sensible one—she had no intention of showing up at Gianmarco's to meet Dr. Jensen that evening. It was a crazy idea. She hadn't seen him for years. She didn't really know him. She wanted his help, sure, but how much serious academic discussion could she realistically expect in a candlelit restaurant? And she had Devereaux to consider. Their relationship had gotten a little ragged around the edges over the last week or so. It wasn't the first time that had happened. But was she really ready to throw it away? Over something that may not even be his fault?

To Alexandra's surprise, she realized that the part of her on the other, wilder track was already making arrangements for the evening. She'd texted the babysitter—the only one she trusted with Nicole, who was hardly ever available these days but just happened to be free that night. She'd prepared enough activities to keep Nicole occupied when her friend Trixie popped by to blow her hair out. She was even mulling over combinations of dresses, shoes, and bags. It had been years since she'd been out anywhere formal. She'd loved it when she'd worked at the law firm. But consulting, which she'd switched to so she could homeschool Nicole, offered far fewer opportunities. She hadn't dated much between her two spells with Devereaux, so she'd had no reason to visit many fancy places recently. And she hadn't even been to many restaurants since she'd been back together with Devereaux. He was strange. He could afford to go anywhere. He had the contacts to get in anywhere. But he was happier at home, eating something simple they'd whipped up together. Or getting carry-out 'cue. Just as long as it wasn't chicken. He was very traditional, that way.

Without planning to, Alexandra found herself delving into the back of the storage closet at the end of the landing. She pulled out her old cassette tape player. She'd had it since college, and had hung on to it after Nicole was born because she thought it would be fun to show her one day. Modern kids only know about MP3s and downloads, she figured. So what would her daughter make of the ancient machine and the box of cassettes that went with it? Alexandra ran her finger along the edge of their cases, all cloudy and cracked with age. She settled on one in the middle of the box. It was one she'd recorded herself. A mix tape of eighties hits. She popped open the tape deck, slipped the tape into place, and went back to her bedroom. Plugged the machine in. Hit Play. And was greeted by Cindi Lauper's manic voice, reminding her that *girls just wanna have fun* . . .

Damn right, Alexandra thought. Why shouldn't she have fun? She worked hard. She deserved it. And maybe it would be fun to have a night out with someone who didn't get called away every time another grisly discovery was made somewhere in the city.

Chapter Twenty

Saturday. Evening.

DEVEREAUX FOUGHT THE URGE TO DUMP FLYNN'S BODY AND FLEE THE flames that had engulfed the jumble of fallen wooden beams and blocked his escape route to the front doorway. He forced himself to take a breath, despite the agony the smoke caused as it grated against the red-raw tissue of his throat, and think. He'd moved around most of the house. There had to be another way out. But where? There was no access to a deck. No way through to a garage. What about the kitchen? Could there be a door from there to the backyard? He hadn't seen one. But the room had been full of smoke, and his eyes had been streaming. That didn't mean there wasn't one. It had to be worth a try. Anything was better than standing there, waiting to burn to death.

Devereaux turned. He started to move. Then he changed his plan. He swerved back into the living room, still weighed down by Flynn. He made for the window, stumbling and slithering over the DVD cases and fragments of broken ornaments. He went down on one knee, then struggled upright again and forced himself to keep going. He was moving by memory now, pushing on through the impenetrable smoke. It was growing thicker by the second. His eyes were streaming and sore. He was worried about slamming into the unstable wall and bringing another ton of flaming timber crashing down around his head. He slowed to a snail's pace, inching forward, one arm held out in front. His hand found one side of the window frame. He shifted to his right, then gathered the last of his strength, aiming to pitch Flynn's body through the center of the gap and throw himself out after it. He leaned forward, muscles tense, ready for this one last crucial effort. Then he felt the weight disappear from his shoulder. Hands were suddenly reaching in. Grabbing him. Lifting him out.

The deep ridges in the gnarled surface of the bark dug into Devereaux's skin as he sank back against the ancient tree in Flynn's front yard, but he couldn't have cared less. He was in the open. He could breathe. The water the fire crew guy had given him—after yelling at him for going inside the burning building—was soothing his throat. A little bit, at least. His vision had cleared enough to see Flynn being driven away—still alive, although still unconscious. And he'd watched Garretty being lifted into a second ambulance, a temporary bandage on his cheek and a thick wad of absorbent gauze taped tightly to his gut in place of the blood-soaked jacket. Because the hours Devereaux thought he'd spent in the house had turned out to be only minutes.

Devereaux was confident that if he waited long enough, the ability to move would eventually return. How long that would be was another question. Years ago he'd have taken hauling one guy a few yards through some smoke in stride. Maybe he was getting too old for this kind of thing. Maybe he should think about turning in his shield. Watching his daughter grow up. Spending more time with Alexandra. Assuming she ever spoke to him again . . .

Three pairs of uniformed officers had handled the evacuation of the surrounding houses and three more had set up a hasty perimeter to hold back the throng of onlookers that had rapidly assembled. Several people were taking pictures and filming video on their phones, and as Devereaux watched, a TV crew arrived and pushed to the front with its equipment. This caused a temporary gap to open up in the center of the crowd, allowing Devereaux to spot a woman on the far side of the street. She was alone, except for the little boy she was clutching in her arms, and unlike all the other people in the area she was standing stock-still. And instead of excitedly looking around, eager for the next inferno to break out, her eyes were locked on the shell of the house Devereaux had just escaped from.

Devereaux heaved himself to his feet, ducked under the police tape, and skirted the edge of the crowd. He made as if he was heading for one of the parked patrol cars until he was sure no one was paying him any attention, then crossed the street.

"Are you Mrs. Flynn?" Devereaux approached the woman, but kept one eye on the crowd. "Billy Flynn's mom?"

The woman nodded. "What happened? Where's my son? Is he OK?"

"I won't lie to you." Devereaux paused to make sure the woman wasn't too shocked to understand him. "Billy's banged up pretty bad. He's been taken to the hospital. The doctors are going to do everything they can to help him. As soon as he's well enough to have visitors, I'll make sure you're the first to see him. In the meantime, I'm going to need you to answer a few questions. It looks like Billy could have been wrapped up in something pretty bad. He could be in serious trouble. But I've heard he's a good guy. I'd like to help him if I can. And with him in the hospital, he needs someone out here to speak for him."

Chapter *Twenty-one*

Saturday. Evening.

IT'S ONLY A MILE AND A QUARTER FROM ALEXANDRA'S HOUSE TO Gianmarco's restaurant, but the usual three-minute taxi ride took the best part of half an hour due to a nasty three-car accident on Broadway Street. Alexandra hated being late. She could feel her heart rate increase with every extra second it took the cab to squeeze between the police cruisers and ambulances that were blocking their path. But it wasn't just the delay that was causing her anxiety. It was the question she couldn't stop asking herself: What on earth was she doing?

Going to the restaurant was a crazy idea. She decided to tell the driver not to stop. To keep going to Forest Drive and loop back around that way. To take her home the long way via Saulter and Rockaway, to avoid the traffic. But when he finally pulled up next to the cars that were parked neatly end-on at the side of the street outside Gianmarco's, she didn't say a word. She just paid her fare and climbed out. Made her way toward the wide ivy-covered brick building, squeezing between two expensive German sedans. Saw herself reflected in the restaurant's glass doors. Knew it was her last chance to walk away.

And went inside anyway.

Tim Jensen was already at the table when the maître d' showed Alexandra to her seat. The moment he saw her approach he put down the anthropology book he'd been reading and got to his feet, a broad smile spreading across his face. He was wearing a silver-gray jacket and narrow-cut black pants. He had patent brogue shoes with contrasting crocodile leather inserts, and a white shirt that was carefully tailored to show off his trim waist. Without his glasses his eyes seemed unnaturally blue in the subdued, slightly pink light that was cast by the chunky glass chandelier above his head, and his hair was artfully styled to look like it hadn't been styled at all.

"I'm so sorry I'm late." Alexandra stepped around the table to hug him, and she couldn't help but admire the subtle elegance of his sandalwood cologne. "I hope I didn't keep you waiting too long."

"Don't mention it." Jensen waved his hand dismissively. "This is a lovely place. I brought my book, which has some very interesting material relating to your area of interest, by the way. I printed some stuff out for you, too. We'll get to all that later, though. In the meantime, I hope you don't mind but I ordered us some wine . . ."

A waiter stepped forward with a bottle of Billecart-Salmon Brut Rosé and poured a little for Jensen to taste.

"Delicious." Jensen nodded and gestured for the waiter to continue. "I said wine, but it's really champagne, obviously. I first had this one in Reims, France, years ago. I'd just finished a research project at the Sorbonne, in Paris, and decided to travel a little before coming home. I knew nothing about wine at the time, of course, so I picked it for the name. It made me think of a fish in a cart being pulled by a billy goat, which seemed kind of funny. And it was *way* cheaper in France, too, believe me. They were practically giving it away, back then."

Alexandra took a sip and smiled as the tiny bubbles danced on her tongue. "It's fabulous. Great choice, Tim. Thank you."

"My pleasure." Jensen smiled, revealing his cosmetically perfect teeth. "It's not every day I get to reconnect with an old friend. Specially one who's so smart. So accomplished. So beautiful . . ."

Chapter *Twenty-two*

Saturday. Evening.

LIEUTENANT HALE WAITED FOR DEVEREAUX TO FINISH QUESTIONING Billy Flynn's mother, then told him to go home. Normally Devereaux would have resisted any move to make him stand down like that, but his exertions in the burning house had left him feeling drained. His exposed skin was filthy with ash and soot, and he was conscious that his clothes and hair must stink of smoke. Plus there was nothing else for him to stay there for. The Fire Department would have to give the all clear before the crime scene guys could get to work and comb through the wreckage of the house. They had to be sure the structure was safe. They had to check that no hazardous or explosive gasses had built up, and test for asbestos and other dangerous materials. And if anything led them to suspect the fire had been started deliberately, they'd have to sweep the area even more thoroughly in case there were any other devices, which had failed to go off right away. Or which had been designed to go off later, specifically to injure the emergency crews.

Devereaux was conscious of a couple of reporters snapping his picture and filming him as he headed for his car. He let that go—it wasn't worth creating a scene over—but he did make absolutely sure that no one followed him back to the City Federal. He left the Porsche in the building's underground garage and went straight up to his apartment. He stayed there long enough to take a decent shower. Grab some clothes off the rack in his bedroom, including his favorite *I Fought the Law* T-shirt, which was still just this side of wearable despite a hole it had sustained in a fight a few years back. Get dressed. Fire up the coffee machine and make two double espressos. Pull a stainless steel hip flask—one engraved with a fancy version of the original French Devereaux family coat of arms that a girlfriend had bought him when he'd graduated from the Police Academy—out of a kitchen drawer. Fill it with Blanton's. Slip it into the hidden section of a King James bible, where the center portion of the pages had been cut away. And head back down to the garage.

The traffic was light so Devereaux made short work of the mile drive to the UAB Hospital. There was plenty of legal parking at that time, too, so for once he didn't leave the Porsche in an ambulance-only zone. Instead he picked a spot in the far corner of the surface parking lot on Sixth, opposite the main entrance, and strolled across toward the revolving doors. There was no one else around so he took his time, pausing by the reflecting pool and enjoying the warm, still evening air.

No one was on duty at the reception desk, either, when Devereaux approached—he had to look twice to be sure, thanks to the forest of indoor ferns that threatened to overwhelm the whole booth—but he wasn't worried. He knew the basic layout of the hospital pretty well from all the times he'd been there to visit other cops, and was fairly sure he'd find Garretty in one of the general wards on the top floor of the main building.

Garretty was propped up against a pair of pillows, watching a football game on TV with the sound switched off, when Devereaux walked into his room. He was wearing sky blue hospital pajamas with tiny white silhouettes of Vulcan dotted all over them, and a fresh bandage had been taped to his injured cheek. "This is ridiculous, Cooper. They're making me stay here overnight."

Devereaux slid the room's sole visitor's chair closer to the bed and sat down. "What's wrong with you?"

"Nothing!" Garretty pulled a fearsome scowl, then winced and touched his hand to his bandaged cheek. "They say it's standard procedure, because I got beaned by that stupid satellite dish. Bullshit, is what I call it."

"How's your stomach doing?" Devereaux shuffled the chair a little closer.

"Fine." Garretty rolled his eyes. "OK. It's a little sore. I needed a couple of stitches, I guess. But they say there are no internal injuries, which is the important thing."

"That's all good, but maybe this will help you recover a little faster." Devereaux handed Garretty the bible. "I thought you might be in need of some spiritual refreshment."

A flash of confusion crossed Garretty's face, then he opened the cover, found the flask, and smiled. "Cooper, you old dog. Nightcap?"

"Better not." Devereaux frowned. "Don't think my throat could take it. I breathed too much smoke at Billy Flynn's house."

Garretty unscrewed the cap and took a long swig. "I told you not to go in there."

"You did." Devereaux held up his hands. "And you were right."

"You did get Flynn out, though?" Garretty took another swig. "So did he make it?"

Devereaux shrugged. "He's hanging in there, I guess. He was still unconscious, the last I heard. He's got some bad burns and his lungs are damaged from the smoke he inhaled. Apparently they have to kind of hoover them out, due to a bunch of fluid that built up inside them. It sounds gross. But they're hopeful he'll pull through."

"And what do you think?" Garretty closed up the flask. "Is he the guy?"

"The lieutenant's called a case review, first thing in the morning, to put it all together." Devereaux closed his eyes and shuddered in mock terror. "She said Emrich's coming. You can bet he'll be slavering to get in front of the cameras and hand them Flynn's head on a plate. And if Flynn's not the guy . . ."

"He's got to be the guy." Garretty put the flask back inside the bible. "Doesn't he? I mean, he's got no alibi, right?"

"Not that we know of."

"OK. And the time line fits. He had access to the Escalade. And you've seen his face. What do you think? Does he match Mrs. Goodman's description of the guy who snatched Siobhan O'Keefe off the street?"

"He does." Devereaux frowned. "Pretty much. But on the other hand, what's his connection to the victims? Nothing jumps out. We can't question him. Not until he wakes up, anyway. *If* he wakes up. And his house is one big pile of ash, so we'll get nothing from forensics."

"What about his van?"

"It's at the lab. There's nothing obvious, but they're combing through it. You never know. They might find something."

"And if they don't?"

"We wait for the morning." Devereaux sighed. "And see if another body shows up."

Chapter *Twenty-three*

Saturday. Evening.

TIM JENSEN HAD FINISHED BARELY HALF OF HIS TIRAMISU WHEN HE laid down his fork and flopped back in his chair. "Wow. That meal was amazing. So was the wine. But the best part of all? The company." He checked his watch. "You know, Alex, it's still early. What do you say? It seems a shame to bring such a perfect evening to a premature end . . ."

They could go for one drink together, right? Alexandra thought. That wouldn't do any harm. They'd just be two old college buddies, reliving old times. Plus Tim had been helping her. It would be rude to take what she wanted, then blow him off. Alexandra giggled to herself. That was an unfortunate choice of words. Maybe she'd drunk more of the champagne than she'd thought. Still, she could have one more drink with Tim. A nice cocktail, perhaps. Then she'd go home. Alone.

Jensen paid the bill—tipping a scant fifteen percent, Alexandra noticed—then he stood back to let her leave first. He held the door for her, then touched her left elbow to steer her toward the side of the building.

"I parked around back." Jensen released Alexandra's arm so that they could scoot past a pale blue Bentley coupe. It had been tacked onto the end of the line, beyond the last of the marked bays, and its nose was almost touching the restaurant's rustic brick wall. "Look at this guy. He should have parked around back, too. But I bet he wanted to show off his fancy ride. You know Bentleys are really Volkswagens now, right?"

"Are you sure you're OK to drive?" Alexandra was starting to wish she'd chosen a pair of shoes that was easier to walk in. "I don't think I would be."

"Of course I am." Jensen paused on the far side of the Bentley. "I only had one glass. I'm fine. Come on. My car's just over here."

Alexandra looked up to see where he was pointing and stumbled slightly, catching her heel on the uneven pavement. Jensen shot his arm around her waist, stopping her from falling but holding on to her a little tighter than strictly necessary. He pulled her closer still and led her across to his car—a silver Lexus sedan. He took her around to the passenger side, slipped his hand into his pocket, and worked the key fob. The car's lights flashed and Alexandra heard a solid *clunk* as the door unlocked. Jensen reached out to open it for her. But before he could touch the handle he jumped back, pulling his other arm away from her waist. Alexandra was confused. She almost lost her balance again. Then she saw a guy moving toward her. He was wearing motorcycle boots. Black jeans. A black long-sleeved T-shirt. Black leather gloves. His face was hidden by an ice hockey mask. It was plain white apart from the holes for his eyes and the perforations around the mouth and nose, leaving it eerily impersonal, and making it seem to almost float above his body.

And he was holding a gun.

The guy shoved Alexandra aside, stepped past her, grabbed Jensen by the neck, and pushed him against the car. "Give me the keys."

His voice was slightly muffled by the mask. "Give me the keys, and no one gets hurt."

Jensen didn't react, but Alexandra could see from his eyes that he was frozen by fear, not defiance. The other guy's gun was still low down at his side. A threat to Jensen, but not an invitation for a passerby to call 911. Not that anyone was passing by.

Alexandra drew breath, but she didn't scream. There was no point, as there was no one there to hear her. Instead she looked around for something to use as a weapon. There was nothing. She could feel the desperation building inside her, and then she remembered her shoes. They had three-inch heels. Narrow, with sharp metal tips. She could hit the guy with one. In the back of his head. His throat. His eye . . .

"Don't be a hero." The guy tightened his grip on Jensen's shirt. "That'll just get you killed. It's only a car. You can get another one. Now, do the smart thing and give me the keys!"

Alexandra was close enough to see the tendons bulging at each side of the guy's neck. She figured his vision would be restricted by the mask. She could whack him and he'd never see it coming. She took off her shoe. Picked her spot. Tried to move her arm . . .

"Last chance." The guy leaned in close, his mask almost touching Jensen's face.

Alexandra knew her opportunity was slipping away. She had to hit the guy right away. She couldn't delay any longer . . .

The guy turned sideways and whipped up his arm, bringing the muzzle of the pistol level with Alexandra's head. "Drop the shoe."

Alexandra unclenched her fingers and let the shoe fall, and was suddenly bathed in blinding light. Behind her she heard the squeal of tires.

"Birmingham PD." The man's voice was tinny and impersonal through the squad car's external speaker. "Drop the gun. Get on the ground. Do it now!"

The guy released the gun and Alexandra watched it fall, then bounce off the pavement before landing finally near her bare foot. The sound it made was light and insubstantial. She poked it with her big toe, and it moved easily. It was made of plastic. It was just a toy . . .

Chapter *Twenty-four*

Saturday. Late evening.

DEVEREAUX HAD REJECTED FOUR PHONE CALLS WHILE HE WAS IN GAR-
retty's hospital room. Each time the handset buzzed he'd taken a
peek at the screen, hoping to see Alexandra's name. Each time he'd
been disappointed. And increasingly annoyed. Because each time it
had been Kendrick who was trying to reach him.

His phone buzzed again as Devereaux was walking through the
hospital's main entrance. Again, it was Kendrick's number that appeared. Devereaux rejected the call and fought the urge to fling the
phone into the center of the reflecting pool. The fountain had been
switched off, and the surface had settled out as smooth as polished
glass. Devereaux perched on the low surrounding wall for a moment,
wondering whether he should just call Alexandra and get it over
with. He'd given her time, as she'd asked. How much longer did she
expect him to wait? He hated waiting. Waiting for her to decide if
they had a future together. Waiting to find out if Flynn really was the
killer. Waiting to see if another body would be discovered in the
morning. He slammed his palm against the surface of the water,

splashing his pants and sending ripples radiating in all directions. Some of them went straight, disrupting the reflection of the moon which was hanging lazily above the white buildings behind him. Others bounced off the walls and changed their course. Some once. Others—those near the corner—twice. Even so, it was relatively easy to anticipate which way they'd go, he thought. But once they were off and running, almost impossible to work out where they'd begun . . .

"Devereaux?" It was Kendrick's voice, somewhere behind him. "What are you doing here? Why don't you ever answer your phone?"

Devereaux closed his eyes and counted to ten. "All right, Tim. What do you want?"

"I have good news." Kendrick came right up close. "My grand-dad's woken up."

"And the good news would be . . . ?" Devereaux folded his arms.

"He's woken up!" Kendrick took a step back toward the entrance. "He's ready to talk. He has the proof you wanted. So come on. Let's go!"

Devereaux didn't move. "Now?"

"Why not?" Kendrick took another step. "You said you wanted proof your father was innocent. My granddad has it. He's two minutes away. What are you waiting for?"

Chris Lambert was sitting upright in an armchair next to his neatly made bed when Devereaux followed Kendrick into his room off the basement corridor. The scent of the air was as nauseating as usual. The underground environment, as oppressive. But Lambert was looking much healthier. His skin seemed less transparent. He'd been shaved. His face even looked a little plumper than it had a couple of days earlier.

"Nearly dying seems to agree with you, Lambert." Devereaux stayed near the door. "Why not take it a step further next time?"

"Devereaux, don't—" Kendrick's hands balled themselves into fists.

"It's all right, Tim." Lambert's voice was stronger now, too. "Let him get his snarkiness out of the way. He'll be thanking us in a minute. And paying us a lot of money."

"Don't hold your breath." Devereaux leaned against the doorframe. "Or on second thought . . ."

"Tim?" Lambert nodded. "Go ahead. Show him."

Kendrick took an iPad from the shelf under the nightstand, called up a picture—a copy of an old Polaroid photograph—and handed it to Devereaux.

"A desk." Devereaux studied the image for a few seconds. "With some papers on it. Damn. If only I'd brought my checkbook . . ."

"Look closer." Lambert leaned forward in his chair. "Enlarge the picture. You see the folder? The page sticking out from underneath it?"

Devereaux zoomed in on the center of the image. He saw that there was a piece of paper, its lower three-quarters covered by a plain manila file. Someone had added four column headings in flowing, old-fashioned handwriting. The first was labeled *Date*. Then *Officers*. *Summary*. And *Source*. Devereaux scanned across the top row: *April–May 1973. HT & JJ. Dealer disappeared—body found in abandoned furnace—no arrests. Scorpio.*

"You know who *HT* is, right?" Lambert shot Devereaux a smug smile.

Devereaux tossed the iPad back to Kendrick without saying a word. He guessed that the entry referred to Hayden Tomcik, the detective who—along with his partner Jim Jenner—had broken the news of his father's death. Tomcik had looked out for Devereaux in the years that followed, eventually pulling the strings that enabled Devereaux to enter the police academy at a time when life behind bars had seemed a more likely fate. Devereaux owed Tomcik his life. But he also knew that Tomcik was no angel. He'd read Tomcik's private files. He knew that back in the day when officers had a little more latitude to play with, Tomcik wasn't one to stand back and watch while a violent criminal slipped through the cracks in the system. If the law failed to deliver justice, Tomcik would find another way to ensure it was served. A drug pusher found dead in a furnace? Sure. If a witness had been bribed, say, or jury members intimidated, putting an untraceable nine in the scumbag's head and leaving his body to rot was something Tomcik could have lived with. He wouldn't have welcomed it. But he'd have preferred it to the alternative. Devereaux didn't condone it. But he certainly wasn't happy about Lambert trying to profit from it by peddling the gory details.

"H. T." Lambert left an exaggerated gap between the initials as if spelling them out for an idiot child. "Hayden Tomcik. Asshole extraordinaire. Bane of my existence, for more than half my life. Corrupt piece of shit. And the guy you treated like a hero—even though he's the one who killed your father. You did know that?"

"I know everything there is to know about Tomcik and my father." Devereaux thrust his hands into his pockets. "There's no mileage in it for you. You're wasting my time, just like I knew you would. As for Tomcik—he was a thousand times the cop you ever were. You want to build yourself up by knocking down a dead man's memory? That's between you and your conscience. If you have one. If you weren't so washed up and I thought you could take it, I'd give you an ass kicking you'd never forget. As it is, I'm out of here. Don't send your grandson after me again. If you do, maybe I'll give him what you deserve."

"You still don't get it, do you?" Lambert shook his head as if genuinely surprised. "This list of Tomcik's crimes. It doesn't come from the department. Tomcik was too well connected for any of his activities to see the light of day. This comes from an independent source. It's thoroughly researched. It's based on firsthand testimony. And it's comprehensive. It doesn't just cover the odd missing drug dealer, who no one was ever going to lose sleep over. No. It contains the mother lode. It proves that what I told you Thursday night is true. That Tomcik was the worst kind of scumbag there is. That he murdered a fellow cop."

"Which fellow cop?" Devereaux's voice was loaded with skepticism. "When?"

"John Devereaux. 1976. I think you know the exact date."

"Rubbish." Devereaux was scathing. "Raymond Kerr killed John Devereaux."

"Sure." Lambert nodded. "That's what the report said. What the Officer Involved Shooting Board signed off on. But it's not what happened."

"So what did happen?" Devereaux couldn't resist taking the bait.

"It's simple. John Devereaux was on to Tomcik and his partner, so they killed him. Then they set up Raymond Kerr to take the fall. They pegged Kerr as a notorious serial killer. But he was no such thing."

"The killings were real." Devereaux levered himself away from the wall. "There are crime scene photos. I've seen them. So have you."

"Right." Lambert nodded again. "But the killer was a young guy Raymond Kerr had been trying to help. John Devereaux had recently shot the kid, creating the perfect apparent motive for Kerr to take revenge."

"Raymond Kerr was not the innocent party here." Devereaux folded his arms.

"He was." Lambert was insistent. "The poor guy had a hell of a life. His wife had died, leaving just him and a little boy. Aka, you. Who was now orphaned. Which was a problem for Tomcik. What was he to do? Who'd take in the spawn of a mass murderer? The embodiment of evil? No one would. But the kid of a hero cop? That was a different proposition. How did he get away with fudging the paperwork? I guess he had experience with that. It was easier in those days. And the circumstances helped, like you being young and never having been to school."

Devereaux was silent.

"Don't deny you know. I spoke to Bronson Segard." Segard had taken over as Tomcik's partner after Jim Jenner was killed.

"Raymond Kerr was my father." Devereaux spoke quietly. "But you're wrong about the rest."

"Why would you cling to that?" Lambert made as if to slam his palm into his forehead. "Why would you choose to believe that your father was a monster? I guess if you think that's true, and you're OK with it, then walk away. But I know this: Any normal person would want to know the truth. And I can prove what that is."

"You've shown me part of one page." Devereaux rubbed his eyes. "That proves nothing. What more is there?"

"There's plenty more." Lambert grinned. "Pay me, and I'll give it to you."

"Where did you get it?"

"That doesn't matter."

"Yes it does." Devereaux paused. "You're asking for a lot of money. I need to know what you're selling is genuine. Think of it like art. You've got to prove the provenance."

"Fair enough. I got it from a journalist."

"I'm walking away . . ."

"Wait." Lambert held up his hands. "It wasn't just any journalist. It was Frederick McKinzie."

Frederick McKinzie was a legend in Birmingham. He'd been the main man at the *Tribune* throughout some of the most tumultuous decades of the twentieth century. When McKinzie spoke, people listened. Even cops. They simply didn't make reporters like him anymore.

"Frederick McKinzie's been dead for years, and none of this was ever published. How did you get hold of his material? How do you know it's real?"

"I saw it with my own eyes. I took that picture myself. In his study. You see, he was investigating police corruption, back in the late seventies. Naturally, Tomcik was a main focus. Not many people dared to tell the truth, but I did. Frederick heard about me. He reached out. He asked me to help. And he interviewed me, more than once."

"And you repaid that trust by stealing his work?"

"I'd have been stupid not to. Most revelations about Tomcik got buried. I hoped McKinzie would be different, but look what happened. His story got squashed. I don't know how. Tomcik must have gotten to him. Or one of his buddies did. That guy was like an octopus—he had arms everywhere."

"What did you do? Break into his office and copy his files?"

"No." Lambert couldn't resist a smug smile. "I did it when he invited me to his house, to do the first interview. He got called to the door, and I took pictures."

"He just got called to the door in the middle of an important interview?"

"It could be that a uniform happened to call round with something that couldn't wait. Tomcik wasn't the only one who knew how to work an angle. The picture you saw—that was a polaroid, so I could put everything back in the right place. The rest are of McKinzie's research. Every detail. Every page."

"So there are hard copies? It's not all just in your head?"

Lambert winked. "You don't expect me to show all my cards on the first hand?"

"If you have all this information, why did you sit on it for so long?"

"That wasn't my plan. I intended to use it right away. So I told Tomcik what I had, to give him the chance to do the right thing."

"To try to blackmail him, you mean."

"Tom-ay-to, tom-ah-to. Whatever. That's water under the bridge. The point is, he refused. Certain threats were made. On my side, I was committed to exposing the truth. And I figured, how could I do that if the next body to show up in an abandoned furnace was mine?"

"So you're a chicken. You waited for Tomcik to die, then came after me."

"It wasn't like that." Lambert shook his head. "The truth is, I didn't realize exactly what I had. I'd kept the copies of the files in case a chance ever came up to use them against Tomcik. When he died, I figured I might as well clear them out. But first I read through them, one final time. And I noticed something that had escaped me when I was just focusing on Tomcik. It was in your dad's case. There were several mentions of Raymond Kerr having a little boy, named Cooper. There were no records of John Devereaux having any children. Not until after he was killed. Then there were all kinds of stories about his one orphaned son. That didn't raise any red flags when I thought Devereaux had been killed by Kerr. But when I discovered that both of them had been killed by Tomcik, and connected that with the way Tomcik took so much interest in Cooper *Devereaux*? It was a lightbulb moment. It got me thinking. Was this more of Tomcik's shenanigans? But why would he bother with it? Did he have a guilty conscience? Or was it a more practical issue? Because of a cute little orphan boy? That's a loose end. And if there was one thing that Tomcik never did, it was leave a loose end. That's one reason he stayed out of jail."

"So you figured this out and thought you'd use it to blackmail me?"

"Not blackmail, no." Lambert took a moment to think. "*Blackmail*'s far too cynical a word. It was more like making valuable information available to the person who'd benefit the most, at a reasonable rate. People pay for family trees and DNA tests, don't they? What I'm offering you is much more significant."

"Except that I already know."

"No." Lambert was emphatic. "You only have half the story. The sad half. I can give you the happy ending. I might not like you, Devereaux. But I don't believe you're the kind of cop who can walk away from cast-iron proof of murder. Specially when the victim is another cop. And the truth will redeem your own father."

"You're certain McKinzie's material is genuine?"

"One hundred percent. I saw it with my own eyes. And Frederick McKinzie wasn't a guy who made stuff up. You know that. So. Do we have a deal?"

"Maybe." Devereaux turned to leave the room. "Give me a couple of days."

Chapter *Twenty-five*

Saturday. Late evening.

ALEXANDRA COULD NOT LIE STILL.

She'd given her statement to the officers who'd intervened in the carjacking—her lawyer's brain kicking in and marshaling the facts into a clear, succinct, and above all brief account of what had happened after leaving the restaurant—and politely declined their offer of a ride home. She realized it was probably illogical, but was hoping that the less time she spent with the police, the lower the chances would be of word reaching Devereaux about her involvement. When she got to her house she paid the babysitter, giving her a huge tip and practically bundling her out the door. She checked on Nicole, resisting the temptation to wake her daughter and hug her closer and tighter than ever before. She hurried to the bathroom, dumping her clothes in the laundry and rapidly removing all traces of makeup. Then she dove into bed and pulled the covers high up over her head.

It was the images of movement that were agitating her now, crowding into her head, causing her to jerk and twist as she tried in vain to escape them. She kept seeing the guy in the hockey mask, appearing from nowhere. Over and over. Then she saw the gun in his hand, snapping upward and pointing at her face. And she saw Tim Jensen, pulling his arm away from her waist and scuttling out of harm's way. Trying to hide behind her. Practically using her as a shield. Had he just pulled his arm back? Or had he actually pushed her forward? She hadn't fully registered it in the moment, but now the individual scenes were running in a continuous loop in her memory, and she couldn't be sure.

Alexandra summoned every ounce of self-control she possessed and gradually managed to slow the images down. Finally she stopped them altogether. But that didn't bring the relief she was hoping for. Because she was left with another picture in her head. Something she'd seen on the TV display in the back of the taxi that had brought her home. A segment from the local news. A report about a house fire. The subtitles described how a police officer had run into the burning building and rescued its owner. They were superimposed over footage a neighbor had taken of the aftermath, using his cellphone. The film was grainy and unstable, but the officer's smoke-stained face was clearly recognizable.

It was Devereaux.

Devereaux had run into the flames to save a stranger. Jensen had run away from a man with a plastic gun, to save himself.

Alexandra didn't need one of Nicole's puzzle books to spot the difference between those two pictures.

Chapter *Twenty-six*

Saturday. Late evening.

DEVEREAUX REACHED THE LINE OF TREES AT THE SIDE OF SIXTH AVE-
nue, put his hand in his pocket to find his keys, then paused. Two
guys were standing next to his Porsche, in the far corner of the parking lot. They were taking far too close an interest in it. They were
probably in their late teens, and both were wearing jeans and black
leather jackets with the sleeves cut off. The taller one leaned in close
to the passenger-side window and cupped his hand at the side of his
face to defeat the reflection and get a better view inside. Then he
straightened up and started talking to the other guy. He was looming
over him and making a series of exaggerated gestures with his hands
like a high school football coach explaining a play to a freshman
quarterback. Devereaux couldn't hear the words—he was too far
away—but the game plan looked simple enough. The smaller guy
was to wait for the owner to return then step out from behind the
nearest tree, pretending to be hurt and attracting his attention. The
taller one would hit him from behind. Then they'd take the keys and
drive away. A reasonable approach, Devereaux thought. No unneces-
sary complications. And car security was comprehensive these days.

Locks were solidly shielded, and keys had built-in transponders that were needed to activate the engine's electrical systems. It wasn't like back in his day, when a coat hanger and a screwdriver could get you pretty much any ride you pleased.

Devereaux gave the two guys time to get situated, then strolled slowly toward his car. He drew level with the rear fender and right on cue the smaller guy staggered out in front of him, clutching his gut like a movie cowboy who'd lost a shootout in an old-fashioned Western. Devereaux ignored him, focusing on the reflection in the Porsche's gleaming blue paintwork and using it to time a perfectly delivered elbow to the face of the onrushing taller guy.

"Stand still!" Devereaux glared at the shorter guy. "Move, and you get the same treatment. Are we clear?"

The shorter guy nodded, but Devereaux still didn't take his eyes off him while he called Dispatch and asked for a patrol car to be sent to escort prisoners in an attempted carjacking. "I have one confirmed suspect. Possibly two."

Devereaux ended his call and looked down at the taller guy, who was still writhing on the ground, blood and snot pouring from his shattered nose and covering his chin and neck.

"It's too late for your friend, I guess." Devereaux turned to the shorter guy. "He's made his choice. But I'm not sure about you. I was watching when he was telling you what to do just now. You seemed hesitant. Like you needed some persuading. Am I right? Or am I just a hopeless optimist?"

"No, you're right." The short guy's eyes were bulging. "I didn't want to do it. I told him it was a bad idea, but—"

"A bad idea because you thought it wouldn't work?" Devereaux paused. "Or a bad idea because you thought it was wrong?"

"I thought it *would* work. He's done it before." The guy looked up at the sky. "I just . . . taking someone's car? That's too much."

Devereaux opened the Porsche's passenger door. "Get in."

"Why?" The short guy backed away. "Where are you taking me?"

"The patrol car will be here in . . ." Devereaux checked his watch. "Sixty seconds. Max. If you're still standing there when it arrives, you'll be going to jail."

The guy climbed cautiously into the car. Devereaux closed the door and stood in the parking lot until the patrol car arrived. He talked to the officers for a minute, watched as they scooped the taller guy up off the ground and drove away, then got in behind the wheel.

"Good decision." Devereaux slid the key into the ignition, but held off from starting the engine. "Now, let's start with your name."

"Taylor. Taylor May."

"All right, Taylor, let's see some ID."

The guy pulled a driver's license out of his pants pocket and handed it to Devereaux.

"This says you're twenty-one. Is that right?"

The guy nodded.

"And you live in Chicago, Illinois?"

"No." The guy looked away. "Not anymore. I'm from Chicago, but I just moved here a month ago. I haven't gotten around to swapping out my license yet."

"You don't sound like you're from Chicago." Devereaux stressed the middle syllable.

The guy shrugged. "I pick up accents quick, I guess."

"I guess you do." Devereaux gestured to the license. "So, Lakeview Avenue? Sounds like a nice address. I went to Chicago once. Good city, I thought. I don't remember that street, though. Where is it? East side, I guess? Not the west side, where all the gang problems are?"

"Right. East side."

"Good. And how about those skyscrapers? I loved them. But remind me, which is the crazy tall one—the Citicorp, or the Chrysler?"

"The Citicorp."

"OK. So that gives you two problems. First, do you know another name for the east side of Chicago?"

"Uptown?"

"Try Lake Michigan. There is no east side. And those two buildings? They're both in New York. So you know what I think? You're not twenty-one. You bought a fake ID to get into bars. And it's from Illinois because they're the easiest to forge. Am I right?"

The guy closed his eyes, then nodded.

"OK." Devereaux kept his voice calm and level. "Let's start again with your real name."

"It's Mike Jedinak."

"And your address?"

"1902, 3rd Avenue, Pleasant Grove. Are you going to tell my parents about this?"

Devereaux pulled out his notebook and wrote the guy's details down. "How old are you, Mike?"

"Seventeen."

"Then, no. I'm not going to tell them. There'd be no point. You're at an age where you have to figure things out for yourself. You've obviously made some poor decisions, up to now. Surrounded yourself with the wrong kind of people. Which means you have to decide—do you want to carry on down that same path? In which case you'll end up either dead, or in jail. I guarantee. Or do you want to turn your life around? Which won't be easy, but will at least give you a shot at a future."

Jedinak stared out of the side window.

"I know." Devereaux paused. "You're thinking, *who does this old guy think he is, telling me what to do?* Well, I'm not telling you what to do. I'm offering to help, if you want me to. Because believe it or not, I've walked in your shoes. Only the shit I waded through was way deeper. I had no parents, for one thing. And some of the crap I pulled? You simply couldn't get away with it these days. The only reason I survived was that I had help. A guy—a police officer, actually—looked out for me. And I'm willing to do the same thing for you."

Jedinak turned to look at Devereaux. His face was blank, and he still didn't say anything.

"Here." Devereaux held out his card. "Take this. Memorize the details. And if you ever need help, call me. OK?"

"I guess." Jedinak reached out his hand.

"Just be clear about one thing." Devereaux didn't let go of the card right away, holding it tight until Jedinak met his gaze. "This isn't a free pass. I'll be talking to the officers who patrol this area, all the time. And if you put one toe over the line, I'll come back and throw you in jail myself."

"I get it." Jedinak jammed the license back into his pocket, along with Devereaux's card.

"Good." Devereaux's finger hovered over the button that unlocked the doors. "Because this isn't a one-way street, either. If you see my number come up on your phone, you better answer. I might have a little job for you to do, from time to time. And you better not ever let me down."

Chapter Twenty-seven

Sunday. Early morning.

SICK BUILDING SYNDROME IS A THING, RIGHT? DEVEREAUX THOUGHT as he rode up in the elevator. *So what about Sick Room Syndrome? Could that be a thing, too?*

Devereaux didn't loathe the whole headquarters building. Parts of it were fine. The spacious suite on the third floor where the detectives had their desks, for example. But the fourth-floor conference room? It was an appalling place. Devereaux hated going to it. Maybe all the boring bureaucratic briefings he'd been subjected to over the years had left some kind of psychic residue behind. Maybe the crime scene photographs and other pieces of evidence they taped to its walls at the height of their most complex cases had tainted it with the implied human wickedness. Or maybe it was just because the room was so badly furnished and equipped. Take the blinds that were supposed to cover the wide expanse of windows as an example. They were hopelessly twisted and broken, leaving everyone on one side of the long conference table with no protection from the sun. And everyone on the other side with nothing but their willpower to stop them from gazing outside.

Never look out of the window in the first half of a briefing, a long-serving detective had told Devereaux the day he'd got his shield.

Why not? Devereaux almost blushed to think how naïve he'd been back then.

Because then you'll have nothing to do in the second half . . .

With Garretty still in the hospital, Devereaux was first to arrive. He took a seat, sipped his coffee, and was joined after a couple of minutes by Lieutenant Hale and two visitors: Special Agent Linda Irvin, profile coordinator with the FBI's Birmingham Field Office, and Donald Young, Battalion Chief with the Birmingham Fire and Rescue Department. Devereaux had worked with both of them before— recently—so Hale skipped the introductions and got right down to business.

"Did anyone see the papers this morning?"

Everyone shook heads.

Hale pulled a copy of the *Tribune* out of her briefcase and held it up in front of her. "They started with the Birthday Killer. Now the press is calling him B/DK, after that BTK asshole Dennis Rader in Kansas. It's all over the web, too, of course. And there have been pictures. The way the bodies were wrapped up has really caught people's imaginations. Speculation is running wild. It's turning to panic. Twenty-year-olds with birthdays coming up are freaking out. So are their parents. Even people who've recently turned twenty-one. Parties are getting canceled. Bars are complaining. So are restaurants and stores. We've had all kinds of false reports phoned in. The mayor's putting pressure on the captain, and you all know what that means. He wants to announce that we've caught the killer. Which I'd be delighted for him to do—as long as we really have. Which is why I asked you all to come in this morning. I need to know—is Billy Flynn our guy? And what about the fire at his house? Was that a coincidence? An accident? Arson? Or what? Chief? Maybe you could get the ball rolling."

Young pulled a sheet of paper out of his messenger bag, stood, and stuck it on the wall, near the door. "This is a floor plan of Flynn's house. The degree of damage is indicated by the color: Red is the most severe, through orange, to yellow. As you can see, the rear of the house was hit the hardest. That's where the kitchen was. But we don't think that's where the fire started. The point of origin was most likely the living room, where the victim was found. That's where the initial ignition occurred, and then the flames spread from there."

"Was it started deliberately?" Hale asked.

"I'm not signing off on this yet because I still need the results of more tests, but the preliminary indications are consistent with the fire resulting from a gas leak. It started high. It spread fast. And the worst of the damage was in the kitchen, where the range was. This is what I think happened. It's pretty simple. Mr. Flynn came home. He went into the living room. Lit a cigarette. And—boom."

"And the gas leak," Devereaux said. "Was it accidental? Or was something tampered with?"

"It's too soon to say. I'm waiting on the lab. We sent them the remains of the range, and they're still examining it. Don't hold your breath, though. It was badly dinged up. And the perennial problem with arson investigation, as you know, is that fire destroys its own evidence. And if this was something as simple as opening a gas tap, there won't even be any evidence. This isn't like searching for traces of accelerant, which is much easier to find."

"Don't ranges have some kind of safety feature to stop gas pouring out and collecting?" Irvin rubbed the small of her back.

"Newer ones have. Or should have. But Flynn's range was old. And that kind of safety mechanism can easily be defeated, with just a little technical knowledge."

"This whole question is really bugging me." Devereaux frowned.

"We show up to arrest Flynn for murder, and his house chooses that exact moment to blow up? Try and sell me a coincidence like that, and my hackles are up instantly. But on the other hand, what motive could there have been for someone to torch the house?"

"Could a relative of one of the victims have figured out he was the killer?" Irvin said. "Or found out we were looking at him? And decided to take matters into their own hands?"

"Possibly." Hale sounded hesitant. "I'll have some uniforms canvass the neighbors, see if they noticed anyone going in or out. But causing a gas leak is so indiscriminate. What if someone else triggered the explosion?"

"Flynn's mother doesn't smoke," Devereaux said.

"But she could have been in the house when Billy lit up," Irvin said. "So could the kid brother. That would mean at least running the risk of taking both of them out, as well as Flynn. That indicates a whole other level of ruthless. Let me think about that. See how it fits the profile."

"So are we leaning toward it being an accident?" Hale asked. "How about you, Chief? If you were pressed, which side would you come down on?"

"It's impossible to say, Lieutenant. It's even money. I can't do better than that."

"I understand. Thanks anyway, Chief. I really appreciate you giving up your Sunday morning to help us. You'll let us know when you hear from the lab?"

Young nodded then excused himself, and when the door had closed behind him Hale turned to Devereaux.

"Any word on Flynn's condition?"

Devereaux shook his head. "There's no change from yesterday. He's still unconscious. They have no idea how long he'll be out for. And he's pretty messed up. There's no guarantee he'll wake up at all."

"Did you get anything useful from the mother?"

"Nada. She claims he didn't know either victim. Aside from that, it was the usual mother crap. He was a hard worker. He did what he was told. He wouldn't hurt a fly. You get the picture. I did press her on his juvie record, though. According to her, when Flynn was fifteen, he broke into his high school. Surprise, surprise, he got caught. He was accused of B and E, vandalism, the usual stuff. The public defender had him play it like a prank gone wrong, which might not have been a terrible idea because Flynn got off with a warning. But his mother had a different explanation for why he did it. She said he was tired of the other kids always calling him stupid, so he was trying to sneak a peek at the questions for an upcoming test. She said he just wanted to get a better grade."

"So he was enterprising, at least," Hale said.

"Did you ask her about the significance of the twenty-first birthdays?" Irvin asked.

"I did." Devereaux shrugged. "She had no idea, so I tried prompting her a little. I suggested that maybe he'd been dumped by a girlfriend on her twenty-first birthday. Or rejected by a girl at her twenty-first-birthday party. Or bought a girl a really thoughtful present, which she'd scorned. Things like that. But she said Billy had never had anything to do with any girls. Cars, yes. Guns, yes. Girls, no. That was her verdict. I asked about male friends, too, and she said he didn't really have any. Only Lucas Paltrow, who's obviously older. She said Paltrow is about the only person ever to be nice to Billy, or to try to help him."

Irvin pressed her fingertips against her temples for a moment, then dropped her hands to the table. "I just wish we could talk to him. I have to say, though, he does sound like a candidate. From what I can tell from the crime scenes and the victims themselves, we're looking for someone who can be overtaken by anger that is driven by feelings of rejection and not being appreciated. But not someone who has no conscience at all. Whoever he is, he feels deep remorse after the frenzy has worn off. We can tell that by the way he wraps his victims, covers their modesty, and leaves them in places associated with taking care of the dead."

"Cooper?" Hale brushed a loose strand of hair away from her eyes. "You don't look convinced."

"No." Devereaux held up his hands. "It's not that. Everything Linda said makes perfect sense. I'd just be happier if we could tie up some of the loose ends, and the fire makes that so much harder. What if Flynn killed the women at his house? Without a confession we'll never find out. Their clothes and possessions could have been there. We haven't found those yet. And the bedding. Now we can't match his sheets with the ones from the crime scenes. It's so frustrating."

"Here's an idea," Hale said. "It might be crazy, but we've heard that Flynn might have been a couple sandwiches short of a picnic. What if he realized we were closing in, tried to torch the house himself to get rid of the evidence, and blew himself up with it by mistake?"

"That's possible," Irvin said. "But unless Young pulls a rabbit out of his hat, we'll never know without talking to Flynn."

"What about the witness?" Hale asked. "Didn't she report seeing Flynn abducting the second victim?"

"Mrs. Goodman described someone generically similar to Flynn," Devereaux said. "We'd need to show her a photograph to be sure. Any photographs that were in the house were burned up. And his face is all covered with bandages now, so we can't get a new one."

"What about the car?" Irvin asked. "The one that belongs to that celebrity guy? Were Flynn's prints found in it?"

"They were." Devereaux nodded. "But he drove it to the celebrity guy's house. And that's another weird thing. His were the only prints. There were none of the owner's. And none of the victim's. So that doesn't help us, either."

"OK." Hale rubbed her chin. "I still have a good feeling about Flynn, but I agree there are too many unanswered questions for us to be certain. I'll keep the captain away from the press for as long as I can. Linda, can you keep working on the profile? See if you can pin down why these particular women were targeted. Cooper, see if you can figure out where their paths crossed with the killer's."

"Will do, Lieutenant. I'll talk to Deborah Holt's mother again. We're trying to track down Siobhan O'Keefe's parents as well, so I'll chase them up."

"Good. Any other ideas?"

"Yes," Devereaux said. "Two things. I've reached out to some fences I know to see if we can get any hits on the women's missing jewelry. And I'm going to take another look at Lucas Paltrow's alibi for Thursday afternoon, when Deborah Holt disappeared. He showed me tickets for the movie theater, but that doesn't mean he necessarily went."

"Good. Keep me posted. And Cooper—one more thing. If you see any more infernos, stay away from them. The captain wanted to suspend you for ignoring departmental protocol. And honestly, for once he had a point. It wouldn't have helped Fire and Rescue if you'd given them a second body to drag out of there. And it wouldn't have helped me if you were benched again. We're just lucky the press showed up when they did. It wouldn't have looked good to punish Birmingham's newest TV hero."

Chapter *Twenty-eight*

Sunday. Morning.

ALEXANDRA CHOSE THE REARMOST PEW AT THE TRINITY PRESBYTE-rian Church for the second week running.

That day she knew Devereaux wouldn't be joining her, so she wasted no time hanging around in the shade of her favorite oak tree, waiting for him. She just parked her Range Rover at the side of the lot, dragged Nicole past the line of spherical bushes at the side of the driveway that she normally liked to run and hide between, and hurried inside the simple, single-story building. There were still ten minutes before the organ was due to begin playing. Nicole had no problem passing the time. As usual she'd brought a couple of Barbies with her, and quickly set about continuing whatever scenario she'd sketched out for them. Alexandra glanced at her daughter to check that everything was OK, and after dismissing a flash of frustration when she noticed that one of the dolls had lost an arm—they were made far more robustly when she'd been a child, she was sure, because none of hers had ever broken—she settled herself and tried to clear her mind ahead of the sermon.

The preacher's words were a disappointment to her. Normally

she found that whatever topic he chose, however obscure it may seem at the outset, it wound up shining a helpful light on some aspect of her life. Often she hadn't even realized it was something she was struggling with and marveled at his almost telepathic ability to sense the areas that were troubling her before the symptoms came to the surface. But that day, his message missed the mark. It was as if she'd strayed into a lecture on some obscure branch of science—she recognized the words as English, but none had any discernible meaning. She felt only numbness on the drive home rather than the . . . what, relief? absolution? she'd hoped for, though she was beginning to give the preacher the benefit of the doubt as she turned in to her street. What words could compete with what had happened the night before? She was so distracted by the question that it took her a moment to recognize the Lexus that was parked at the curb in front of her house.

Alexandra opened the door from the garage to the backyard, sent Nicole out to play, then reluctantly made her way to the driveway.

Tim Jensen climbed out of the Lexus holding a folder that was a good half-inch thick. "How are you doing this morning? I was worried about you after last night. Then when I got here I was worried you'd left town!"

"I'm fine." Alexandra crossed her arms. "I was just at church. It was nice of you to think of me. But you were there last night, too. How are you doing?"

Jensen shivered despite the warm morning sun. "I'm still a little freaked out, to be honest. When that guy pulled a gun on us? It was horrible. I couldn't sleep a wink. I gave up trying in the end. So I pulled this together for you instead." Jensen held out the folder. "I hope it'll help with the thing you're working on. I should have focused on that all along, instead of tricking you into coming to dinner with me. I'm sorry I put you through that, Alex."

"Thank you." Alexandra took the folder. "I appreciate your help. I'll read this cover to cover as soon as I've given Nicole her lunch. But listen. Last night, you didn't put me through anything. And you didn't trick me. I chose to come."

"I guess." Jensen looked thoroughly miserable. "I just keep replaying the whole thing in my head. And part of me feels so stupid. The guy didn't even have a real gun. I had no idea."

"The gun looked real enough to me, too." *When you were trying to use me as a human shield,* Alexandra was tempted to add.

"And he was so young. Did you see his face when his mask fell off? He couldn't have been more than seventeen or eighteen."

"Why does that matter? Do you think someone can't pull a trigger just because they're—" Alexandra stopped herself. All she could think of was Devereaux, eight years before, seeing a teenager with a gun—a real gun—pointing at his partner's head. How Devereaux had responded. And the damage the fallout from that incident had caused to their lives. "You know what, Tim? I think we should leave this here. Thanks for getting involved. I truly appreciate your assistance. But I don't think I can be around you for a while."

Chapter *Twenty-nine*

Sunday. Morning.

DEVEREAUX LEFT THE CONFERENCE ROOM WHILE LIEUTENANT HALE was still wrapping up some small talk with Agent Irvin. His plan was to leave the building and go knock on some doors, but before he was halfway along the fourth-floor corridor his phone rang. It was the officer on duty in reception. Devereaux had a visitor.

There was only one person waiting when Devereaux stepped out of the elevator, sitting on the first of the four pale blue chairs opposite the counter. A woman, in her early twenties. She was thin without being skinny, and when she stood up to shake his hand Devereaux guessed she was no more than five feet tall. She had on a dark blue cardigan over a flowery sundress with an embroidered neckline, as well as a pearl necklace and matching earrings. Next to her, tucked in neatly at the side of her chair, was a floral-patterned rolling suitcase.

"Detective Devereaux?" The woman pushed a long braid of brown hair back over her shoulder. "I'm Niamh O'Keefe. Siobhan's sister. Is there somewhere we could talk?"

The interview rooms were all available, but Devereaux chose not to use any of them. Not right away, at least. Instead he led the woman back up in the elevator to his desk, wheeled Garretty's chair around for her to use, and gave her a moment to settle herself.

"Thanks for giving up your time this morning, Ms. O'Keefe." Devereaux gestured to the suitcase. "Did you have far to travel?"

"From Atlanta." O'Keefe blinked several times. "I live there with my parents. I was with them when we got the news about Siobhan . . ."

"That must have been very hard on you all." Devereaux paused for a moment. "I was hoping to talk to your parents, as well. Did they come to Birmingham with you?"

"No. They stayed home. I came on my own."

"Are your parents older? Not up to the trip?"

"No. It's not that." O'Keefe looked away, blinking rapidly. "It's just—they kind of disowned Siobhan. They refuse to have anything to do with her. Even now. But I figured someone should come. Oh God. Her body. Will I have to identify her?"

"We'll get to that. Try not to think about it for a moment. First of all, I'm sorry to hear that things have been rocky at home. I'm grateful you came here anyway. Now, we're still trying to piece together exactly what happened to your sister. We have someone in custody— well, in the hospital—who we think is responsible, but we have to be sure. So, would it be OK if I ask you a few questions? The more we know about Siobhan, the better we understand her as a person, the sooner we can wrap everything up. Make sure we have the right guy."

"Sure. I guess." O'Keefe fumbled in her purse, took the last Kleenex from a multicolored travel pack, and blew her nose. "What do you need to know?"

"Let's start with your family situation, if that's OK? What happened between Siobhan and your parents to make them disown her?"

"It was the baby. You have to understand, my parents are weird. They're totally old-fashioned. So when Siobhan told them she was pregnant—they just couldn't handle it. They weren't trying to be mean. It's just—they're from a different world."

"Your sister was pregnant? When was this? There was no sign of a baby or a child at her house."

"It was two years ago. She had the baby, if that's what you're driving at. A beautiful little boy. I was with her at the birth. Only with everything that was happening—her boyfriend was a complete flake, our parents were so down on her, she'd just started a new job—she couldn't keep him. So she gave him up. She had him adopted. I think part of her hoped that if she did that, our parents would come around. Maybe they would have, given more time."

"Do you know which adoption agency she used?"

"I'm sorry." O'Keefe wiped her eyes. "I don't remember. I met the woman who was organizing the whole thing, and I know she was very nice, but I can't recall her name. Is it important?"

"Probably not. Just covering all the bases. What about Siobhan's boyfriend. The baby's father. Is he still on the scene?"

"Goodness, no. They split up before the baby was born. Siobhan decided to go the adoption route, and Kevin was furious. He wanted them to keep the kid. Get married. The whole nine yards. Can you believe it? When she broke the news, he went totally AWOL. She didn't see him for weeks. Had to do all the prenatal stuff on her own, because I was in Atlanta and of course Mom wouldn't get involved. Then he reappears with all kinds of unrealistic expectations and was pissed when she wouldn't go along with them."

"Did he contact her afterward? Try to get back together? Threaten her? Anything like that?"

"At first he did. She said he called her sometimes, when he was drunk. Sometimes he was mad at her and wanted to yell. Sometimes he was sloppy and begged her for another chance. But I don't think he's done it for a while. Probably lost interest, or found someone else."

"What was this guy's name? Kevin?"

"Right. Kevin McAuley."

"Do you remember his address?"

O'Keefe nodded. "I have it in my phone."

"Excellent." Devereaux passed her his notebook. "Can you write it down for me? Just in case we need to ask him any follow-up questions."

"I guess. But I don't want to get him in any trouble, if he hasn't done anything wrong."

"Don't worry. If he's done nothing wrong, then he's got nothing to worry about."

O'Keefe scrawled the details in Devereaux's notebook and handed it back to him.

"Thanks. I know this is hard, but I just have a couple more questions. You mentioned Siobhan had a job. Where did she work?"

"At the McWane science place. She was a receptionist. It wasn't her original plan. She came to Birmingham to go to college, but dropped out. Daddy didn't approve of anything that smacked of giving up, so she started working there temporarily to buy some time to figure out how to tell them. Turned out she liked it there. She decided to stay on."

"Was there anyone there she didn't get on with?"

"I don't think so. We talked on the phone all the time, and she never mentioned anything like that."

"What about socially? Did she have problems with any other boyfriends?"

"No. After the baby thing she pretty much stopped socializing. She did go to a party a couple Saturdays ago at a coworker's house, but she didn't like what was going on there. She was home in bed by nine-thirty."

"What was going on? Did she say?"

"She did, but I don't know if I should tell you. She wouldn't have wanted to get anyone in trouble. She was . . ." A tear dripped down onto the collar of O'Keefe's cardigan before she could wipe it away. "She was such a kind person."

"Don't worry." Devereaux opened his desk drawer, took out a

fresh box of Kleenex, and handed it to her. "You can tell me. The only thing I'm interested in is making sure we've caught the guy who killed your sister. Anything else, it goes no further than here. I guarantee."

"OK." O'Keefe took a moment to blow her nose and compose herself. "Well. The thing is, Siobhan said there were people at the party who were smoking drugs. In fact, she said everyone there was smoking drugs. Apart from her. She didn't want to. There was pressure. She felt uncomfortable. That's why she came home. She wasn't judging. And like I say, she wouldn't have wanted to get anyone in trouble."

"That's it? People were smoking at the party?"

"Isn't that a bad thing?"

"Well, yes. It is. Your sister was right not to participate. Walking away was the sensible thing to do. She was obviously a very strong person."

"She was."

"Did she ever mention knowing a guy named Billy Flynn? He could have gone by William, or Bill?"

"No. I don't think so. Who is that?"

"What about her car? Did she ever have work done on its audio system? Any upgrades? Or electrical repairs of any kind?"

"No." O'Keefe sniffed. "She liked her car. She took it in for oil changes and what have you religiously, every six months. And she didn't need a new stereo. The car already had a good one. And it never broke down or anything."

"What about a woman named Deborah Holt? She was the same age. She lived in Birmingham. And worked at a company called Invetrade, in the Empire building downtown."

"That name doesn't ring a bell, either. I'm sorry."

"It's no problem. I just have one more name for you. Oliver Casey. He plays the guitar. Mainly goes by *Thor,* apparently."

"Thor? No way. I'd have remembered him."

"OK. You've been very helpful, Niamh. I just have one last question. Friday was Siobhan's twenty-first birthday. That's kind of a big deal. Did she have any plans to celebrate it?"

"No. We talked about it. She didn't want to do anything with her coworkers, because of the drug problem. She couldn't come home to Atlanta, because of our parents. I offered to come here and take her out to dinner, but she said no. She wanted us to save up, instead. She had this crazy plan for next summer." O'Keefe looked away and dabbed her eyes, struggling to hold back more tears. "Siobhan wanted us to go to Europe. She is—was—a huge *Game of Thrones* fan, you see. So she wanted to go to Dubrovnik, which is in Croatia, I think, and visit the places where they film it."

Devereaux let Niamh O'Keefe reminisce about her sister for another few minutes, and when he was confident she had nothing else to add that would help the investigation, he escorted her back to reception. Then he returned to the third floor and knocked on Lieutenant Hale's office door.

"Lieutenant, we need to call Linda Irvin back. There's another overlap between the victims. It's not just the age thing. They both gave up babies for adoption. That can't just be a coincidence . . ."

Dear Mom,

Lucas Paltrow is the worst person in the world. He literally is. You wouldn't believe how mean he is. How thoughtless. Inconsiderate. Manipulative. He's just a taker! I mean, sure, if he's doing something fun he'll include me. But beyond that, if he wants something done, who does he ask? Me. Well, <u>ask</u> probably isn't the right word. It's not like I could say no. Not unless I want to be left out altogether. So I help. I do what he <u>asks</u> me to do. But here's the thing. It has to be exactly on his terms. If I do something like, say, ask him <u>why</u> he wants me to do something, what does he do? Does he tell me? Let me into the secret? No. He gets mad. He yells at me. Like when he told me to babysit the halfwit who works for him while he went out for half an hour. He was so specific. Stay here, he said. Make sure Billy stays here, too. DO NOT LET HIM LEAVE. Not even for a second. Don't let him out of your sight. OK, Lucas, I say. No problem. I'll do that. But how come? Where are you going? Honestly, Mom, I thought he was going to hit me. It's OK to leave me shut in with a cretin who has the conversational skills of a wheelbarrow, but not to tell me why? What's the point? Why leave me in the dark? What does he get out of it?

Chapter *Thirty*

Sunday. Morning.

DEVEREAUX SUMMONED UP HIS MENTAL MAP OF THE CITY AND TOOK A minute to figure out how best to adjust the route he'd planned for the day, now that he had an extra stop to make. He definitely wanted to end up at an address in Vestavia Hills, so that he could take his time on the final task he had in mind without feeling pressure to hurry off somewhere else. He'd already factored in stops at Deborah Holt's mother's and Dean Sullivan's—the guy who Lucas Paltrow claimed to have gone to the movies with—but those would both be follow-up calls. The information about Kevin McAuley, Siobhan O'Keefe's ex-boyfriend, was new. The guy sounded like he had a temper, so Devereaux figured it was worth having a conversation with him first.

McAuley was blinking like a zoo animal that had been woken too early from hibernation when he finally answered Devereaux's knock.

"I didn't buzz you in," McAuley grunted, somehow managing to sound indignant and half-asleep at the same time. "How'd you get in the building? Who the hell are you?"

It was true that McAuley hadn't responded to his buzzer. None of the building's residents had. There were eight, and Devereaux had tried them all. But that wasn't a problem. The entrance to the building was halfway down a narrow driveway leading off the street. No windows overlooked it, and there was no sign of any cameras, so it had only taken Devereaux a few seconds to open the outer door with a credit card he carried specially for the purpose. Then he'd picked his way through the mounds of bills and catalogs that were scattered across the black-and-white-tiled floor of the entrance lobby and turned his attention to the inner glass door that led to the stairwell.

"Kevin McAuley?" Devereaux showed his badge. "Birmingham PD. I need to ask you a couple of questions. Mind if I come in?"

Devereaux pushed the door, forcing McAuley to move back, and stepped after him into the apartment's inner hallway. The floor was covered with paper-thin brown carpet. The walls were pale green. They looked recently painted, and there were no pictures or posters hanging anywhere. The one bedroom was to the right. The shades were pulled across its window, but Devereaux could still make out a queen bed beneath a knot of unmade turquoise sheets. There was a built-in closet, its door open, nothing on the rail but a bunch of clothes heaped on the floor, some spilling out into the space at the foot of the bed. Four beer bottles were perched haphazardly on the nightstand. And there was a ceiling fan, slowly spinning.

"Hey!" McAuley grunted.

Devereaux continued as far as the living room. A bay window looked out over the street, and the trees that lined the sidewalk made the room feel dark and enclosed. It was hard to see out. Or in, Devereaux guessed. The fireplace was filled with giant candles. There was a bookcase on either side, though McAuley had just one book—a thick, hardcover bible. A narrow couch was the only other piece of furniture, with a filthy tartan blanket flung across it. A TV was balanced on an old packing crate by the opposite wall, and a door in the far corner led to a dark kitchen. Devereaux could smell the odor of rotting food. He didn't want to think what the countertops or refrigerator would be like.

"Come in." McAuley gestured sarcastically. "Make yourself at home. And tell me. What do you want?"

"I have a couple of questions for you. About Siobhan."

"I don't know who that is." McAuley inched back toward the door.

"It's Sunday today, and on the Sabbath I normally try not to beat anyone senseless until after lunch. In your case, though, I'd be happy to make an exception. Siobhan had your child. So don't be disrespectful. And don't lie to me again."

"Oh—you mean *Siobhan*." McAuley threw up his arms. "I always called her Vonnie. That's why I was slow to catch on. What do you want to know?"

"When did you last see her?"

"Oh, wow. It must have been, like, two years ago. When she was pregnant. Her parents didn't approve of me and she didn't have the backbone to stand up to them, so we pretty much parted ways."

"And when did you last speak to her?"

"I don't know, exactly. Somewhere around the same time, I guess."

"You're lying again, Kevin. I know you called her. More than once. Sometimes you threatened her. Sometimes you begged. Depending on—" Devereaux sniffed the air "—whether you were drunk or stoned."

McAuley leaned against the wall. "OK. We talked on the phone. Sure. I thought you meant, like, face-to-face, when you said *talked*."

"I'll let that go if you tell me when you last saw Deborah Holt."

"I don't know who that is." McAuley brought his arms up to protect the sides of his head. "Really! I don't. Please don't go crazy."

"OK. In that case, where were you on Friday afternoon?"

"Why?"

"Where were you?"

"I was here."

"What were you doing?"

"Watching TV."

"What was on?"

"*Survivor.* I DVR'd it."

"Who got voted off?"

"I don't know. I fell asleep before the end."

"Can anyone confirm you were here?"

"No. I was on my own."

"OK. What about Thursday afternoon? Where were you then?"

"Same thing. I was here."

"Alone again?"

"That's right."

Devereaux picked up a coffee cup from the floor next to the couch. The dregs were congealing in it, but were still semi-liquid. And there was lipstick on the rim.

"So I had female company." McAuley took a step toward Devereaux. "So what? She's married, so we're keeping it on the DL. What's that to Siobhan? What's she saying I've done? Because let me tell you, she's no angel. How do you think we met? But listen. I was ready to give all this up for her. Straighten myself out. Get a job. Be a father. And a husband, if she'd have me. I wanted that kid! But she wasn't interested. She gave my baby away so she could carry on partying, or whatever she's up to these days."

"This female who was keeping you company. She was here Friday afternoon?"

"Yes." McAuley slumped back against the wall. "She leaves work early Fridays. Comes over at lunchtime and stays all afternoon. That way she can get home at her regular time, and her husband doesn't suspect a thing."

"I'll need her name and contact details."

"No way." McAuley held his hands out. "Her husband's a monster. If he finds out, he'll kill me."

"You should have thought of that before you started sleeping with his wife." Devereaux took out his notebook. "Here are your options. Give me her name and contact details. Or I'll take you to jail."

"For what?" McAuley crossed his arms. "I haven't done anything illegal."

Devereaux crossed to the bookcase and picked up the bible. "This looks familiar. I have one around the same size." He opened the book and revealed a compartment full of bags of dope and pills. "It looks like we're going with option B. Taking you to jail."

"No, wait." McAuley moved closer to the bookcase. "I can explain. That bible's not mine. I didn't know there was anything inside. It was here when I moved in, and I never even opened it."

"This is your last chance, Kevin." Devereaux took his handcuffs out of the leather pouch on his belt. "Give me the name of someone who can alibi you for Friday."

"OK." McAuley's body sagged. "OK. I'll tell you. Just please, try to be discreet. Why's this so important, anyway?"

"It's important because Siobhan was murdered on Friday."

"Holy shit." McAuley stepped back, his eyes suddenly wide and full of fear, and he reached out to lean on the wall for support. "And you think I did it?"

"Maybe." Devereaux dangled the cuffs from his finger. "You were pissed about what she did with your kid. You said so."

"Not that pissed!" McAuley's eyes bulged even wider. "I'm over it. I've got a good thing going here. No way would I risk it over paying back some ex."

"We'll see." Devereaux stopped swinging the cuffs. "In the meantime, give me a good reason not to take you in for the dope."

"Come on, Detective." McAuley sounded like a kid wheedling for more candy. "That's just for personal use. It's not like I'm a big-time dealer or something."

"You never help out a friend? Or a friend of a friend, maybe?"

"You know how it is. A buddy might come over, once in a blue moon. We might get a little mellow together. But nothing beyond that. I swear."

Devereaux moved back to the couch and took hold of a sleeve that was peeping out from underneath. He pulled it out. It belonged to a hoodie. The pink camo pattern was similar to ones he'd seen in the kids' and teens' sections of clothing stores he'd been to with Alexandra and Nicole. And it was small. It would barely fit a fifteen-year-old, if that.

"Does this belong to your female companion?" Devereaux grabbed McAuley by the throat. "Are you sure it's not school she's missing, not work? And her mom she's keeping you a secret from, not her husband?"

"No!" McAuley tried to wriggle free. "No. Someone else left that. She was here for a different reason."

"A customer?" Devereaux didn't loosen his grip.

"No." McAuley grabbed the hand Devereaux was holding on to him with. "She's a buddy's little sister. He was supposed to be watching her, but his girlfriend—"

"Forget it." Devereaux spun McAuley around and grabbed his wrist. "You're getting arrested."

"OK." McAuley stopped struggling. "Go ahead. Take me in. How long do you think I'll be in the cell for? I have a lawyer. He'll get me straight back out. And then I'll sue you for wrongful arrest."

"You know what?" Devereaux secured the first cuff. "You might be right. You might get straight back out. But I have to give the system a chance to do its job. After that, all bets are off."

"What does that mean?"

"My partner's not with me today. He's in the hospital. He got hurt trying to catch the scumbag who killed Siobhan. But if he was here, I'm pretty sure he'd tell you a story about one of his first cases. So I'll tell you a story about one of mine, instead. Actually, it's about a cop I once knew. He was a big influence on my career. The biggest, in fact. Now, this guy, he had a particular way of working. He under-stood that justice and the law aren't always the same thing. Some-times the system needs a little help. Here's an example. He once locked up an asshole who sold drugs to kids. The asshole beat the rap. The cop came back after a couple of days. The asshole was up to his old tricks again. And then he disappeared. His body was found in an abandoned furnace. No one knows how it got there. No one wasted any time trying to find out. Because here's the thing. No one cares about small-time asshole dealers. They can take major ass kick-ings—or wind up dead—and no one even notices."

Chapter *Thirty-one*

Sunday. Late morning.

DEVEREAUX HAD CALLED FOR TWO BACKUP UNITS. ONE TO TAKE MCAU-ley into custody and another to secure his apartment until the crime scene guys could process it. The second patrol car had taken forever to arrive, which left Devereaux seething with impatience, so as a result he took 20 and 280 to get to Mrs. Holt's house. Avoiding the residential streets in that way added a little distance, and given the lightness of the traffic due to most people still being at church, there was no guarantee it saved any time. But it did enable Devereaux to be more generous with the gas, and the sensation of moving fast always made him feel better.

Devereaux eased the Porsche into the narrow driveway and rolled down the gentle slope, coming to a stop just in front of the entrance to Mrs. Holt's garage. The structure was framed by tall, mature trees, and their leaves splashed four distinct shades of green against the clear blue of the sky. Devereaux sat for a moment and gazed up at the star-shaped pattern left by half a dozen planes' contrails. He was suddenly reluctant to get out of the car. He hated dealing with griev-ing relatives. They could be so unpredictable. He wished Garretty was there. He was so much better in situations that called for high degrees of sensitivity. As it was, all Devereaux could do was hope that whatever the outcome—strike out, or hit the jackpot—the visit wouldn't drag on for too long.

There was no answer when Devereaux rang the doorbell.

"Mrs. Holt?" He tried knocking, instead. "It's Detective Devereaux. We met on Friday. I have a couple more questions I need to ask you. It won't take long, I promise."

There was still no response from inside the house. The driveway had been empty when he arrived, but it had also been that way on Friday when Mrs. Holt was home. Plus it was dotted with oil stains, suggesting that was where Deborah used to keep her old Chevy. Devereaux moved to the side of the garage and peered in through the window. The glass was grimy, but he could make out the shape of a car parked inside. A Toyota Camry. Not the latest model. Was it possible that Mrs. Holt had taken a walk somewhere? Devereaux doubted it. She'd told him she wasn't a churchgoer, and there weren't any stores nearby. Or parks, if you assumed that Mrs. Holt didn't have the legs for the climb up to Vulcan, which was the only place nearby worth visiting.

Devereaux returned to the front door and rang the bell one more time. Then he pulled out his phone and dialed Mrs. Holt's number. He could hear the old-fashioned jangle of the ringer coming from somewhere inside the house, but the call tripped over to an answering machine without being picked up.

Mrs. Holt didn't have any family. She hadn't mentioned any friends. She hadn't driven anywhere. And there was nowhere to walk to. Where could she have gone? If she'd gone anywhere. Devereaux hurried across the lawn toward the street. The neatly cut, brownish grass crunched slightly beneath his feet, and he noticed that scrawny strands of ivy were trying to make their way up the post that supported Mrs. Holt's mailbox. He reached it and looked inside. There was a late birthday card for Deborah. Two bills. And an event invitation from the Civil Rights Institute. They must have been there since the previous day, as there's no delivery on Sunday. Was Mrs. Holt the kind of person to leave her mail out for twenty-four hours? She hadn't struck Devereaux that way. Although grief can change how people behave, of course.

Another thought struck Devereaux as he walked back toward the house. He took his phone back out of his pocket and pulled up the photograph he'd taken of the text Deborah had sent her mother. That showed Mrs. Holt's cell number, so he tried giving it a call. It took much longer to connect than the landline had, but as he reached the front door once again he could hear ringing from somewhere inside the house. Ringing, but no answer. He waited for voicemail to kick in, then followed the path around the side of the building. The first window he came to looked into the living room. The room seemed neat and cozy, just as it had on Friday. Next up was the kitchen. Everything in there looked orderly, too. There was a bowl on the draining rack, and a mug and a spoon. Two bananas and an apple nestled in the fruit basket. A clean tea towel was hanging on the rail. Nothing was broken. Nothing was out of place.

Still uneasy, Devereaux turned and started to make his way back to his car. He was probably worrying about nothing, he told himself. Mrs. Holt probably just wanted some privacy, after what had happened to her daughter. She was probably too grief stricken to talk to anyone. He took a deep breath and let it out slowly, trying to shake the feeling that he was missing something. Then he stopped dead. The cats! Where were they? There was no sign of them. Or their litter trays. Their water bowls. The pretty embroidered mats where Mrs. Holt gave them their food . . .

Devereaux found Mrs. Holt in her bed, in her room next to Deborah's on the second floor. She was propped up on a mound of pillows, looking for all the world as if she was peacefully asleep. Except that her eyes were open and her gaze was locked forever onto a photo album that was lying open on her lap. The pages were full of pictures of Deborah as a baby. Other albums were stacked up on the floor. Baby clothes were fanned out on the empty side of the bed. A soft toy was on the nightstand. A threadbare rabbit. It was lying next to an empty bottle of pills and a glass. Of water, Devereaux noted. Not whiskey.

At least she was no longer alone, he thought, as he reached down to close her eyes.

Chapter Thirty-two

Sunday. Early afternoon.

DEVEREAUX COULD HEAR THE VOICES FROM THE ELEVATOR LOBBY, long before he was close enough to knock on the apartment door.

"Answer it, then, jackass!" The woman's voice was ferocious.

"You answer it, you lazy bitch." The man's was equally hostile. "Why should I have to do everything?"

"Don't make me laugh. You don't do anything. If I didn't—"

Devereaux knocked again, harder. "Birmingham PD. Open up."

Footsteps approached from inside the apartment and a second later the door opened and a man peered around the edge, his face a little flushed. He was around six feet tall, slim, unshaven, with untidy brown hair.

"Dean Sullivan?" Devereaux showed his badge. "I have a couple of questions, if this is a good time?"

"You know, Detective, it's a terrible time. Could we maybe do this later? Maybe tomorrow? It's like a war zone in here right now."

"Let me explain something to you, Dean." Devereaux took a step closer. "When I asked if now was a good time for you? That's what's known as a social nicety. What I really mean is that I'm going to ask you some questions. Right now. You're going to answer them to my satisfaction. Or you're going to have a problem. Is that clear enough for you?"

Sullivan opened the door the rest of the way and stepped back. "Just be careful. Watch where you walk. Don't slip."

There was a white U-shaped countertop to the left, with a polished surface that glittered with silver flecks. A teakettle sat on a stove top. Next to that was a coffee machine. A stand mixer. A packet of cereal that had been knocked over. An empty knife block. Two empty wine bottles and one used glass. Two newspapers were spread out, open to reports of the murders. A woman had been reading them. She was heavily pregnant and was now patrolling the kitchen area like a boxer in a ring, waiting to see if her opponent would get up from the canvas.

Beyond the countertop was the living area. There was a brown leather couch facing a large, wall-mounted TV. Extra speakers perched on the shelves on either side, which also held fifty or sixty books. Devereaux could see volumes of poetry. Art encyclopedias. Psychology texts. Computer manuals. All with colorful jackets that were psychedelically reflected in a sliding door that led to the balcony.

Between the two spaces a broken vase lay on the blond wood floor. Water had pooled around it, along with shards of glass and a handful of broken stems and crushed petals that were all that remained of a bunch of multicolored tulips.

"You better clean that up." The woman stepped forward, her weight on her front foot as if she was ready to attack.

"I'm not cleaning it up." Sullivan sneered at her. "You clean it up. You broke it!"

"Only because you made me! If you hadn't—"

"No one's cleaning it up!" Devereaux stepped between them. "Not until I'm done here. Then you can sort it out between yourselves. Miss—what's your name?"

"Hayley King. Why? What did I do?"

"Miss King, would you give us a moment?"

"Happily." She flounced away through an arch to the right of the room, continued into the bedroom, and slammed the door.

"Let's sit for a minute." Devereaux nodded toward the couch. "This is a nice place. How many bedrooms do you guys have?"

"Two." Sullivan sat at the far end.

"That's good. It'll be useful when the baby comes. How much longer to go?"

"Two weeks. Anyway, how can I help you, Detective?"

"You can start by telling me where you were on Friday afternoon."

"Why? What's this about?"

"Things will move a lot quicker if I ask the questions and you stick to the answers. Friday afternoon. Where were you?"

"At the movies."

"What did you see?"

"*Rush*. It's a motor racing movie. About Formula One, in Europe in the 1970s. The action sequences are unbelievable. The sound, the cinematography—it's like you were really there, at the racetrack. And the crashes? The fires? They take your breath away."

"How did Hayley like it? I'm not sure my girlfriend would be so enthusiastic. She prefers musicals."

"Hayley didn't come."

"Oh, now I'm really jealous. It's been years since I got to sneak off to the movies on my own."

"Who said I was on my own?"

"Weren't you?"

"No. I went with a friend."

"What was his name?"

"Lucas Paltrow. He picked the movie, actually. It's up his alley, him being an auto electrician. I wasn't expecting to like it much, but it blew me away. There were these two guys, two drivers, they were total rivals, and the movie kind of focused on their stories and there was this accident, a huge crash, and a fire, and the one guy—I'm rambling, aren't I? Lucas is always yelling at me about that."

"Don't worry about it. What time did you get home?"

"I'm not sure. It was pretty late. I hung out at Lucas's for a while after we got back from the movie theater. I don't know the exact time. Hayley might, though. You could ask her. She remembers that kind of thing."

"You mentioned that Lucas Paltrow's an auto electrician. He employs a guy named Billy Flynn, isn't that right?"

"Yeah. Flynn's a kind of charity case. He's a complete moron. A trained seal would be more useful than him."

"What kind of things does he do?"

"I don't really know. Sweeps the floor. Cleans things. Fetches drinks. The most complicated thing he ever does is sometimes return cars to their owners, after Lucas has done the hard part and fixed them or done an upgrade to the sound system, or whatever."

"Is Flynn allowed to drive the customers' cars at other times, when he's not returning them?"

"No. Lucas is very strict about that. But I wouldn't be surprised if Billy did drive them anyway. He's a total freak. I don't trust him."

"Why not?"

Sullivan shrugged. "I don't really know. It's a feeling I get. Specially if I ever have to spend time alone with him. He's creepy in some weird way. He kind of stares at you with his mouth open a little bit and doesn't say anything."

"When did you last see him?"

"Yesterday morning. At Lucas's."

"What time did he leave?"

"Quite early. Lucas had him dropping off an SUV—an Escalade, I think—for some celebrity. Then he went to his other job. He works at a bar, somewhere out of town."

"This is good." Devereaux flashed Sullivan a brief smile. "You're being very helpful. Just a couple more questions and I'll be out of your way. The name Siobhan O'Keefe. Does that mean anything to you?"

"Of course." Sullivan nodded enthusiastically. "It's all over the papers. She was murdered on her twenty-first birthday and her body was wrapped up like a birthday present. Creepy!"

"Did you ever see her at Lucas's workshop?"

"No. I've only seen her picture in the *Tribune*. Never in real life."

"What about with Billy Flynn?"

"That imbecile with a woman? Never going to happen, Detective. Impossible."

"OK. One last name. Deborah Holt?"

"I've never seen her or met her. But I do know her name. She was the first victim, right? Lucas told me he'd met her once. About a year ago. He fixed her car. Is this why you're asking? Because Lucas knew one of the women who was killed?"

"I can't say too much about the investigation while it's still ongoing. But you've been very helpful. I'm going to leave you my card. I need you to call me if anything comes to mind regarding Billy Flynn and either of the dead women, OK?"

Devereaux was waiting for the elevator to arrive when he heard more sounds from Sullivan's place. First the *crash* of breaking glass. Then the shriek of Hayley's voice.

"What do you mean, you're going to see Lucas . . ."

Chapter *Thirty-three*

Sunday. Afternoon.

DIANE MCKINZIE HAD GOTTEN A NEW DOOR FITTED TO HER HOUSE, midway down a quiet cul-de-sac near Lunker Lake in Vestavia Hills. The new door was a good thing, Devereaux thought. Given that the last time he'd been there, on a case involving an arsonist who was targeting the city's schools, he'd had to kick the old one down.

Devereaux hesitated before walking up the path. He'd gone easy with his right foot on the way over from Sullivan's building to give himself extra time to think through some possible approaches. He hadn't come up with anything he was happy with—there was simply no leverage, unlike when you're dealing with a suspect—so he decided to just ring the bell and wing it.

Diane—daughter of the legendary journalist Frederick McKinzie and an accomplished reporter in her own right—was wearing pink satin pajamas with a matching robe when she answered the door. She didn't speak for a moment, but Devereaux thought she actually looked pleased to see him.

"Are you checking up on me, Detective?" The hint of a smile played across Diane's face. "Or is this a work thing?"

"It's definitely not work."

Diane stepped back and opened the new door the rest of the way. "What personal service! I'm impressed."

Devereaux followed her into the hallway and saw that more repair work was under way. The dents in the floor had been filled and sanded, though not yet stained, and the framed newspaper articles had been taken down from the walls and their hooks removed.

"One of the frames was damaged." She knew he'd noticed the absence. "It broke when my son, Daniel, flung something, a couple years ago. They couldn't match the glass, so I'm having them all refinished. My life's changed whether I like it or not, so I may as well take the chance to draw a line and move on. Fix anything that needs to be fixed. Make up for lost time, if you know what I mean. Come on in. Make yourself at home."

Diane led the way to the living room. Patches of that floor were also mid-repair, and the chandelier—which had a cracked globe when Devereaux last visited—was missing, with just a clump of wires sticking out in its place. Diane sat in the corner of the couch and indicated that Devereaux should join her.

"Would you like a drink?" Diane ran a hand through her hair. "Then give me a minute to change and we could go grab some dinner? Still no ring, I notice . . ."

"Coffee would be nice." Devereaux glanced down at his left hand. "And honestly, dinner sounds good, too. I'm starving, and this hasn't been the best of days. I could use some interesting company. But that's not why I'm here. The truth is, I need to ask for your help."

Diane's back stiffened. "You want my help? Seriously? After everything that happened following the fires? Maybe you should just leave."

"If that's what you want, I will." Devereaux clasped his hands together. "But let me tell you what I have in mind, first. Because it concerns both of us. It's an opportunity for us to help each other."

"Really. How's that?" Diane's hand shot out like she was a traffic cop. "But let me warn you. If this is leading up to you asking to see my father's files, you can forget it. I won't just throw you out. I'll shoot you with my father's gun. I can't even count the number of people who've crawled around here spouting pathetic convoluted excuses for needing to get their hands on his research. I always say to them, if you want the reward, do the work for yourself. That was his rule, too."

"That's fair." Devereaux nodded. "But it does leave me between a rock and a hard place. It's a weird situation—not of my making—and it impacts your father, too. I'd thought there might be an answer in his files, but it hadn't occurred to me you'd be bombarded by this kind of request. So, let's do this. I'll explain what's happened, and you tell me what you think we should do about it. OK?"

"I guess." Diane pulled the robe tighter around herself. "But no promises."

"Understood." Devereaux took a breath. "All right. Here's the background. A guy I know—an untrustworthy asshole who's had it in for me for years—says he has new information about my father's death. Information that, if it were true, would be massively important to me. He says if I give him a bunch of money, he'll hand over the proof."

"So what's the problem?" Diane glared at Devereaux. "Just pay him. Everyone knows you're loaded."

"It's not just about the money. It's not that simple. The guy's theory is that another cop—who's dead now, but was the only guy who ever helped me when I was growing up—was crooked and framed my father for his own crimes. So if I don't pay there's a risk he'll release his story and smear the old guy I care about."

"But also clear your father?"

"Potentially." Devereaux shrugged. "But I don't think he's right. I know who my father was, and I've made peace with it. I think the guy's got his wires crossed. Which is where the next problem comes in. His theory is based on your father's research—he showed me a picture of a file he took when your father met him for an interview."

"Then why didn't my father break the story, if it's true? Crooked cops? That would have been right up his alley."

"That's part two of the guy's theory. And these are his words, not mine. Your father knew the truth, but didn't take the dirty cop down because he was crooked, too."

Diane was straight on her feet. Her eyes wild. Her fists clenched. "Who is this asshole? He thinks he can destroy my father's reputation? I'll kill him! I'll burn his damn house down with him inside it."

"Both good options. But the way I see it, first we need to look in your father's files and figure out how this guy put two and two together and made a thousand. That way your dad's name will be protected if any of this somehow leaks out. What do you say?"

"I don't know." Diane sat back down. "We're talking about police corruption. You're a cop. How can I trust you not to destroy evidence, or something? Maybe I should find someone independent to look into this?"

"There's no time for that. And it's like I told you—I already know my father was a very bad man. My girlfriend knows. My job knows. There's no reason for me to destroy anything, or cover anything up."

"What about the old cop? Your friend. It sounds like you want to save his reputation."

"I just want to make sure no lies are told about him, not hide the truth. So how about this? Why don't you sit with me. Keep your eye on me the whole time. See for yourself that I don't tamper with anything."

"I don't know . . ." Diane shuffled closer to the front of the couch.

"Here's another thing to think about. One way or another, there's a story here. Help me get to the truth, and I'll make sure you get the exclusive. The chance to build on your father's work, rather than let some asshole taint his legacy."

Diane didn't reply.

"How are things going at the paper, by the way? Does your boss still have you working on that blog you hate so much? Big City Nights?"

Diane led the way down the corridor, through the kitchen, and into her father's study. She paused for a moment, relishing as always the decades-old aroma of ingrained tobacco smoke, then gestured for Devereaux to sit behind the giant mahogany desk and wait. Then she pulled out a large cardboard archive box from the closet and set it in front of him.

"You're probably wasting your time." Diane perched on the corner of the desk. "I've looked through this a couple of times since . . . recently and didn't come across anything that sounds relevant to what you were describing."

"I've seen a picture of one of the key documents, remember," Devereaux said. "That gives me a head start."

Devereaux methodically sifted through the contents of the box. There were stacks of notes in Frederick McKinzie's own hand, along with photographs and cuttings from his and other newspapers. Roughly half the documents related to Raymond Kerr and half to John Devereaux. The inference that Frederick had been suspicious about Devereaux's lineage was clear. But he hadn't pursued it all the way. The entries stopped a few months after Devereaux's father had died. Diane was right. There was nothing related to Lambert's claims. Devereaux felt disappointed. Then confused. Then suspicious. Could Lambert have been so caught up in his vendetta against Tomcik that he hadn't just copied McKinzie's papers, but stolen them?

"Wait!" Diane slid down from the corner of the desk. "We're idiots. We're looking in the wrong file."

Diane returned to the closet and disappeared inside. It must have been an old dressing room, Devereaux guessed. He was wondering what else could be squirreled away in there when Diane emerged with another box.

The contents painted a bleak picture of Tomcik. Devereaux knew about most of the episodes from Tomcik's own files so he saw them in a different context, but could still appreciate how wrong it could all look. He was imagining the way a committed anti-corruption campaigner would respond when, halfway down, he found the page that Lambert had photographed. McKinzie must have kept working on it after interviewing Lambert, because additional handwritten notes had been scrawled in the margins. Some were in pencil, making them hard to read after so many years.

"This is what the guy showed me." Devereaux handed the page to Diane. "Does it mean anything to you?"

Diane scanned the notes. "No. But it must have related to something complex. This is how Dad organized his research. He wanted me to do the same. I remember him teaching me. He liked to make a kind of summary. That helped him to focus, and to get back up to speed if he got pulled away in the early stages by more urgent stories. Here—let me see what I can find."

Diane rummaged through the contents of the box once again, forming the documents into two piles. The first, taller one she ignored. When she reached the bottom of the box she picked up the second pile and retreated to an armchair in the corner of the room. She read every page carefully, cross-referencing and comparing with the other sheets. Eventually she looked up at Devereaux, concern and confusion etched into her face.

"Detective, trust me on this. I've read a lot of my dad's papers over the years. I know how to interpret them. And these—the conclusion he reached? Your father really was framed. He was innocent."

Chapter *Thirty-four*

Sunday. Afternoon.

FAULTY REASONING!

Alexandra laid Jensen's folder down on her kitchen table and despite everything that was going on in her life, she smiled. Those two
words had sprung into her head, and they reminded her of another
friend from Notre Dame. Melissa, who she'd met in freshman phi-
losophy class. Melissa was a woman who could spot an invalid argument at a hundred paces. In Alexandra's defense, the information
that Jensen had collated for her was a welcome diversion. But it was
still crazy that it had taken her all afternoon to recognize the logical
error her frightened subconscious had been pushing her toward. Just
because Jensen was wrong for her, it didn't mean Devereaux was
right. Melissa would have seen that immediately.

There was nothing in Jensen's file that meant Devereaux was
wrong for her, either, she conceded. There were plenty of theories,
and lots of speculation, but nothing to prove that Devereaux's character was inherently flawed. Nothing to tie his behavior to his father's. No irrefutable proof for her to base any decisions on. So
maybe it was time for a different approach. Maybe it was time to

listen to her gut. Because her gut wasn't flip-flopping. It had been telling her the same thing from the moment she saw a photograph of the four-year-old Devereaux standing next to his dad. Whether there was empirical evidence to support her or not, she simply wasn't comfortable in a relationship with the son of a mass murderer.

Chapter *Thirty-five*

Sunday. Afternoon.

THE DISCOVERY IN HER FATHER'S FILES ENERGIZED DIANE. IT SENT HER bouncing around the room in a sudden burst of irrepressible energy. She was awash in ideas. For articles. Books. Social media tie-ins. People to interview. Her journalist's brain had been thrown into overdrive and she just couldn't stop moving. Or talking.

The discovery had the opposite effect on Devereaux. He fell silent, still sitting behind Frederick McKinzie's desk. The original revelation about his father had felt to Devereaux like crashing through a thick crust of ice into the freezing water of confusion and doubt. He'd dragged himself out of that. Now he'd been plunged back in. He needed calm. Quiet. A place to isolate himself and think. He needed his cabin.

Devereaux had traced the ownership of the decaying one-room structure in the woods outside Birmingham using the city archives and then bought it, fifteen years ago, in the belief that the original owner had been his great-grandfather. He'd paid well over the odds, hoping that the place would help him connect with his family history. Now he knew that his history was a sham, as flimsy and shot through with holes as the cabin itself. But even leaving the family angle aside, he'd forged his own ties to the place. There was a straightforward, rustic honesty to it that he'd never found anyplace else, and in his darkest moments it was always where he wanted to be.

When Devereaux stood up to leave, he still had the presence of mind to thank Diane for her help and to ask if he could come back and see her again if any more questions arose. Still buzzing, she agreed. But before she could walk him to the door, his phone rang.

"Cooper?" It was Lieutenant Hale. "Billy Flynn's awake. Tommy's not cleared for work till tomorrow, so I'll meet you at the hospital. This could be huge, so it has to be done by the book. Don't try to talk to Flynn without me."

Devereaux stopped at the City Federal for just long enough to grab a bag of basic clothes. Then he completed the drive to the hospital, parked in the same spot in the Sixth Street lot as the previous night, and hurried to Garretty's room.

"I'm going mad in here, Cooper." Garretty turned the TV off when Devereaux appeared in the doorway. "Have you brought me more bible study material?"

"No." Devereaux dumped the bag on Garretty's bed. "Something better. Flynn's ready to talk. Get dressed. I'll wait outside."

Devereaux and Garretty arrived at the nurses' station outside the burn unit two minutes before Lieutenant Hale got there. She was wearing jeans and a plain blouse, but her hair was up and her face showed tiny traces of makeup. Devereaux was dying to find out where she'd been, but he knew better than to ask.

"Tommy?" Hale put her hands on her hips. "What are you doing here?"

"I'm just out for an evening stroll, Lieu." Garretty kept his face relatively straight. "It's part of the physical therapy rehab routine they have here."

"I see. And since when do you like The Who?"

Garretty looked down at the roundel logo on the shirt he was wearing. "Always. My favorite band."

"OK. Name me—"

"Excuse me, Officers?" A nurse had arrived to escort them to a pair of anterooms so that they could prepare for their visit. The environment in the burn unit was strictly controlled due to the increased risk of infection for the patients. Nothing from the outside world was allowed unless it was sterilized or carefully covered up, which meant each of them would have to wear a hat, mask, scrubs, and disposable slippers.

"You're Detective Devereaux?" the nurse asked, when the detectives emerged. "Mr. Flynn asked to see you first."

"Why?" Devereaux adjusted his mask.

"He was very confused when he woke up this afternoon. He didn't know where he was, or what had happened to him. Dr. Mason told him all about how you saved his life—how you ran into the burning building, and everything—and he was totally grateful. All he could talk about was thanking you."

He won't be thanking me for long, if I arrest him, Devereaux thought.

"What kind of shape is Mr. Flynn in?" Lieutenant Hale adjusted her scrubs. She didn't look happy about how short the pants were on her.

"He's doing surprisingly well." The nurse led the way to the main entrance to the unit and entered her code into a keypad. "He's as strong as an ox. The main problem you'll have is that his larynx is damaged. He'll speak very quietly, so be ready to listen closely. And he might not be able to keep the conversation going for long. If I were you I'd try to think of all my questions up front, make sure they're clear—he doesn't seem like the smartest guy we've ever had in here; but then, we deal with a lot of meth heads, so that's not saying much—and ask them in priority order."

"I think—"

Lieutenant Hale was cut off by the angry screeching of an alarm. It was behind them at the nurses' station, so it was muffled when the door hissed back into place, but was still audible.

"Code blue." The nurse started running toward the corner of the corridor. "This is weird. We only have one patient tonight . . ."

Devereaux and Hale sprinted after the nurse. Garretty followed a few paces behind, wary of his injured abdomen. Around the corner an officer wearing scrubs was waiting outside Flynn's room. He was on his feet, his chair pushed back at a crooked angle. Shock and concern were evident on his face. The glass between the room and corridor was opaque. An alarm sounded from inside the room, too, jarring and insistent.

"What happened?" Worry added a hard edge to Hale's voice.

"I don't know, Lieutenant." The officer drew himself up a little straighter. "Everything was fine. Flynn was awake. I could see him through the window. Doctors and nurses were in and out all day. Everyone was calm. They were moving slow. There was no panic. Then suddenly the alarm went off. A nurse rushed in pushing a cart with all kinds of equipment on it. The window went blank. Then you guys arrived."

One of the nurses they'd seen outside appeared and paused with her hand above the door switch. "Stay here. I'll update you as soon as there's news."

All four cops peered into the room as the door slid open. They caught a glimpse of Flynn lying on the bed. A single, lightweight sheet was tangled on the floor in the corner of the room. Flynn was only wearing pajama bottoms. Much of his head was bandaged, and his face and torso were covered with angry red-purple blisters and clear shiny ointment. A nurse was leaning over the bed. She had a pair of defibrillator paddles in her hands, which were attached with curly leads to a machine on a cart.

"Clear!"

The nurse pressed the paddles onto Flynn's chest. His body jerked into the air for a second, then flopped back down. The trace on his monitor spiked, then returned to horizontal. The door closed, ending their view. A doctor arrived, glared suspiciously at the gaggle of cops, then hurried into the room. A similar scene was visible inside for a moment. Jerk, then flop. Jerk, then flop.

Fifteen minutes later the door opened and Dr. Mason emerged, a grim expression on his face.

"This guy was a suspected murderer, right? Well, I want you to know something. That had nothing to do with what just happened in there. We did everything we possibly could to save him. Nurse Brown, who was the first to respond? She's one of our very best. Last year, she received a special commendation from the CEO for going above and beyond her duty in saving patients' lives. If a relative had a heart attack, she's the one you'd want to find them. She saved a retired cop's life just a couple of days ago. She's absolutely distraught she couldn't do the same thing tonight."

Chapter Thirty-six

Monday. Early morning.

DEVEREAUX DIDN'T NEED AN ALARM CLOCK THAT MORNING. THE RAYS of sunshine that began to stream in through the hole in the roof shortly after dawn were more than enough to rouse him from his sleep. He remained stretched out on his battered leather couch for another five minutes after the daylight had prompted him to open his eyes, breathing in the cool, pure forest air and reveling in the perfect silence of the secluded countryside. Normally he'd have lain there for half an hour or more, but just then he was too fired up to stay still. His cabin had worked its old magic. The confusion and frustration of the previous day were gone. He was feeling calm. Focused. Ready to get down to business—closing the case on Flynn and talking to Alexandra. Telling her the news about his father. And convincing her that there was no longer any reason for them to be apart.

There were no facilities in the cabin—it had been left with just a single room after catching on fire when a moonshine still belonging to the original owner exploded decades earlier—so Devereaux needed to get back to his apartment at the City Federal to shower and change before heading over to Lieutenant Hale's office. He grabbed his boots and his jacket, pulled the door closed behind him, fired up the Porsche, and eased it gently along the rough track that led to the paved road at the outskirts of the woods. Usually he allowed himself a few fast miles at that point before the traffic grew heavier as it approached the city, but he resisted the temptation and kept one eye on his phone. He willed it to pick up a signal. Finally one bar registered on its screen. That jumped up to three. And then a voicemail icon appeared. Alexandra had left him a message.

"Cooper? Damn, I hate to have missed you. Listen. I've been doing a lot of thinking. About us and, you know . . . everything. I think we need to talk. Face-to-face. Not over the phone. So give me a call, let me know when would work for you. Or shoot me a text. Whatever's convenient. Anyway, catch you soon. Bye."

Devereaux pulled onto the shoulder and replayed the message. *We need to talk.* Words that generally don't bode well when it comes to relationships. He knew that from bitter experience. But he wasn't unduly discouraged. When Alexandra dumped him before, eight years ago, she just walked out. There was no warning. No discussion. So the message was actually a step forward. And more importantly, she didn't know what he'd discovered about his father. Once she learned that he was innocent, everything would change. All he had to do was swing past Diane McKinzie's house and get a copy of her father's papers. He should have done that the night before, but with the shock of the revelation and the phone call about Flynn, it had gotten away from him. He'd put that right as soon as possible, then call Alexandra back and fix a time to meet.

"We've had two mornings now." Lieutenant Hale looked at Devereaux and Agent Irvin over the ever-deepening mound of paperwork on her desk and took a long sip of coffee. "Two mornings when we haven't had a gift-wrapped body turn up somewhere in the city. Billy Flynn was out of the game on both occasions. I think it's safe to say that can't be a coincidence. I think it's safe to close the case. But I don't want to just think. I want to know. I want some evidence that's non-circumstantial. Even if it's just one piece. So, Cooper. Linda. What's left to work with?"

"I have one piece of news." Devereaux pulled up a picture on his phone. "I just heard from Tech Services. Deborah Holt's new car's been found. It was at the end of a narrow, twisting track up on the Red Mountain, where teenagers typically go to make out. They need a little while to work on it, so I'm going to break Tommy out of the hospital, meet with the ME for his final word on the bodies, then head over to the workshop and see if they've come up with anything."

"Was the hospital able to help us with Flynn's prints?"

"No luck there. His hands were both too badly burned."

"How about a photograph? It would be good if we could get a positive ID from Mrs. Goodman. Or a fence, if any of the victims' possessions ever resurface. Did you get anything from his mom?"

"No. Not yet, anyway. She's reaching out to her friends and family. All her physical photos were destroyed in the fire, and she only has a few old baby pictures on her phone."

"It's interesting that she doesn't have anything more up to date." Irvin scratched her ear. "She must have gone to some trouble to scan or copy the old pictures. It would have been much easier to take a few newer ones. That suggests she doesn't appreciate him as an adult and harks back to a time when she thought he had more potential. That in turn could contribute to him feeling unappreciated, which is certainly consistent with the profile."

"Sounds good." Hale took another mouthful of coffee. "In theory. Now let's get out there and find some proof. I want this wrapped up. And then I never want to think about the Birthday Killer ever again."

Chapter Thirty-seven

Monday. Morning.

Dr. Liam Barratt was the most cheerful person Devereaux knew, and yet he worked at the most miserable place in the city. The Jefferson County morgue. A gloomy, gray concrete structure that could easily have been mistaken for a parking garage with its sides blocked in. It was surrounded on three sides by other grim concrete buildings, and Devereaux made a point of only going there when he absolutely had to.

Barratt could have sent an assistant to open the door—being the longest-serving ME in the city has its perks—but he went down to the staff entrance himself when Devereaux buzzed the intercom.

"Cooper!" Barratt wiped his palm on the leg of his faded blue scrubs before shaking Devereaux's hand. "It's a pleasure, as always. But why don't you ever stop by for coffee? Or to chat about sailboats, like you keep promising? Sometimes I think you're only interested in me for my bodies . . ."

Devereaux forced a smile onto his face, then gestured to his companions. "You know Tommy, right? And this is Special Agent Linda

Irvin, with the FBI. She works out of the Birmingham Field Office. This is her second case with us."

"Pleased to meet you." Irvin held out her hand. "I'm working on the profile of the guy who brought you those bodies. I thought it might help me to see his handiwork firsthand. I hope that's OK."

"Are you joking?" Barratt's smile grew even larger. "Of course it's OK. The bigger the audience, the happier I am. You should see me in a lecture theater. Although I am a little confused about one thing. I thought you'd caught the asshole who killed these women."

"We have." Irvin hitched her laptop bag higher up onto her shoulder. "We just have to make sure the case is water tight before we put it to bed. And that's a little harder than normal. Our suspect is dead. His fingerprints are all burned off. His face is totally disfigured. And his house—which is most likely the principal crime scene—and all his possessions are incinerated. Lieutenant Hale asked for my input, so before I sign off I need to check that there are no red flags in the victimology."

"In that case, I have two things to say." Barratt beamed at her. "First, never let the lieutenant trick you into playing any form of racket sport with her. She's ridiculously good at all of them. You'd be lucky to escape with your life. And second, come on inside. I'll help you any way I can."

Barratt's rubber work boots squeaked on the tile floor as he led the way across the autopsy room. He paused at the far side, in front of a wall of square steel doors. There were twelve in all, like giant storage lockers. Which, in a macabre way, they were.

Three stainless steel dissection tables with sturdy, tubular legs were lined up along the center of the room. Their sides were raised four inches to contain their contents, and a Y-shaped channel molded into their bases led to the drain, which was covered by a heavy-duty mesh strainer.

One of the tables was empty. It was scrupulously clean, but covered in parallel scratches. They were concentrated in certain areas, like on a platter that's used for carving a family's Thanksgiving roast. Devereaux pictured the procedure of chopping and slicing and separating the samples, then switching them into dishes or jars full of harsh-smelling chemicals. He shivered, then his attention shifted to the hose assembly above the tables, each supported on a giant spring. That was the part that creeped him out the most. But not because he was squeamish. It was due to a strange superstition that had developed. At the end of the first autopsy he'd witnessed, he was convinced that he saw the soul of the victim being washed away down the drain along with their blood and leftover body parts.

The other two tables were occupied. The first by Deborah Holt. The second, Siobhan O'Keefe. Their bodies were covered with pale green sheets. Their eyes were closed. Their necks were supported by porcelain wedges, like tiny pillows. You could almost have believed the women were asleep, if it weren't for the indefinable, preternatural stillness that separates the dead from the living.

Barratt gestured for the officers to gather around. Devereaux stayed as close to the door as he could. Barratt pulled back the sheets. The women's skin was pale, almost transparent in the harsh, even light thrown by the round overhead rigs. The coarse blue thread clashed horribly with the skin where their bodies had been sewn up following the probing of their organs.

"Let me tell you their stories, since they're in no position to do it themselves." Barratt's voice was quiet, almost reverential. "This makes a fascinating comparison. We have two Caucasian females of exactly the same age. Twenty-one, to the day. They could almost be twins. They've both given birth. Both were in generally good health. Neither smoked. Neither shows signs of drug use, or excessive alcohol intake. Then we come to the less palatable similarities. First, neither had any defensive wounds or restraint marks on her wrists or ankles."

"That suggests a couple of possibilities." Irvin frowned. "They could have been victims of a blitz attack, being overcome by their attacker before they had the chance to react. Or they could have known their attacker. Or trusted him for some reason."

"Mrs. Goodman's account of Siobhan being coerced into a vehicle makes it sound like either a threat or a trick was used," Garretty said.

"It may be a combination of the two," Irvin said. "A trick to get them into the vehicle and a blitz attack at the secondary crime scene when they were killed."

"They were both assaulted, as well." The smile had disappeared from Barratt's face. "By someone incredibly fastidious. Not a single hair or trace of fluid was left behind. They're the cleanest—if that's the word—victims I've ever examined."

"No trace at all?" Garretty shook his head. "We're catching no breaks—none—in this case."

"And of course the final, tragic similarity." Barratt frowned. "Both were killed by manual strangulation. Though there is a significant contrast between the two cases. Look at the first vic, Ms. Holt. You can see from the marks on her neck that the attack was quick and brutal. There was no hesitation. No adjustment. Her larynx was completely crushed. But the second vic, Ms. O'Keefe, has a different story. Her end was slow. Drawn out. Can you see the overlapping marks on her neck? And the way the blood vessels in her eyes are shot across a wider area, but with less intensity? I wouldn't be surprised if he strangled her till she lost consciousness and then revived her several times before finishing the job."

"That's just sick." The expression on Garretty's face was murderous.

"I know this is a long shot, but is there any chance of recovering a print from either of their necks?" Irvin asked. "The killer kept his fingers nice and still with Deborah. It looks like a constant contact. And she wore plenty of lotion. What do you think, Doctor?"

"There's no chance at all. I was just coming to that. It's my final point. The killer wore gloves. The texture is imprinted on the victims' skin. Look closely, and you'll see."

"What kind of gloves were they?" Garretty leaned in close to Deborah Holt's neck. "Leather?"

"No." Barratt shook his head. "Synthetic. Some kind of protective work gloves, would be my guess."

Dear Mom,

You'll never believe what just happened! My car just got repossessed! My damn car! I have no idea how they even found it. I knew I was a couple of payments behind—I mean, come on, who hasn't been a little in the red, one time or another?—so I kept it locked up. Well not actually locked, because the garage technically belongs to Chorlton (Do you remember him? Nice guy. I went to high school with him. He did live in my building, but he's in jail right now so he doesn't exactly need full use of his parking spot) and I don't have the key. But no one could see it, or know it was there. Except for when I _had_ to take it out, like when Hayley wouldn't let me drive her car. The selfish bitch. That's probably how they got on to me. Someone saw me when she forced me to break cover one time. God, I hate selfish people. And I'm totally surrounded by them. There's her. And Lucas. Don't get me started on Lucas! It's his fault I was behind on the payments in the first place. I asked him to spot me a few bucks when I lost my job—which totally wasn't my fault, by the way. I _am_ sick! How is it my fault if the doctors are too stupid to find out what's wrong with me? OK, so I said "asked" but actually I begged Lucas to help me out. And you know what? He turned me down flat. Wouldn't even consider it. After everything I've done for him? And after he screwed up our extra income with his idiotic overreaching, which I did warn him about? Honestly, the man's a disgrace. And he's rolling in cash!

He has mountains of it! Because, let's face it. It's easy for him to make money. He's a journeyman. Tinkering around with people's cars. That's not hard. Anyone could do that. But not just anyone can be an artist in their field. Not like I am.

Chapter *Thirty-eight*

Monday. Morning.

ALL OF THE MAJOR FUNCTIONS THAT FELL UNDER THE UMBRELLA OF THE Police Department's Support Services Bureau had now been consolidated in the recently extended building on Fourth Avenue. Several had been relocated from relatively new facilities around the city. The one notable exception was the vehicle inspection unit, which was still based in the former warehouse near the airport that had been its "temporary" home for the last fifteen years.

Irvin elected to return to the FBI Field Office after leaving the morgue, so she only followed Devereaux and Garretty as far as First Avenue and then continued straight on 18th Street after the detectives peeled off to the right. Devereaux chose to stay on First rather than loop around onto Stephens, in part because that took them right past Sloss Furnaces. Sloss had been one of his favorite places to hide as a kid whenever he'd run away from a foster home, and he still felt drawn to its bold shapes and raw, uncompromising industrial character. The road is raised at the point it passes the site, and the border of trees obscures some of the maze of pipes and trusses that run at ground level. The chimneys are still visible, though, as are the tops of the rust-red silos that Devereaux used to imagine being parts of a demented giant's chemistry set.

Devereaux continued for another mile, then jogged left on 41st Street to Messer. He cut under 20/59, skirted around Forest Hill Cemetery, then turned right into Aviation Avenue and pulled up in the small lot at the side of a bleak, soot-stained brick structure. There were no signs or notices to advertise what the building was. The only clues to its purpose were the heavy bars on its blacked-out windows, the heavy-duty vehicle and personnel doors, the plethora of security cameras, and the oversize stainless steel chimney that protruded eight feet from one corner of the roof. The department had learned the hard way that there are times when it pays to be discreet. Confiscated vehicles are often valuable. Sometimes in themselves. Sometimes due to the contraband that's hidden inside them. And sometimes because of the evidence they contain.

Inside, Devereaux found the smell of oil and grease mixed with a hint of stale exhaust gas a welcome change after the chemically tainted atmosphere of the autopsy room. He paused for a moment, gratefully filling his lungs with air that he didn't feel would corrode him from the inside out. Garretty had the opposite reaction, coughing and scowling unhappily at the technician who'd let them in.

"Bill Scott." The technician shook the detectives' hands and then turned away. "Come on. Follow me."

Scott led the way through the receiving area, where vehicles were held when they first arrived, and continued toward a row of six work bays that had been created between the rows of vaulted pillars that ran the length of the structure, supporting the roof.

"Tell me you found something good." Devereaux nodded toward the car in the bay nearest the entrance. It was a vintage TR6 in British Racing Green, completely dismantled, its pieces neatly laid out in functional groups on a plastic sheet on the ground as if to be photographed for an exploded view in an owner's manual. "Look at that leather. The wood. It would be a tragedy to trash such a beauty for no result."

"I can't give you details." Scott surveyed the parts with a look of quiet satisfaction on his face. "But I will say, it didn't die in vain."

"Is this Deborah Holt's Mercedes?" Garretty had moved ahead to the next bay, where a gleaming red SLK was positioned over an inspection pit.

"That's right." Scott cast his eyes over its long, sculptured hood and nodded approvingly. "What a beautiful car."

"I prefer the Triumph." Devereaux glanced back over his shoulder.

"Those sure were pretty." Scott shrugged. "But assuming you ever want to go anywhere without having to call a tow truck first, this would be a better bet."

"I guess." Devereaux frowned. "But leaving aesthetics aside for a moment, what else can you tell us about it?"

"Not much." Scott scratched his forehead. "It's got eighteen miles on the odometer, and frankly it looks like what it is—a car that's fresh out of the showroom. Fresher, actually. There's not a scratch on the outside. And no prints on the inside."

"No prints at all?" Devereaux stepped past a red tool chest on wheels and peered through the driver's window.

"None." Scott shook his head. "The car's been wiped totally clean. Even the tires and the inside of the wheel arches are spotless. And there were no personal possessions. Or keys. The only thing inside it was the owner's manual. We sent that to the lab to check for prints, but I'm not holding my breath. I know a sterile vehicle when I see one. The only weird thing is that all the systems—engine management, navigation, that kind of thing—have been reset to the factory defaults. Not many people know to go to those lengths. Remember that guy, in the spring? Whose ex-wife was murdered in her sleep? He claimed he didn't even know where she'd moved to."

Scott pointed to a computer that was fixed to a steel table at the side of the booth. "But when we hooked that baby up, we could see the last destination he'd searched for was her house."

"That was in the paper, right?" Garretty ducked under the vacuum hose that was hanging from the ceiling and moved to the rear of the car. "Maybe our guy read about it. Or maybe he did his homework. When you go on a killing spree, the stakes are pretty high."

"It's a shame the same trick didn't work this time." Devereaux took a step back from the car. "But we could check with the dealer. See if they recorded the delivery mileage. Maybe some of the total will be unaccounted for. That could give a clue whether Deborah drove anywhere else. Maybe give us a search radius for where she crossed paths with the guy who killed her."

"Good thinking." Scott stepped out of the bay. "Now, is there anything else you want to see while you're here? We still have the TV guy's Escalade and the suspect's Nissan." Scott pointed to the area on the other side of the booths. "We'll be releasing the Escalade in a couple of days—we could have done it today, but the owner called up and yelled at our civilian aide, demanding it back immediately, so unfortunately the paperwork got misplaced—and the Nissan will go to long-term storage on the next transporter."

"What about the property from the Nissan?" Devereaux's eyes momentarily narrowed. "Do you still have that?"

"No." Scott shook his head. "That went to the lab. We have pictures, though."

Scott stepped back into the booth, called up a file on the computer, and showed the detectives a series of photographs showing exactly where in his vehicle Flynn's possessions had been found.

"Were those gloves already in a Ziploc bag?" Devereaux gestured for Scott to pause on one particular shot. "Or did you guys put them in for transport to the lab?"

"They were already in it." Scott straightened up. "If we'd bagged them, we'd have used paper. That's the correct procedure. It reduces the risk of the evidence deteriorating due to trapped moisture or condensation."

"So why would Flynn bag them himself?"

"Probably because he wouldn't always need them. Most gas stations, they have dispensers with disposable gloves next to the diesel pumps. Maybe he carried these as a backup, in case he was at a place where the dispenser was out?"

"Something here's not quite making sense. Have you filled up diesels yourself before?"

"Sure. Not often. But a few times."

"And the procedure's basically the same as gas, right?"

"Right. You hit a different button and use a separate line, but otherwise it's the same."

"Did you wear gloves?"

"Sure. Diesel's horrible stuff. You don't want it on your skin."

"Right. Now, this is important. Glove? Or gloves?"

"What do you mean?"

"You hold the nozzle with one hand, right? Just like with a gas pump?"

"Right."

"So why would you need gloves on both hands?"

"Oh. I see. Yes. Thinking about it, I only wore one. On my right hand. Because I'm right-handed."

"So here's my real question. If you only need one glove to fill a van with diesel, why did Flynn have a pair?"

Scott shrugged. "No idea. Maybe they come in pairs, and he didn't bother separating them."

Devereaux turned back to the image on the computer screen. "Or maybe he needed the complete pair for another reason . . ."

Chapter *Thirty-nine*

Monday. Morning.

THE OPENING CHORDS OF "WHOLE LOTTA LOVE" BEGAN TO BLARE from Devereaux's pocket just as he pulled up outside Police Headquarters. He reached for his phone, willing Alexandra's name to appear on the screen and hoping he hadn't jinxed himself with his choice of ringtone.

The call was from Diane McKinzie.

"Sorry, Tommy." Devereaux turned to Garretty. "I need to get this. I'll be inside in a minute."

Garretty slid out of the car and Devereaux hit the answer key as soon as the passenger door had slammed shut behind him.

"Devereaux?" Diane's voice had an anxious edge to it. "Have you told anyone about . . . my father's research?"

"No. Not yet. But I'm planning to."

"Can you come over? There's something I need you to see first. It's important."

"Sure." Devereaux checked his watch. "I have one thing to take care of, then I'll head to your place. Be there in, say, an hour?"

Lieutenant Hale had more questions than Devereaux had expected, and the traffic on 280 was worse than he'd hoped, so close to ninety minutes had passed by the time he knocked on Diane McKinzie's door.

"What took you so long?" Diane ushered him inside. "Never mind. It doesn't matter. You're here now. Can I get you a drink?"

"I thought this was about your father's work?" Devereaux stayed near the door.

"It is." Diane gestured for him to follow her. "But I thought, you know, a drink might be a good idea."

"You're worrying me, Diane." Devereaux started after her down the hallway. "What's this about?"

"Come on." Diane reached the entrance to her father's study. "I'll show you."

The filing box Devereaux had searched through the night before was back on Frederick McKinzie's desk. The papers that detailed the way Devereaux's father had been framed were in a tidy pile, in front of it. Next to it was another box. It was the same size. The same color. It was in better shape, with fewer dings and scuffs. And lined up neatly beside it was a second stack of papers.

"After you left last night, I couldn't get to sleep." Diane started to pace back and forth in front of the desk. "Something was bothering me. I couldn't stop thinking about what my father had discovered about your father being innocent. It was great news for you, obviously. But a problem for me. If my dad had uncovered police corruption, why hadn't he written about it? Passing on a story—especially an exclusive—just wasn't like him. He lived to expose scandal and injustice. I began to worry. I thought, what if someone got to him? What if he was in someone's pocket? What if my dad isn't the hero I thought he was? So I came back downstairs. Pulled out his files, box after box. And prayed the answer was in one, somewhere."

"I'm guessing it was." Devereaux glanced at the second box. "Diane? What did you find?"

"Sit." Diane stopped moving and perched on the edge of the desk. "See for yourself. I've pulled out the pages you need to read."

Devereaux had heard that Frederick McKinzie was an old-school journalist, but he hadn't fully appreciated what that meant until he leafed through the stack of papers Diane had selected from the second box. As Devereaux began to read, it was clear that Frederick had come across a juicy story. He'd gotten wind of dirty cops breaking some very serious laws. He'd interviewed witnesses. Gathered evidence. But when he'd reached a conclusion, he hadn't rushed straight to his typewriter. He'd cross-referenced the claims people had made with alternative accounts, to ensure no one was lying. At first everything checked out. Frederick's early notes had been made in a steady, solid hand. But then he'd found a loose thread. He pulled on it. And found an inconsistency in something a key source had said. His writing had become hurried and untidy, and Devereaux recognized from each new scribbled entry the excitement of a fellow investigator sensing there was more to be revealed.

At the bottom of the fourth page, everything came into focus. When Diane had found it, she'd understood why her father never published the story. Now Devereaux did, too. It was because the case against Hayden Tomcik was a sham. A well-constructed sham, to give it its due. Its foundation checked out. The first few accusations held water. A less conscientious reporter might have stopped looking and gone to his editor, ready to publish and be damned. But Tomcik's transgressions up to that point were relatively minor. The victims were vile characters who should already have been in jail, if the system had done its work. The events took place in the 1970s, when the police had a lot more latitude to take matters into their own hands. And Frederick was an experienced interviewer, with a good ear for notes that didn't quite ring true.

Frederick kept digging. It took him months. He went down more than one blind alley. But he noticed that with each subsequent claim made against Tomcik, the quality of the proof diminished. He traced each successive accusation and found they all led back through a series of aliases and fronts to a single person. A woman. Davina Davis. The fiancée of a man named Dave Bruce, who was currently serving twenty-five to life for two brutal murders.

"Do you see?" Diane leaned forward and turned the page. "Tomcik and Jenner arrested Bruce a month after your father was killed. Jenner was dead, too, by the time the case came to court, meaning Bruce's conviction depended on Tomcik's testimony. So Davis set this whole thing up as a ruse to destroy Tomcik's credibility. All the smaller incidents were to dirty him up, make him seem like the kind of cop who routinely bent the rules. And the coup de grâce was the idea that he'd already framed one guy—your father—for murder, so could plausibly have done it again. She couldn't go to the cops herself—they'd never have believed her. So she used her contacts to drip feed the story to my father, knowing his reputation for having zero tolerance for corruption. She tried to get him to do her dirty work for her. She just didn't count on his thoroughness."

Devereaux leaned back and gripped the arms of the chair, fighting the sensation that the world was spinning around him. "First your father built the case, as it was revealed to him. That was the first box. Then he demolished it. That was the second."

"Right." Diane lifted the lid of the second box and dropped the new stack of papers inside. "That's how he worked. He was so methodical. He always had a system for everything."

"It's lucky he was. This stuff's pretty convincing." Devereaux picked up the summary pages from in front of the first box and flicked through them. "Lucky for you, anyway. For me, not so much."

"Cooper, I'm so sorry." Diane reached out and touched Devereaux's shoulder. "I feel awful for you. It nearly killed me suspecting something bad about my father for half an evening. Having to deal with that, then think it wasn't true, then have the hope snatched away from you again? I think my head would explode. Are you OK? Seriously? You can drop the tough detective act when you're here, you know. God knows you've seen me at my worst. If there's anything I can do . . ."

"How about that drink I stupidly turned down?" Devereaux leaned forward and lifted the lid from the first box. "Have you got any scotch?"

"I think that can be arranged." Diane smiled warmly, slid off the desk, and made for the door.

Devereaux waited until she was out of the room and replaced the lid on the box. Then he folded Frederick's papers—the ones that made his father look innocent—and slipped them into his jacket pocket.

They may not be true, he thought. *But if I found them convincing . . .*

Chapter **Forty**

Tuesday. Morning.

THIS TIME, THE SHEETS WERE PINK.

Devereaux, Garretty, Isringhausen, and Ryan stood in silence. None of them moved. The technicians had taken their photographs—more than were strictly necessary, to drag the proceedings out because no one wanted the job of untying the bow. Unlike on previous mornings, the parcel lying in front of them was intact. It was laid out on the steps of the Prince of Peace church, in the outskirts of Hoover. A lay minister named John Anderson had found it on his way to unlock the front door. Anderson kept up with the news. So he had a good idea of what would be inside. And he had no desire to see another dead body. He'd encountered more than his share as a Marine in Vietnam, and despite the passage of almost fifty years, he had no wish to come face-to-face with even one more corpse.

Another minute crawled past in silence. And another. Then Isringhausen sighed, pulled on his gloves, tightened his mask, and stepped forward. Ryan joined him, and together they loosened the wrapping. Inside, to no one's surprise, was the body of a young woman. She looked about twenty-one. Maybe twenty-two, or twenty-three at a push. She was naked. Her short black hair was neatly combed. Her arms were positioned in the same way that Deborah Holt's and Siobhan O'Keefe's had been. But there were burns on the back of both this woman's hands. Her forearms, elbows, and knees were bruised. A jagged gash had been torn in her abdomen. And there was a small, angry, purple wound on the left side of her neck.

Ryan scanned the woman's prints and sent them to the lab, then picked up his camera and began to photograph her injuries.

"What do you think?" Isringhausen stepped back, out of the way. "A copycat? A bastard who's even more sadistic than the dead guy was?"

"Maybe." Devereaux frowned. "But do one thing for me. When Ryan's done with the pictures, examine her neck. Real close. Tell me if you see anything."

As soon as his colleague was finished with the camera, Isringhausen took a flashlight and a magnifying glass from his tool kit and crouched down next to the woman's head. "OK. There are no deposits. Nothing transferred. No . . . wait a minute. Whoever did this, he was wearing gloves. I can see faint texture marks imprinted in her skin."

"Leather gloves?" Devereaux shot a glance at Garretty.

"No." Isringhausen stood up. "I don't think so. The pattern's too fine. I'd say they were some kind of synthetic material. Is that what you were expecting I'd find?"

Devereaux shrugged. "Whoever killed Deborah and Siobhan, he was also wearing synthetic gloves. We just found out from Dr. Barratt, yesterday."

"That detail wasn't in any press report." Garretty shoved his hands deep into his pockets. "See where we're going with this?"

"Oh, shit." Isringhausen's eyes opened wider.

"Shit is right." Garretty ran his hand through his hair. "Think about it. Same MO means it can't be Flynn. And whoever it was, he killed a woman two nights running. Had two nights off. Then killed another last night."

"Maybe that explains the extra violence?" Isringhausen glanced down at the body. "He stopped for two days and couldn't hold it in any longer."

"Maybe," Devereaux said. "But the real question is, what's the guy going to do tonight? Keep the pattern going? Escalate?"

"We need to make sure he's in a jail cell before he gets the chance." Garretty scowled. "Or in a body bag."

"Let's think this through," Devereaux said. "Go back to the one solid lead we have. The Escalade. Mrs. Goodman saw a guy coercing Siobhan to get into it. We figured that guy must be Flynn. If it wasn't, the killer must be someone else with access to it."

"Paltrow." Garretty practically spat out the name. "He's a similar height. Build. Hair color. All we had was Mrs. Goodman's description."

"Right." Devereaux nodded. "We need to take another look at him."

"Excuse me, Detective." A uniformed officer approached from inside the church. "Mr. Anderson—he's not doing so well. Shock, I think. Do you need to talk to him again? Because I'm thinking we should get him to the hospital. A doctor needs to take a look at him."

"We don't need him. Make sure someone takes care of him."

"Thanks, Detective. Oh—"

"What?"

"Nothing. It's just, the victim—I recognize her."

"Who is she?"

"I don't know her name. But I've seen her before. A couple of months ago. My partner and I, we were called to a disturbance at a hotel. The Petite Maison. A party had gotten out of hand in one of the rooms. Other guests complained. The management did nothing, so someone dialed 911. We showed up, and a couple of guys tried to book out of the window—some wiseass businessmen from Miami had ordered some girls then tried to not pay, and so their minders had shown up to collect. Anyway, a couple of the girls tried to blend in with the suits. She was one of them. Her name should be in the report."

"Thanks, Officer. Good work. Now go look after Mr. Anderson."

The officer turned to leave and almost knocked over Ryan, who was holding his phone.

"We've got an ID on our vic." Ryan steadied himself. "Emma Noble. She had one prior for solicitation."

"Age?" Devereaux asked.

"She turned nineteen two weeks ago."

"At least she wasn't killed on her birthday. I would have sworn she was older than nineteen, though." Devereaux turned back to Ryan. "Any indication she's had a kid?"

"I couldn't tell." Ryan shrugged. "The ME will know."

"So what's next?" Garretty frowned. "Shall we pick up Paltrow?"

"Not yet." Devereaux shook his head. "What have we got on him? The Escalade thing. That's not enough. We need more. And something doesn't sit right here. There are too many deviations from the signature. The additional violence. The age. And neither of the other vics were hookers. It feels like there's something else going on. So this is what we should do. Call the lieutenant. Have her get Colton or Levi to find Paltrow and watch him. Emma Noble was a call girl. Let's find out who called her last night. Whoever did, they're due a serious conversation. We'll start with the hotel bust two months ago. I want the precise date and the name of the guy whose room the party was in."

Chapter *Forty-one*

Tuesday. Morning.

DEVEREAUX SWUNG BY HIS APARTMENT AT THE CITY FEDERAL TO COL-
lect his favorite battered leather Jekyll & Hide suitcase, threw a
bunch of T-shirts inside to make it look realistically filled out, and
headed to the Petite Maison. He left the Porsche under the entrance
canopy—ignoring the valet—and made his way to the reception
counter.

"Good morning, miss." Devereaux kept a friendly smile on his
face and discreetly showed the receptionist his badge. "Here's what I
need you to do. Act like I'm a regular guest checking in. Imagine that
I have a room booked for tonight. Do whatever you normally do with
the computer. Then give me one key for the largest suite you have
available. And don't mention this to anyone at all."

"I'm sorry, sir." The receptionist glanced at her computer screen
and then back to Devereaux, looking alarmed. "We're a small hotel.
We only have one suite, and it's already booked. I could offer you a
standard room on the first floor?"

"That won't work. I need the suite. Are the guests who booked it
already here? Or do they check in later today?"

"The notes on my screen say they're flying in from New York and are due early this afternoon. But—"

"Good. Then give me the key. And don't worry. I only need the suite for half an hour. It won't come to any harm. When these New Yorkers arrive they'll never know I was there. I guarantee. And you have to understand—this is part of a very important investigation. I'm not taking no for an answer. So don't make this difficult."

Devereaux declined the offer of help with his bag. He took the elevator to the fourth floor. Let himself into the suite. Took a moment to see what $400 a night could buy you. Texted the room number to Garretty. Then settled himself in one of the suede chaises by the window and called the number he'd been given by the duty officer in Dispatch.

The phone was picked up after one ring. "Make this quick. I'm heading into a meeting. What do you need?"

"Peter Bromley?" Devereaux pictured a twenty-something in a $4,000 suit with overcoiffured hair and a Bluetooth earpiece, trying to emulate Leonardo DiCaprio in *The Wolf of Wall Street*. "This is Detective Devereaux with the Birmingham Police Department. I have a question for you."

"Can it wait?"

"No, it can't wait."

"Well, I'm very busy, and—"

"Let me explain something. I'm investigating three homicides. I don't have a lot of patience. So you can either answer my one simple question right now on the phone. Or I can have some uniformed officers come to your office. Drag you out of your meeting in handcuffs. Put you on a plane to Birmingham. And you can answer me in person."

"All right. Calm down. I get it. What do you need to know?"

"July twenty-first. You were staying at the Petite Maison hotel, here in town. You had a party in your room. Call girls were involved."

"Hold on, wait a minute. That was a misunderstanding. I explained to the officers at the time, we didn't realize they were call girls. No money changed hands. When we found out what they were doing, we—"

"Cut the crap, Pete. And don't worry. I'm not looking to cause you trouble over the girls. I just need to know who supplied them. That's all."

"Supplied them? No. We just . . . my buddies and I . . . we were walking down the street, and—"

"You weren't walking down any street. We both know how this works. You're fixing to party at a fancy hotel, you don't go to the street corner and round up the first bunch of hookers you see. You talk to someone. They take care of it. I need to know who that some-one is. Right now."

There was silence on the line.

"Are you married, Pete?" Devereaux kept his voice matter-of-fact.

"Yes. Why?"

"Because if I have to send those officers around to arrest you for obstructing my investigation, it's going to be hard to keep the full details of the case quiet. Word might spread . . ."

"You bastard."

"Whatever. The name of the guy who arranged the girls?"

"Art."

"Art?"

"That's all I have. He's one of the bellmen at the hotel. A buddy of mine stays there all the time. He told me—talk to Art. Art can hook you up. He's some kind of European dude. The service was supposed to be discreet."

"What's your buddy's name?"

"Easton. Ken Easton."

"Where does he live? What town?"

"Mobile, Alabama. But you'll have to take my word for it. Ken's out of town. He's in Ecuador. All month. He owns a half share in a hotel there."

"All right. That's good. I'm going to leave you to your meeting now, Mr. Bromley. You won't be hearing from me again. Unless you're lying, of course. If you're lying, and the three homicides turn into four, I'm going to come to Miami and find you. And trust me. You won't like what happens next."

Devereaux returned to the lobby and hung out by the newspaper stand at the entrance to the gift shop, checking the employees' name badges until he spotted a guy in his mid-twenties with a bellman's uniform that was noticeably smarter than his coworkers'.

"Art?" Devereaux strolled across and fell in step with him as he returned from one of the elevators. "Got a minute? I need your help."

"Of course." The guy had a noticeable French accent. "Please, come with me." He led the way to the vacant concierge station, opposite the reception counter and to the left of the main sliding glass doors. "How can I be of assistance today?"

"Well, Art, let me introduce myself. My name's Devereaux. I just drove up from Mobile, and I'm only in town for the night. I'm staying in the suite, on the fourth floor. I've got meetings all afternoon, then I'm taking some clients to dinner. Some very important clients. It's going to be a very intensive few hours. Very stressful. So when it's done, I'm going to be ready for some entertainment. Some very special entertainment, if you know what I mean. And I hear you're the guy who can make that happen."

"You would like me to recommend a nightclub?" Art's expression gave nothing away. "Or perhaps tickets to a show? The Alabama Theatre on Third Avenue North seems to be very popular with our guests."

"No, no, no." Devereaux shook his head. "You misunderstand me. I'm talking about some entertaining company. Female company. For me and one of my associates."

"You have been misinformed, sir." Art remained impassive. "This is not the kind of thing I know anything about."

"Come, come, my friend." Devereaux leaned in close. "Maybe I should have mentioned this before. My buddy Ken stays here all the time. Ken Easton. He told me to find you. He said, *Devereaux, Art will hook you up.* He did say you might be a little wary after that fiasco with Pete Bromley, a couple months back. But listen, don't worry about that. I'm nothing like that jackass. I'm discreet. I pay my bills. And I tip. Very generously."

Art didn't respond.

"Here's a thought." Devereaux pointed outside, to the Porsche. "See that car? The blue one? Look at the license plate." He watched as Art took in the letters *DVRX*, and waited for the penny to drop. "Why don't I give you the key? Have yourself a little fun when your shift ends. I won't be needing it for a while. Then you can give it back to me in the morning, assuming our business is concluded to everyone's satisfaction."

Art didn't answer, but his eyes lingered on the Porsche.

"What do you say?" Devereaux took the car key out of his pocket and held it just out of Art's reach. "Have we got a deal?"

Art nodded. "OK. I can make that work."

"All right, then!" Devereaux smiled. "Outstanding. Let me tell you what I need. First of all—"

"Not here." Art held up his hand. "Upstairs. In your room. Ten minutes."

Devereaux opened the door to the suite when he heard a sharp knock, twelve minutes later. Art was standing outside carrying two pillows, freshly wrapped in crisp white tissue paper.

"You don't have to use these." Art came in, tossed the pillows onto the nearer bed, and looked quizzically at Garretty, who was sprawled on one of the chaises by the window. "You must be Mr. Devereaux's associate?"

"In a manner of speaking." Garretty sat up straighter.

"Here you go." Devereaux wheeled a blood-red Aeron chair from a desk by the wall and positioned it facing the chaises. "Make yourself comfortable."

Art sat down and released the latch so that he could recline the back of the chair. "Well, gentlemen. Let's talk about tonight. Why don't you outline your requirements, and I'll see what I can do to help. I believe you're interested in the company of some accommodating young ladies?"

"That is what I suggested." Devereaux perched on the edge of the empty chaise. "But I have some news for you. Our requirements have changed. As has our method of payment." He reached into his pocket, took out his shield and a small digital voice recorder, and laid them on the coffee table that filled the space between them. "What we require now is information. And we'll pay you for that information by deleting the recording I made of the conversation we had downstairs. The one where you agreed to participate in a felony."

Art grasped the armrests of the chair and his face twisted into a mask of pure hatred. "You cocksucker." He practically spat the words at Devereaux.

"It's OK." Devereaux crossed his arms. "You're upset. We get it. So take a moment. Get it out of your system. Then focus. You have a decision to make. This thing can work out well for you. Or it can work out badly. It's your choice."

Art stood up and moved to the window, stared into the distance for thirty seconds, then spoke without turning around. "This information you require. Be more specific."

"On July 21st, Peter Bromley asked you to arrange some girls for him. We need to know who you called to make that happen."

"No." Art turned around, his eyes open wide. "Forget it. Arrest me. Deport me. Do what you need to do. But I'm not telling you that."

"Why not?"

"Simple." Art shrugged. "I want to stay alive. The guy you want? He's a *bête*. He kills people with his bare hands. Crushes their skulls till their eyeballs pop out. He showed me pictures . . ."

"So you're frightened of this guy." Devereaux nodded. "That's good. Because it shows you know who he is. That saves us the trouble of wading through a whole other layer of bullshit. Now let me explain to you what's at stake. One of the girls you brought to the hotel on July 21st is dead. Emma Noble was her name. She was nineteen years old. Last night she was murdered. She was beaten. Burned. Stabbed. Raped. And strangled. Whoever did it has already killed two other women. We think he'll kill another one tonight. Unless you help us stop him."

"You think the guy I work for did it?"

"No. We think the guy who hired Emma last night did."

"Even if he didn't, we need to trace Emma's movements in the hours before she died," Garretty said.

"So when we go see your boss, we're not going to be talking about anything that happened back in July. Or anything connected to the hotel. Or to you. We're just going to ask him where he sent Emma last night," Devereaux said.

"There's no way anything will link back to you. There's absolutely no risk. You'll be completely safe," Garretty said.

"And if you don't help us now and another girl dies, you'll have that on your conscience the rest of your life." Devereaux paused and let that settle.

"That's not the easiest thing to bear." Garretty sounded sincere. "Let me tell you about a case I worked, years ago. A young woman had been murdered. She was completely torn apart. It was a horrible, horrible crime. My partner and I, we got wind that a guy might have seen the killer leaving the scene. We went and talked to him. He denied having been anywhere near the place, let alone seeing anything. The trail went cold, leaving the killer on the loose. He took two more lives before we caught him. And do you know what? That first witness? He'd lied to us. He had seen the killer. He could have identified him. Stopped the murders. But the guy was driving a stolen car at the time. He was afraid that if he talked to us and we looked into his story, we'd find out and he'd get in trouble for it. So he kept quiet, to save his own skin. And when he realized his selfishness had cost those two other women their lives, he couldn't live with himself. Two weeks later he locked himself in his garage, fired up his old Camaro, and checked out."

"Of course, if you don't help us, you won't have access to garages or Camaros." Devereaux tapped the voice recorder. "Because we'll be taking you to jail."

Dear Mom,

I hate Lucas! He's the most selfish asshole I've ever met. You won't believe this, but he still won't give me my video camera back. It's totally outrageous. Why doesn't he buy his own, if he wants one so much? He's rich enough. He could buy ten. He knows I can't afford to replace it. And it's not like he's even using it anymore. He doesn't have anything to use it for now. He's just holding on to it to torment me. He knows I want it. He knows not having it is causing me problems with Hayley. And I can't blame her. The baby will be arriving soon. She wants me to document everything. And I mean, everything—going to the hospital, the room, the birth, the baby's first bath, coming home. Everything. It's really important to her. To me, too. So I want to test the equipment. Make sure everything's in top shape. Charge the batteries. Be certain I'm ready. These aren't unreasonable things to want to do, in the circumstances. And I'm running out of excuses for not doing them.

   I wish I knew where the damn thing was. I'd just take it. But he keeps everything in his place so neat. He'd know if I'd been searching for it. But all isn't lost. I have a plan. If he doesn't return it by Friday, I'm going with the nuclear option. I'm going to take one of his client's cars. Whatever he has in the shop at the time. It doesn't matter what kind. They're all valuable. Except for that girl's Nova, last year, and he won't be working on that thing again. But that's irrelevant. The *point is, Lucas is so uptight about his reputation, he'd do anything to avoid finishing a job late. We could have a hostage exchange. Like in that movie with Tom Hanks. There are plenty of bridges in Birmingham, after all . . .*

Chapter *Forty-two*

Tuesday. Late morning.

IT DIDN'T TAKE ART LONG TO REACH A DECISION. HE TALKED.

When a hotel guest made it known he had certain needs, Art explained that he'd call a particular number. It had been given to him by a guy who went by the name Igor. Art didn't know if Igor was the guy's real name. He'd never asked or tried to find out. Because he was terrified of him. All he knew was that one day, eighteen months before, his coworker Darwin—the previous point man for the guests' nocturnal requirements—hadn't shown up to work. Then as he left the hotel at the end of his shift, Art was intercepted by the driver of a black S-Class Mercedes. He was invited to get into the back seat. Igor was already there. He showed Art a photograph. It was of Darwin's head, crushed like a watermelon. Igor invited Art to take Darwin's place in his organization. Art hadn't felt that refusal was an option. And besides, he'd seen the motorcycle Darwin drove. The jewelry he'd worn. The girls he occasionally went home with. The wad of notes he carried, rolled up in his uniform pocket. And he'd wanted some of that for himself.

The number Igor had given Art undoubtedly belonged to a burner phone, so Devereaux made a call to his old friend Spencer Page in Support Services.

It took him twenty minutes, but Page was able to narrow the phone's location to a building on Fourth Avenue. The information would have been useless in court—worse than useless, as it would have put Page and the detectives in the dock themselves—but Devereaux wasn't worried. The priority was finding the killer before he added a fourth victim. If any legal feathers needed to be smoothed over afterward, there were ways to do that. It could turn out, for example, that Art remembered Igor mentioning the address. He could write a statement to that effect. Whether he wanted to or not.

"Which one first?" Devereaux paused in front of the directory notice in the building's foyer. There was a hair salon. A greeting card store. A tax accountant. And a combined temporary service/modeling agency.

"The top one." Garretty started toward the stairs. "If the girls ever need to show up for any reason, a modeling agency would be a great cover."

The double doors at the top of the stairs gave way to a semi-circular reception area. A black line woven into the carpet divided the space into two quadrants. The one on the right was fitted out with a sleek, blond wood couch and two matching chairs. They had ink blue suede cushions. The walls were sky blue, and above each piece of furniture were large, framed black-and-white photographs of emaciated women in a variety of uncomfortable-looking clothes. The furniture on the left was laid out the same way, but it was made of mahogany and brown leather. It was more traditional in style, and on the magnolia-colored walls behind it was a set of prints showing groups of people happily working in half a dozen different settings.

A phone began to ring as Devereaux and Garretty approached the reception desk, which was opposite the doorway, straddling the divide between the two zones.

"Good morning, gentlemen." The receptionist—a woman who appeared to be in her early sixties with a 1960s-style beehive hairdo—picked up her handset. "Bear with me one moment."

Devereaux reached over and disconnected the call. "Birmingham PD. We're here to see Igor."

"There's no one by that name here." The woman slammed the handset down, almost crushing Devereaux's fingers. "You must be in the wrong place."

"Maybe." Devereaux took out his cell and dialed the number Art had given him. A few seconds later the chorus from one of Borodin's Polovtsian Dances rang out from behind a door on the blue side of the room. "Or maybe not." Devereaux ended the call. "Don't get up. We'll introduce ourselves."

The detectives didn't knock. The door opened onto an office that had clearly been set up with interviewing in mind. There was a daybed against the left-hand wall. A couch on the right. And straight ahead, facing back into the room, was a desk with a single visitor's chair next to it. Behind the desk, a man got to his feet. He was easily seven feet tall. His blond hair was cropped close to his skull, which somehow accented his radiant blue eyes and high cheekbones. He was wearing black suit pants and a white dress shirt, with seams that were struggling to contain his chest and biceps.

"Igor." Devereaux crossed to the desk, picked up the iPhone that was lying there, and slipped it into his pocket. "This is your lucky day."

Garretty showed his badge, then wedged himself in the corner of the couch. "You see, normally we'd have spoken to our buddies in Vice before coming to visit with you. They'd be waiting outside to scoop you up, once we were done with our questions. In fact, we can still call them. But if you give us the one little piece of information we're looking for, we're willing to walk out of here and leave you in peace."

"Where did you send Emma Noble last night, Igor?" Devereaux asked.

"Who?" Igor's voice was surprisingly soft for a guy his size.

"Maybe you knew her by a different name." Devereaux took out his phone and called up a picture of Emma lying on the church steps.

"She's dead?" A flash of alarm showed on Igor's face.

"Correct." Devereaux kept the picture up on the screen. "You sent her somewhere last night. Don't waste time denying it—we know she worked for your service. You sent her somewhere, and she wound up dead. Tortured. Then murdered. We want the guy who did it. For now, we don't care about you. If you want it to stay that way, tell us where you sent her."

"You can't connect this to me." Igor pulled his eyes away from the gruesome image. "You take me in, and I'll be free in twenty-four hours."

"Maybe." Devereaux shrugged. "So here's a couple of things for you to think about while you're in the holding cells. First, we might just whisper in a couple of ears that the girls you're running are underage. Pimping out kids? Not great for life expectancy in the joint. But you're a big guy. You'll probably make it through, as long as you don't close your eyes. So here's the second thing. The guy who murdered Emma—he's done it twice before. He started out with regular women. Then he figured out how to work a little smarter. Why snatch someone off the street and risk getting seen, when you can call a number and have a victim sent wherever you want her? And this guy? He likes to kill on consecutive nights. We know that for a fact. So which of your girls will be next? And when two of them are dead, how many of the others will continue working for you? I hope you haven't got any big spending plans, Igor. 'Cause your cash supply's about to dry up."

"Just tell us where you sent Emma," Garretty said. "That's all you have to do."

"I don't remember." Igor leaned forward with his palms on the desk. "I'll have to check. I'll—"

"It's OK." A woman had appeared in the doorway. She was in her mid-forties. She was short and slim, and was wearing a plain black knee-length dress with black pumps. Her hair was cut short. It was dark and shiny. She had a sheet of paper in her hand. "Igor, you can go. I can help these gentlemen."

The woman stood aside to let Igor pass, then closed the door and stepped into the center of the room. "My name's Linda Marshall. This is my . . . agency. I was listening to your conversation just now. I can help you with the details you need."

"OK." Devereaux stepped around from behind the desk. "Let's have them."

"One moment." Marshall held the paper close to her body. "As you can see, I'm cooperating with you here. It's just awful, what you said happened to poor Emma, so I'm making things as easy for you as I can. And I'd appreciate it if you could return the favor."

"What have you got in mind?" Devereaux crossed his arms.

"Janice, my receptionist, she doesn't know anything about this side of the business. None of my other employees do. My other companies—they're totally legitimate. I wouldn't want to see any of them go down with the ship."

"What about Igor?"

"He knows a little bit. But he's mostly window dressing. It's hard to make the kind of impression that keeps people awake at night when you're four foot eleven without your heels."

"We heard he crushed a guy's skull."

"Ha. The guy from the French hotel? No. He was an idiot. He fell off his Harley on his way to meet Igor one night. He wasn't wearing a helmet, and he went headfirst between a Dumpster and a brick wall. Igor called me. I saw the mess the guy had made of himself, and I thought, why look a gift horse in the mouth. I took pictures. Spread the story. That way, Igor didn't have to break any heads."

"And you?"

"This is a volatile business, Detective." Marshall shook her head. "I've known this day would come for a long time. My bags are always packed. If Vice didn't show up for, say, half an hour, in return for my cooperation . . ."

"They can be a little slow moving, those guys." Devereaux nodded. "So tell us what you know."

"Here's the address we sent Emma to last night." Marshall held out the sheet of paper. "The call came in at 2:33 pm. The appointment was for eight pm."

"The client's name was John Smith?"

"John Smith 17, actually. John Smith's a very popular alias." A flash of amusement faded quickly from Marshall's face. "You don't expect married men to use their real names, do you, Detective?"

"But you do know his real name?"

"How would I?" Marshall shrugged. "This is a cash business. We don't ask clients for ID. All we ask is that they pay and don't smack anyone around."

"And if I have my Forensic Accounting guys take a look at your bank accounts?"

"They'll find money. Plenty of that. But no names." Marshall stepped forward and took hold of Devereaux's forearm. "I swear, Detective, if I knew his name I'd tell you. One of my girls is dead. I take that personally. What do you think I did before I started running this place?"

"If I find out you're lying . . ." Devereaux pulled his arm free from Marshall's grip.

"I'm not." Marshall paused. "But there's another possibility you should take into account. Last night Emma only had one appoint-ment. She arrived OK, right on time. Then five minutes later she texted in a code nine." Marshall registered the blank expressions on the detectives' faces. "That means the client was a no-show. We have codes that the girls use to update their status on a job. To tell us they've arrived at a client's address, for example. When they're leav-ing. If the client gets rough. If he won't pay. And so on. So if Emma never met the client, he couldn't have killed her. Someone else must have jumped her, maybe when she was leaving the premises. It would have taken a strong son of a bitch, though. Emma was a tough girl. And she was streetwise."

"Interesting." Devereaux glanced across at Garretty. "And the code nine—that was the last you heard from her?"

"Right." Marshall nodded. "The appointment didn't go ahead, and she didn't have any other jobs."

"Do you have an emergency code?"

"Of course."

"Any chance she could have texted the wrong one?"

"I mean, it's possible, I guess. But I doubt it. Emma wasn't a moron."

"OK. We'll keep that in mind. Was there anything else that didn't ring true about last night?"

"Well," Marshall's face contorted as if she'd bitten into some-thing sour. "One thing was creepy, looking back. The guy, he was very specific about his requirements. Which is nothing unusual, in itself. But . . ."

"But?" Devereaux prompted.

"He said he wanted a girl who was turning twenty-one that day." Marshall couldn't meet Devereaux's eye.

"And you sent Emma to him anyway?" Devereaux couldn't keep the disdain out of his voice. "Don't you read the papers?"

"Of course I do." Marshall forced herself to look up. "And if that's all he asked for, I'd have turned him down in a heartbeat. But he was just as insistent about something else. He only wanted a girl who had a kid. He really hammered that point home so I figured he was mainly into the kinky stuff—spanking, wearing diapers, whatever."

"Did Emma have a kid?" Devereaux was suddenly uneasy.

"Of course not. And it wasn't her birthday, either. We're not selling reality, Detective. Just fantasy. But whether John Smith 17 is B/DK and he killed Emma, or someone else grabbed her near the address he gave, it was me who sent Emma there. And I'm the one who has to live with that."

Chapter Forty-three

Tuesday. Early afternoon.

On the way out of the building, Devereaux called one of his old partners—Eddie England—who now worked in Vice. Devereaux told him about the setup at the modeling agency and said he should roll on it right away. Then he unfolded the sheet of paper Marshall had given him and handed it to Garretty.

"Recognize the address?"

"No." Garretty handed it back. "Should I?"

"Of course not." Devereaux mimed shooting himself in the head. "You were still in the hospital. But I was just there. It's the building where Dean Sullivan lives. The guy who was at the movies with Lucas Paltrow on Thursday. Or claimed to be."

"That's an interesting coincidence. We should have another conversation with Sullivan while we're there. See why he lied."

The apartment the detectives were interested in was on the first floor, midway along the corridor, on the same side of the building as Sulli-

van's. Devereaux pointed to the slot for a name card below the peep-
hole in the center of the door. It was empty.

"I guess he didn't want her to see his real name." Devereaux
banged on the door.

There was no reply.

"Stay here, Cooper, in case someone shows up." Garretty turned
back toward the entrance to the building. "I'll find the super."

Garretty returned twelve minutes later. He was walking several
feet ahead of a short, round, fifty-something guy who was wearing a
kind of uniform that was made up of beige pants and a matching
shirt with the title *Superintendent* embroidered on the chest. He had
round, wire-framed glasses balancing on his squashed, stubby nose,
a greasy comb-over, and hands like baseball mitts.

"Wait up." The guy was really dragging his feet. "What's your
hurry?"

"This is Anton." Garretty rolled his eyes. "Anton was napping
when I found him. Apparently he's cranky right after he wakes up."

"Thanks for helping us, Anton." Devereaux nodded toward the
door. "We need you to unlock this. Then step away to the side and
remain in the corridor. You are not to set one foot in the apartment
unless we call for you. Do you understand?"

Anton grunted, then pulled out a master key on an extending
wire attached to a drum on his belt and slid it into the lock.

The layout of the apartment was the same as Sullivan's. There
was a U-shaped kitchen on the left. A floor-to-ceiling window straight
ahead, beyond the living and dining area, though this one opened
onto a small private deck rather than a balcony. And an archway
leading to the bedrooms on the right. But there was no furniture. No
personal possessions of any kind. The place clearly wasn't occupied.
There was a closed-up, musty tinge to the air. And along with it, the
hint of a harsher scent with a bitter, metallic aftertaste.

"Blood." Devereaux stepped farther into the room. "Tommy—
over here. Look."

There was a reddish-brown oval-shaped pool on the floor, about eighteen inches long. Its edges were darker and were turning crusty. The center still looked soft and was a richer scarlet. Flies were already buzzing around it, and three were stuck in the slick.

"Looks like that madam was wide of the mark with her random attacker theory," Garretty said.

"That was never going to fly." Devereaux shook his head. "Not with the guy asking specifically for a twenty-one-year-old with a kid. Marshall was just trying to find a little wiggle room for her conscience. You can't blame her, really."

"So our guy calls Marshall's service." Garretty stepped back toward the door. "Gives this address. Emma shows up. He lets her in. She sees the place is empty, realizes there's a problem, maybe tries to get away. There's a struggle. The guy subdues her, but it takes a while and she's hurt in the process. Marshall said Emma was tough. He makes her send the code for a no-show, to make sure no one came looking for her. Then he either finished the job here or took her somewhere else."

"He most likely took her somewhere else." Devereaux looked at the walls as if trying to assess how soundproof they were. "He wouldn't know if anyone had heard them struggling and called 911. It's hard to carry a body to a vehicle without looking suspicious. And my guess is he'd want privacy, and time, to do what he wanted."

"We need to get CSU down here to make sure that is Emma's blood." Garretty checked off the actions with his fingers. "We need to get a canvass going. Someone might have seen the guy coming in. Or leaving, with Emma. We need to figure out who could have had access to the apartment. And who could have known it was empty."

"Tommy, look at this." Devereaux was pointing to the corner of the living area. A piece of wood was propped up against the wall. It was an inch wide. An inch deep. And as long as roughly half the width of the window.

"That shouldn't be there." Garretty narrowed his eyes.

"Right. It should be wedged in the door track, in case the lock gets forced." Devereaux crossed to the window, pulled on a latex glove, and with the tip of one finger he pushed on the door handle. It slid open easily, giving full access to the deck. "Except that it was already unlocked. The guy could have taken Emma out this way. We need to extend the canvass. It should include every apartment with a view across the gardens."

"I'm on it." Garretty pulled out his phone. "Why don't you ask Anton about access. You might have more luck. He didn't seem to warm to me."

Out in the corridor Anton was sitting on the floor, back against the wall, legs pulled in to his chest, arms wrapped around ankles, chin resting on knees, eyes half-closed. Devereaux sat down next to him.

"How long has the apartment been vacant, Anton?"

"Since last Monday. Just over a week."

"Who does it belong to? Do you know?"

"A company owns it. They have four in this building. Maybe fifty altogether, spread out across the city."

"Does anyone from the company ever come and check up on the place?"

"Maybe once in the fifteen years I've worked here." Anton scratched his forehead. "A new tenant moved in. Complained the apartment hadn't been left clean enough. He kicked up a real hullaballoo. Eventually a woman from their office came to see for herself. She was inside all of three minutes, and she didn't even bring a key. I had to let her in myself."

"What about the tenant who just vacated? Or was it a couple?"

"Just the one guy. A German dude. He was here six months. He works for a company that had invented some new kind of laser, he said. The university bought one, for one of the labs. The guy was here to help them get it set up, train them, that kind of thing. He was a nice guy. Very quiet."

"If I wanted to rent the apartment, what would I have to do?"

"There's an agent who handles all that. You call her and arrange a viewing. If you like it, you fill out a bunch of forms. And pay your security deposit."

"Have there been any viewings since the German dude left?"

"One, I think. Yesterday."

"So if I wanted it, how would I know it's on the market? There are no notices anywhere."

"The building doesn't allow notices. You'd have to look on the agency's website, or use one of those real estate search things online. Or if you know anyone who already lives here, they might tell you. All the available units are posted on the building's Facebook page."

"That's good. Thank you. Now, I need to talk to the agent you mentioned. Do you have her details?"

"Oh, well, that's just great." Anton heaved himself up off the ground. "Remind me to thank your buddy for not mentioning that before. I have a bunch of her cards, but they're all in my office. Wait here. I'll be back."

Amy Jarvis, the real estate agent who was handling the apartment rental, answered her phone on the first ring.

"Sure." Her voice was loud and confident. "I remember showing a guy that place. It was only yesterday, Detective. He had a Scottish-sounding name. Alex McLeish. That's it. I have his address in my notebook. I'll text it to you when we're done talking."

"Can you describe him?"

"He seemed like a nice enough guy. Talked a lot. Didn't ask too many questions, but he already seemed to know a lot about the building. I'd say he was serious. He's going through a divorce and wants a place for six months, maybe a year, while he figures out what to do next with his life. He spent quite a while looking around inside, checking that everything worked. I wouldn't be surprised if he calls back today, wanting to go ahead."

"I meant, can you describe him physically."

"Oh. Yes. He was pretty average, I guess. Around six feet tall. Not fat. Not thin. Didn't wear glasses. Dark hair. Kind of ruffled."

"I'm going to send you a picture, so hang up and call me back when you've got it. Tell me if it's the guy you're talking about."

Devereaux messaged a copy of Lucas Paltrow's driver's license photograph to Jarvis.

"Nope." Jarvis called back a moment later. "This guy's not totally dissimilar, but he's not Alex McLeish."

"You're sure?"

"Positive. I have a great memory for faces. I can't always remember names, but if I've seen someone before, even years ago, I always recognize them. It freaks people out sometimes."

"I bet. So, Amy, one final question. Did McLeish ask you about any other apartments?"

"No. I offered to show him some others, but he said he wasn't interested. It seemed like his choice was between the apartment he saw—which he liked—or leaving town. I don't see him leaving town, though, honestly. He has two kids. Twin girls. He'll want to stay close."

"OK. Well, thanks for your help. If you can send me McLeish's address, that'll be great. And if you hear from him again, do me one other favor. Don't agree to meet him. Call me first."

Jarvis sent McLeish's address thirty seconds later, and Devereaux called Dispatch to get his full background.

"Are you sure we're not missing a trick here, Cooper?" Garretty looked concerned. "All this tells us is that McLeish knew the apartment was empty. Well, so what? The thing we really need to know is who had access to it. I say we should talk to the super again. Lean on him a little. See if he's been supplementing his income by selling copies of his master key."

Devereaux's phone rang again. It was the duty officer at Dispatch. "Detective, are you sure the address you gave me is correct?"

"As far as I know it is. Why?"

"Because it doesn't exist. It's bogus."

"All right." Garretty nodded when Devereaux gave him the news. "Let's find Anton. Follow up on the key idea. And we should get Amy Jarvis down to the precinct. Set her up with a sketch artist. Try to get a likeness of this McLeish guy to circulate, if that's even his real name."

"Yes to the sketch artist." Devereaux closed his eyes for a moment. "But before we lean on the super, I want him to let us in the apartment again. There's something I want to take another look at."

The detectives had Anton wait outside in the corridor again, which did little to improve his mood. Particularly when they closed the door on him.

"That's what I thought." Devereaux pointed to the lock. "You can open it from the inside without needing a key."

"But how do you get . . ." Garretty turned and looked at the patio door. "Damn, Cooper. You're thinking the guy didn't just leave through the back. He came in that way, too."

"Right." Devereaux stepped back. "He set up the appointment to view the apartment yesterday afternoon. He moved the wood and undid the latch while the agent wasn't looking. She said he really took his time, poking around the place. Then he gave the address to Emma's service. He sneaked in through the patio door, so he was inside waiting when she arrived. He didn't need a key to open the door. And he reduced the chances of anyone seeing him coming or going, all in one move."

"He's a smart cookie." Garretty took out his phone. "I'm going to put a rush on that sketch. I'll get a unit to pick up Amy Jarvis and bring her in. We need to get his description out there, and fast."

Devereaux moved over to the window and stared outside while Garretty was on the phone. Then he turned back to face his partner. "There's something else about the way this was set up. Whoever the guy is, for his plan to work, he needed a place with the right kind of sliding door at the back and the right kind of lock at the front. He only asked to see one place, and it had both those things. That's not chance. It's not coincidence."

"He must know the building."

"Right. Like Dean Sullivan. He lives here. And he's already lied once to cover for Lucas Paltrow."

Chapter *Forty-four*

Tuesday. Afternoon.

DEAN SULLIVAN WAS STILL IN HIS PAJAMAS WHEN HE OPENED HIS DOOR.

"Sick again, Dean?" Devereaux stepped past him into the apartment.

"No." Sullivan moved sideways to make room for Garretty. "I mean, yes, I'm still sick. Obviously. That's why I can't work. But that's not why I'm still in my pajamas, if that's what you mean. The pajamas aren't my fault. Hayley, my girlfriend, was supposed to wake me up this morning. But instead, she just went out. She can be so inconsiderate. She's gone to see her mother and that always puts her on edge, and there are the pregnancy hormones to think about, so I guess I should cut her some slack. And hopefully she'll be back soon. Anyway, who's this?"

"My partner, Detective Garretty." Devereaux started toward the window. "He was in the hospital when I was here before. Today we were in the building working on another case, so we thought we'd stop by so he could say hello."

Garretty crossed to the couch and picked up a stack of papers Sullivan had been working on. "You didn't tell me Dean was a poet, Detective." Garretty cleared his throat and held the papers out in front of him.

Don't go far off, not even for a day,
Because I don't know how to say it—a day is long
And I will be waiting for you, as in
An empty station when the trains are
Parked off somewhere else, asleep.

"OK. That doesn't suck. Did you write it yourself?"

"Yes." Sullivan folded his arms tightly across his chest. "I did. It's for Hayley. I like to surprise her with something nice every now and again. Is there something wrong with that?"

"Not at all." Garretty winked.

"Safer than flowers," Devereaux added.

"And look!" Garretty shuffled through the pages. "A letter to your mom. The start of one, anyway. You're quite the renaissance man, aren't you, Dean?"

"Give those back!" Sullivan snatched the papers out of Garretty's hands and sat back down on the couch. "Now tell me. Why are you really here?"

"Just to talk. There's nothing to worry about." Devereaux tugged on the balcony door and it slid effortlessly aside. "Wait. You don't keep this locked?"

"Why would I keep it locked, Detective? We're twelve floors up. What's an intruder going to do? Scale the side of the building like Spider-Man?"

"Good point." Devereaux slid the door closed again. "Up here, you probably don't need to worry. But if you move to the first floor, that'll be a whole different story. You'll definitely need to use the lock down there. And the lock might not even be enough. You might need to get a piece of wood and fit it into the track at the bottom of the door. That'll stop anyone from forcing it open. You know about that little trick, don't you, Dean? It's low-tech, but effective."

"What are you talking about?" Red dots appeared on Sullivan's neck and spread up to his cheeks. "I'm not moving anywhere."

"Really?" Devereaux stepped away from the window. "Amy Jarvis will be so disappointed. She thought you were serious. And she really liked you. She went on for ages about what a great conversationalist you are."

"Amy who?" Sullivan's gaze shifted to the floor.

"Bad memory for names, huh?" Devereaux sat at the far end of the couch. "Amy Jarvis. The agent who showed you the apartment, right here in the building, on the first floor. Yesterday lunchtime. You can't have forgotten going down there? You made quite an impression on her, you know."

"No." Sullivan shook his head. "That's not ringing any bells."

"Dean." Garretty sat down on the other side of Sullivan, penning him in. "We showed her your driver's license photograph. She recognized you."

"Oh, well I *looked* at that apartment, sure." Tiny beads of sweat broke out on Sullivan's forehead. "But that doesn't mean I'm moving there. I mean, I thought of moving there, or I wouldn't have wasted her time, and mine, going to look. I decided against the idea, though. I'm staying here. I like this apartment."

"Why did you think of moving, then, if you like this place so much?"

"Well, the baby's coming. She'll be arriving very soon. And when you have a baby, you need more space. This is a nice apartment but it's not the biggest in the world, so I thought maybe a bigger one would be better. For all three of us. But in the end I didn't like it. I decided we should all just stay here."

"How could the first-floor apartment be any bigger? It's directly below this one. Its footprint is exactly the same."

"So?"

"So what do you think? The laws of physics don't apply in this building?"

"Well, no. It's not that. It's not so much having extra space for the baby. It's more that, if I'm totally honest with you, things aren't going too well between me and Hayley. I figure there's a chance I might have to move out. And with a new baby, I won't want to be too far away. I want to be totally involved in her life. Changing diapers. Midnight feedings. Sign me up. The whole enchilada. I'm in. No one will ever be able to say that Dean Sullivan shirks his responsibilities when it comes to his family."

"All right, stop it now." Devereaux shook his head. "Your story changes every two seconds. It makes absolutely no sense. None. Which is a major problem. And I think you know why. A young woman was lured to that apartment downstairs last night. She was tortured. And murdered. The killer got in through the patio door, which had been unlocked by the only person who had prior access to the place."

"Dean, we know that person was you," Garretty said.

"The way we see it, things could have gone one of two ways," Devereaux said. "One, you opened the door for someone else, and he did the actual killing. Or two, you murdered the woman yourself."

"If it's the second one, and you murdered her, then screw you, Dean," Garretty said. "We're going to see to it that you get the needle. I'm just putting that out there, so you know where you stand."

"If it's the first option, and you only opened the door, you've got to be realistic," Devereaux said. "You're still in a whole heap of trouble. *Accessory before the fact,* the DA will call it. You're looking at *life without,* at the minimum. The needle's not even out of the question."

"Unless you work with us."

"Tell us the truth this time."

"Get out in front of this thing, before it gets any worse."

"If you help us catch the guy before he hurts anyone else, that'll be huge for you."

"We'll go to bat for you with the DA. Tell her how you didn't know what you were getting yourself into at first. How remorseful you were when you figured it out. How we couldn't have broken the case without you."

"And you know, that's the kind of thing the press pick up on. They'd be wanting to interview you. Write profile pieces about you. Maybe even a book. There could be a miniseries. A movie . . ."

"All right!" Sullivan leaned forward. "Yes. I'll help you. It was Lucas. He made me do it."

"Lucas Paltrow?" Devereaux asked.

"Yes. My so-called friend. He tricked me."

"Lucas Paltrow killed that woman?" Devereaux said.

"Wait, no." Sullivan held up his hands. "I can't believe Lucas would go that far. That's not what I'm saying at all. All I'm telling you is that he tricked me into leaving the apartment door open. I don't know anything about what happened after that."

"How did he trick you?"

"Let me explain. You see, one thing you should know about Lucas is he has a thing for prostitutes. He just loves sleeping with them. There's no need for dinner, movies, anything like that. They just get straight down to business, which is Lucas all over. He's a very direct kind of guy. Anyway, recently, he's been seeing more and more of them. It's been costing him a fortune. So he came up with a plan. Or so he said. He told me, if he could find an empty apartment to use for his—what's the word?—assignations, he could refuse to pay the girl and her pimp wouldn't know where to find him. He tried that at his own place once, years ago, and he had all kinds of problems with lunatics showing up and threatening him. Which is why he told me to leave that door open. So that he could get set up ahead of time and meet the hooker there."

"Dean—are you lying to us again?"

"No. I swear. This is the truth."

"OK." Devereaux shook his head. "Now here's my problem. You have a major credibility issue, given all the bullshit you've fed me in the short time we've known each other. So to fully convince me, I want you to think back and tell me if there was anything you said in our first conversation that wasn't absolutely true."

"OK." Sullivan covered his eyes for a moment, then looked up. "Yes. I'm not proud of this, but I wasn't completely honest about one other thing. Remember I told you I went to the movies with Lucas? Well, I didn't. We were supposed to go. He even bought the tickets. But at the last minute, he bailed. And he said to me, if anyone asks, to tell them we did go. He was very insistent about that."

"Why did he bail?" Devereaux asked.

"He didn't say."

"Didn't you ask?"

"Of course not. You don't question Lucas when he's made a decision. Not unless you're crazy. That guy's got a temper on him like a shot-at rat. I can't even count the number of times he's threatened to strangle me over the tiniest of things. And I'm his oldest friend!"

"All right." Devereaux took out the pen he'd taken from the Petite Maison and offered it to Sullivan. "This is what's going to happen. You're going to write down everything you just told us and sign it. Then we're going to stay with you until we get word from the detectives who are watching Lucas's place that they have him safely in custody. We wouldn't want him getting any mysterious phone calls, warning him to run."

"OK. I can write a statement. No problem. I definitely won't try to warn him. And after that, I won't be in any trouble, right? I'm helping. I'm overflowing with remorse. I didn't know what Lucas was going to do, if he even did anything. And I'm going to be a father soon. A kid needs its parents, right? You can't punish an innocent newborn baby for something her father did without even meaning to."

"That's not our call. It's up to the DA. But don't worry." Devereaux turned and smiled at Garretty. "We'll make our recommendation."

Chapter **Forty-five**

Tuesday. Afternoon.

SUSPECTS ARE LIKE CATNIP TO THIS GUY, DEVEREAUX THOUGHT AS HE watched Captain Emrich staring through the observation window into the interview room. Nothing could get him out of his office on the fifth floor quicker than the sniff of a possible break in a major investigation. Now he was standing there, practically drooling. When they'd first met, Devereaux had taken Emrich to be a kind of voyeur, getting his kicks at the expense of the criminals whose lives were about to come seriously unraveled. But Devereaux had quickly changed that theory. He realized it was something else that attracted the captain. The chance to share in the kudos if the case ended well. And to deflect the blame if it didn't.

On the other side of the glass Lucas Paltrow sat at the metal table, still wearing his blue coveralls. He was absolutely still. His back was straight. His feet were flat on the floor. His forearms were resting on the scratched and dented surface in front of him. He could have been meditating, if it weren't for his open eyes and the tiny smile that occasionally played around the corners of his mouth.

There was a tap on the door. Garretty opened it, and Agent Irvin hurried into the gallery, followed by Lieutenant Hale.

"How long has he been like that?" Lieutenant Hale instinctively took a position between Emrich and Devereaux.

"Fifty-five minutes." Devereaux checked his watch. "Tommy and I've been here the last five. We wanted to see how he'd react to being kept waiting."

"Has he been calm like that the whole time?" Irvin sounded hopeful.

"The whole time." Devereaux nodded.

"Excellent." Irvin turned back to the observation window. "An innocent man would have been raging long before now. *Let me out. I haven't done anything. Why are you keeping me here?* But look at this guy. He could be at a spa. He's got *guilty* written all over him."

Paltrow turned to look at Devereaux when he entered the interview room, but his expression remained neutral.

"Lucas." Devereaux took the seat on the other side of the table. "Do you know why the officers brought you here?"

"I guess." Paltrow moved his hands to his lap. "But I've got to say, it seems like a lot of trouble over one missed movie."

"You lied about going to see it."

"Not exactly." Paltrow paused for a moment. "I have seen it. Just on a different day. Beyond that, I guess it all depends on what you take the concept of lying to be about. If you're one of those pedantic-type guys who gets all caught up in the details, then you probably would say I lied. But me? I'm more about the big picture. You see, it was clear from the context of our discussion that what you really wanted to know was whether I'd killed that poor girl whose body was found at the crematorium. And as I did not do that, I figured there was no point in casting any unwanted light on another individual who also had nothing to do with the girl winding up dead. Plus I had actually bought the theater tickets. I liked the movie. I was planning to see it again."

"What changed your mind?"

"Do I have to spell it out, Detective?"

"That's kind of the idea of what we're doing here, Lucas. So yes. Spell it out."

Paltrow took a deep breath. "OK. The truth is, I'm seeing another guy's wife. He's one of my customers. She keeps saying she wants to leave him and move in with me. Which is absolutely not what I signed up for. So I keep trying to cool things down. Then Friday afternoon she calls me. She says she's finally going to walk out. Tell her husband everything. So I figure, if there's any chance of getting this woman's finger off the nuclear button, I better head right over there. To her place. To try to calm her down. Make her see sense. Which I successfully did. But it meant missing the movie. And, it would seem, bringing a whole plague of suspicion down on my head."

"I'll need this woman's name and address."

"No problem. I'll write it down for you. She'll confirm what I said."

"We'll see."

"Just do me one favor, Detective. If her husband's around when you're talking to her, be discreet. The whole point of the exercise was to keep him from finding out. And you know, really, I think they could still have a future together. If he could just listen to her more, and maybe occasionally—"

"Can the marriage counseling, Lucas. Tell me this instead. Where were you yesterday? Say, at eight pm."

"Out." Lucas crossed his arms. "Visiting a friend."

"A friend like Dean Sullivan? The guy who lied for you about the movie theater?"

"Dean? That sorry-ass loser? God, no. A female friend."

"The kind who comes with a price tag?"

"Me? With a hooker? Come on, Detective. The day I have to pay for it is the day I'll eat my gun."

"Ever heard the expression *when you're in a hole, stop digging?* Because your friend Dean? He gave you up, Lucas. He told us all about your scheme with the hooker and the vacant apartment."

"Wait a minute!" Paltrow slammed his palms on the table. "The imbecile. He didn't fall for it? That's ridiculous. He totally wasted his time, then. I didn't go near the place. Why would I have to? I mean, for one thing, I could afford as many hookers as I could possibly want. And for another, I don't want any. I don't need them."

"Drop the bravado, Lucas." Devereaux leaned in closer. "It's time to start telling the truth. You convinced Dean Sullivan to leave that apartment unlocked. Admit it."

"Sure. I asked him to leave the place unlocked. But I never thought he would. The truth is, I'm sick of him hanging around all the time. He does nothing but complain about how sick he pretends to be, and how he can't get a job, and how unfair life is. And all the while he's sponging off me. I've tried to be nice and drop some gentle hints. I've tried being blunt and told him to give me space. Neither approach worked. So I thought, seeing as how he's about the vainest guy I've ever met, I'll embarrass him. Trick him into agreeing to do something he's bound to chicken out of. Then he'd be too ashamed to show his face for a while. I'd have bet you a million bucks he wouldn't go through with it. I had no idea he'd all of a sudden grow a pair."

"But the fact remains, you arranged for that apartment to be left open. Then Emma Noble was lured there. Abducted. Tortured. And killed."

"I get it. The whole thing's a terrible shame for this Emma chick. But what's her death got to do with me? Put it this way. What if I'd told dumb-ass Dean to leave his car unlocked instead. If his car then got in an accident, would it follow that I was the one who was driving it?"

"Where were you at eight pm, Lucas?"

"I told you. I was . . . wait. It was wrong, what I told you. I know exactly where I was at eight pm. Well, eight-oh-two, to be precise. I was getting gas. I have the receipt in my billfold. The time stuck in my head because the credit card machine was set to the twenty-four-hour clock. So eight-oh-two pm comes out as two zero zero two, and I liked the symmetry of it."

"I'll need to see that receipt. And we'll be checking the security cameras at the gas station."

"Knock yourself out. And while you're doing that, here's something else to think about. It just struck me. This Emma—her body was left at the Prince of Peace Catholic Church, according to the news. I know that church. I used to do a tai chi class there on Monday nights. It was a great place for meeting women. Anyway, that class ends at ten pm. I got to my friend's house at 9:45, and I was there all night. So whatever happened to the poor woman, it had nothing to do with me."

There was a knock at the door. It opened and Garretty leaned into the room. "Detective? I need you out here for a moment."

Garretty led the way back to the observation gallery where Isringhausen, the technician from the crime scene unit, had joined Irvin, Lieutenant Hale, and Captain Emrich.

"I just got back from Paltrow's house and workshop." Isringhausen handed Devereaux a USB drive. "I copied the video for you. It was a weird place. Unbelievably clean and tidy. Like, OCD-level clean. I've never seen anything like it in real life. Only on training courses and in books."

"Anything to tie him to the murders?" Devereaux slipped the drive into his pocket.

"He had four boxes of synthetic work gloves, which could be similar to the ones that left the texture marks on the dead women's necks." Isringhausen shrugged. "We're having them analyzed, but the guy works on cars. It's natural that he'd have gloves. And there was nothing else incriminating in the rest of the place. No blood. None of the women's missing clothes or possessions. No sheets that matched the ones left at the dump sites. The only other suspicious thing was the second bedroom in the house. It was painted matte black throughout, including the window. The carpet was black. The bed had black iron head and foot rails with straps attached to them. There was one of those kinky sex chairs with all kinds of restraints on it. And there was a false wall at one end, with a cutout for a hidden video camera. I can't give you a guarantee, but if I had to guess I'd say it was a setup for making home porno movies."

"I could see him doing that." Irvin turned back to the window. "Especially with the bondage elements. Look at him. Like a statue. He's obviously all about control."

Devereaux closed the interview room door slowly, drawing out the high-pitched squeal from its hinges, and moved around to face Paltrow.

"The crime scene techs just got back from your place." Devereaux shook his head. "They brought a lot of samples with them. The lab's going to be busy. I just hope they didn't make too much of a mess. They're not exactly house-trained, some of those guys. They can get a bit heavy-handed. And what about your little porno studio, Lucas? Things get a little Fifty Shades at Chez Paltrow, huh?"

Paltrow showed no signs of a response.

"Well, not to worry." Devereaux leaned his hands on the back of the chair. "I'm sure you'll get everything straightened up. Eventually. But for now, the next step is to get you transferred to a holding cell. We need to check your alibis. I hope that won't take too long."

"I was doing some thinking when you were out of the room just then, Detective." Paltrow laced his fingers and placed his hands on the table. "And it struck me, maybe the best way to help myself get out of this situation is to help you find the guy who did kill these women. So I have a question. All the time you were with Dean Sullivan while he was trying to point the finger at me, how much energy did you put into looking at him? Think about it. I wasn't at the movie theater Friday, which means he wasn't there, either. Where was he? Billy Flynn, God rest his soul, had access to my customers' cars. So does Dean. He's always hanging around my shop. He knows where I keep the keys. Deborah Holt came to my shop a year ago, the only time I met her. Dean was there that day, too. He became obsessed with her. He went on about wanting to find her for weeks afterward. And then there's the apartment in his building, left unlocked. That was my idea, yes. But Dean's the one who did it. And yes, I planted the idea of taking a hooker there. Now, clearly I don't need to. But Dean? Whose girlfriend's massively pregnant and mad at him all the time? He's not getting any at home, believe me. And he's just the kind of lazy idiot who'd do it on his own doorstep. Take it from me. I've known the guy since we were kids."

Chapter **Forty-six**

Tuesday. Late afternoon.

"DID YOU ARREST HIM?" SULLIVAN'S EYES WERE RED AND HIS FACE WAS paler than it had been earlier, but his expression brightened when he opened the door for the detectives. "Did he get mad?"

Pieces of ripped-up paper covered the floor between the kitchen and the living area like confetti after a wedding. Devereaux moved across and picked one up. There was a fragment of handwriting . . . *empty station when . . .*

"Chocolates next time?" Devereaux let go of the scrap and it fluttered back down to the ground. "Your romantic gestures don't seem to be hitting the mark."

"Just don't get her a puppy." Garretty moved to the couch and sat down. "Now come. Join us. We have a couple of follow-up questions."

Sullivan shuffled over to the couch and perched on the edge of the center cushion. "What more do you need to know?"

"Who else did you tell about your plan to leave the downstairs apartment unlocked?" Devereaux took a step closer.

"No one." Sullivan shrank back. "Aside from Lucas, obviously."

"Have you ever done anything else like that?" Devereaux asked.

"No." Sullivan shook his head. "I only did it because Lucas asked me to. He's been really cranky with me lately, so I thought if I did what he wanted it would make things all right between us again."

Devereaux put his hands on his hips. "So you did this cool thing, outsmarting the real estate agent, unlocking the door, and moving the wooden pole right under her nose without her having any idea what you were doing? Like you're James Bond, or the *Mission Impossible* guy? And you don't tell a soul? That's crazy!"

"No it's not." Sullivan sounded hurt. "I did it for Lucas. He wanted it to be a secret. If I'd told anyone, he'd have been mad at me again. That's the opposite of what I wanted."

"So there were only two people in the whole world who knew that door was unlocked. Lucas." Devereaux paused. "And you."

"That's right." Sullivan looked up. "Where are you going with this, Detective?"

"Here's the problem, Dean." Devereaux crossed his arms. "Lucas has an alibi for last night. Which means there's only one person who could have lured Emma Noble to the apartment."

"No way." Sullivan stood up. "Not me. I didn't do it."

"So someone else—some random stranger—just happened to pick the one apartment out of thousands in the city that you left open, the very night you opened it, to lure Emma? You expect us to believe that, Dean?"

"No." Sullivan sat back down. "Not a random stranger. How about the rental agency? All kinds of people there could have known the apartment was empty. One of them could have done it. Or sold the information to someone else, who was looking for a great place to commit a crime. And the rental guys? They have keys. Do you even know for sure that the patio door was used?"

"That's a complicated scenario you're painting there, Dean."

Devereaux frowned. "Have you ever heard of this thing, Ockham's razor?"

Sullivan's hand instinctively moved to his chin. "No. Why?"

"An FBI agent told me about it on another case we were working together. This Ockham guy, he had a theory. He said that if there are two possible explanations for something, unless you have concrete proof that shows otherwise, the simpler one is probably right."

"I don't follow." Sullivan looked genuinely confused.

"OK." Devereaux spoke slowly. "Say, for example, your car disappeared from the parking lot while you were at the grocery store. One guy told you it had been taken by car thieves. Another guy said it had been vaporized by space aliens. Who would you believe?"

"The alien guy." Sullivan smiled. "He sounds much more imaginative."

"I guess Ockham wasn't catering to morons." Devereaux sighed. "The point is, forget about real estate guys selling addresses to hypothetical criminals. You knew the door was open. You're the simpler option. So, where were you last night, Dean?"

"This is crazy. I was here."

"Doing what?" Devereaux asked.

"Writing poetry."

"Can anyone confirm that?"

"Yes. Hayley can. My girlfriend. The part about me being here, anyway. Not the poems. I didn't give her those till today. And as you can see, that didn't go too well."

"So if you were spilling your emotions all over the page, where was Hayley?"

"In the bedroom. She gets very tired, with the pregnancy."

"So she was asleep." Devereaux didn't sound convinced.

Sullivan shrugged. "I don't know. I was out here."

"That doesn't make for the greatest of alibis, Dean." Devereaux took out his notebook. "Let's try this. Where were you at 2:33 pm?"

"Why do you want to know about the afternoon now?"

"That's when the call was made to Emma Noble's service. Where were you then?"

"Oh. Let me think. Half past two. I know—I went out. I took a walk. I was thinking over some ideas for a poem, and I needed to clear my head."

"Where did you—"

"Honey?" Hayley had appeared in the archway leading to the bedrooms. A pink sleep mask was pushed up on her forehead. Her hair was knotted on top of her head. And her pink frilly nightgown was struggling to accommodate her baby bump. "Why are you lying? Tell them the truth. Or I will."

Sullivan flopped back on the couch. "Oh God. All right. Fine. We were at the doctor's office. We're doing couple's therapy."

"OK. What time was your session?" Devereaux flipped open his notebook.

"It started at two pm. And it ran for fifty excruciating, cringe-worthy minutes."

"Were you in the office that whole time? Or did you step out at all? For a bathroom break? Maybe things were getting fraught? You needed to calm down . . ."

"No. I was in the witch's lair the whole time."

"Hayley?" Devereaux turned to face her. "Is that true?"

"It's true that Dean didn't leave the office. But Dr. Akinsola's not a witch. She's lovely. She listens, and she gives good advice, and if Dean would only—"

"Thanks, Hayley." Devereaux stood up. "We can leave it there. I don't think we need the blow-by-blow."

Outside, in the elevator lobby, Devereaux jabbed the Call button. "I can't believe—"

Garretty put his hand on Devereaux's arm. "Was that a slap?"

The detectives moved back to Sullivan's apartment door and listened.

The *crack* of skin against skin was clearly audible. The detectives drew their guns. Garretty stepped back, ready to line up a kick where the door lock met the frame. Then he paused.

"You freak!" It was Hayley's voice doing the yelling, followed by another slap. "What's wrong with you? You'd rather let those police think you'd committed some kind of crime than admit to going to counseling with me?" Another slap. "You asshole! I should never speak to you again." Slap. "When the baby comes, I'm kicking you out. You can go and live with Lucas." Slap. "You spend more time with him than me anyway."

Chapter *Forty-seven*

Wednesday. Early morning.

LIEUTENANT HALE WAS SITTING IN HER CUSTOMARY PLACE AT THE head of the table in the fourth-floor conference room when Devereaux, Garretty, and Irvin arrived. She had two empty coffee cups in front of her, and she was halfway through a third. Behind her, she'd taped a large piece of lining paper to the wall. On it, in bold capitals, she'd written:

WHERE?
WHEN?
HOW?

And below that list, underlined and circled twice:

WHO???

Hale waited for the others to sit—Devereaux and Garretty on the window side of the table, Irvin opposite them—and took another swig of coffee before she began.

"OK." Hale pushed her cup aside. "Status report. Where are we with Lucas Paltrow's alibis for Monday night?"

"His credit card was used at a gas station at eight-oh-two, as he claimed." Devereaux frowned. "The woman he said he spent the night with also confirmed he was there. The uniforms couldn't reach the woman from Friday afternoon, though. According to neighbors, she left town with her husband Saturday morning for an impromptu romantic getaway to Paris."

"How about the canvass of Dean Sullivan's building?"

"Nada." Garretty checked his notebook. "Uniforms have three no-responses to call on again, but no one else saw or heard anything useful."

"And Billy Flynn? The fire at his house?"

"Nothing conclusive." Garretty closed his book. "Chief Young's waiting for one more lab report, but he hasn't seen anything so far that proves foul play."

"OK." Hale stood up and moved to the paper she'd taped to the wall. "In that case, as of now, we're going back to square one. We got ahead of ourselves, chasing suspects without covering the basics. So I want all our efforts put into these questions. *Where* were the women killed? *When* did they cross paths with the killer? *How* are they connected? The twenty-first birthday thing and the adopted children? Those details are far too specific to be coincidental. Linda, I really need your input here. If there's some weird psychological component, we need to know about it. And finally, if we fill in those blanks effectively, it should lead us to the big one. *Who* the killer is. Methodical, thorough police work. That's what's going to solve this. But we also need to move fast. More women's lives could be at stake. And the department's taking a serious ass-kicking in the press, which will only get worse the longer this guy's on the streets. All right. Thoughts? Questions?"

"Let's not throw the baby out with the bathwater here, Lieutenant." Devereaux held his hands up as if surrendering. "I agree—

thorough and methodical is good. But I don't think we've gotten to the bottom of what happened with Emma Noble yet. I think there are some important clues there. Most importantly, we need to figure out why the killer changed the way he captured his victim. Calling a hooker is very different from coercing a citizen into a vehicle in the middle of the street."

"Convenience?" Garretty suggested. "Efficiency? He used the call girl service like it was Amazon Prime for murder victims."

"The second woman resisted sufficiently to catch the attention of that witness, the art professor." Hale put her hands on her hips. "Maybe our guy realized the danger of being seen and was looking for a safer option."

"Neither of those ideas flies." Irvin shook her head. "As you pointed out, Lieutenant, the first two victims had an extremely specific profile. We still have to figure out why, but those characteristics are of fundamental importance to the killer. I guarantee that. There's no way he's going to give them up for convenience or safety."

"That's how I read it." Devereaux nodded. "So I was thinking, maybe this was something different. Maybe he killed Emma to try and misdirect us. Making a big point of wanting a twenty-one-year-old with a kid felt bolted-on and clumsy to me. It was too obvious a move. I think he was hoping we'd latch onto it and then waste time chasing down the call girl service or the owner of the vacant apartment."

"Which is pretty much what we did do." Hale pointed to her list. "Which is why we're starting again at square one. We need to be in control of the investigation, not be led by the nose."

"Hold on one more second." Devereaux laid his hands flat on the table. "There's one piece we're ignoring that doesn't fit in this scenario. Professor Goodman's ID of the guy coercing Siobhan O'Keefe into the Escalade. And of the Escalade itself."

"Eyewitness testimony's the least reliable kind of evidence there is." Hale crossed her arms. "First she thought she saw Lawton Vetch. Then she thought it was Billy Flynn. She was wrong both times. It doesn't matter who she thinks it was now. She's not credible."

"No." Devereaux shook his head. "*We* thought she saw those guys because her description vaguely matched them and they fit the circumstances. We thought of Vetch, because of the Escalade's license plate. And Flynn, because we figured out he had access to the vehicle once we confirmed it was out of Vetch's possession at the time of the abduction. We never showed Professor Goodman photographs. There was no point with Vetch, since he was eliminated, and it wasn't possible with Flynn because of the fire. So now we need to show her a photograph of Lucas Paltrow. Put his picture in an array. See if she picks it out."

"What would be the point?" Hale returned to her seat. "Paltrow's alibied out. And the license plate doesn't prove anything. They're simplicity itself to clone."

"There's something wrong about Paltrow." Devereaux was ready to dig in. "You saw him in the interview room. Did he look like an innocent man to you? And what about this porno room in his house? The guy's a freak."

"He certainly is." Irvin scratched her temple with her pen. "But there's another reason he can't be our guy. You just more or less said it, Cooper. Paltrow displayed absolutely no compassion or empathy whatsoever in the interview room, even under pressure when you were questioning him. And yet the killer was completely overcome with remorse about what he did. Every time. Just look at the bodies. How they were wrapped. How carefully he covered the women up. And how he left all of them in places that are associated with caring for the dead."

"Paltrow's creepy, all right." Hale took a mouthful of coffee. "But as far as we know, he hasn't broken any laws. Didn't you say Deborah Holt called the guy her Good Samaritan? When he fixed her car for free? It's a long way from that to becoming the Grim Reaper. So, he goes on the back burner. Unless you're really worried about the porn angle, in which case hand him off to Vice."

"I'm not that worried about it."

"Good. Then let's agree on some actions. I want those no-responses followed up in the building Emma Noble was taken from."

"I'll take that." Garretty scribbled a note in his book.

"And I want everyone working flat out on finding the connection between the first two victims. Let's start with the adoption angle. Follow up on the agencies the women used. See if any staff members worked at both places at the relevant times. Check support groups for women whose babies have gone to new families. Church groups. Online groups. Exercise classes for women who've given birth. If none of those pan out, see if their jobs overlapped in any way. If they had the same hobbies. Shopped at the same stores. Got their coffee at the same cafés. Used the same dating service. Anything. Use your imaginations. If you need more people, tell me. Just find something, before another woman ends up dead."

Back at their desks on the third floor, Devereaux brought Garretty a coffee.

"Of course." Garretty didn't look up from his computer screen. "Go ahead."

"I didn't ask you anything yet." Devereaux put the drink down on Garretty's Roll Tide coaster.

"Cooper, how long have we been partners?" Garretty picked up the cup. "You're not putting Paltrow on the back burner. You were about to ask if I'd handle the adoption agencies while you go sniff around for his buried skeletons."

Chapter Forty-eight

Wednesday. Morning.

DEVEREAUX CINCHED THE BATHROBE CORD IN TIGHT AND PAUSED IN front of the shiny wooden door. "All this steam can't be good for you. Why don't we talk out here?"

The truth was, Devereaux didn't mind the steam at all. Or the heat. It was the size of the room that bothered him. Ever since he was a kid, and his father would make him hide in the crawl space below the hallway closet in their house while he was out *working*, Devereaux had hated enclosed spaces. He did everything he could to avoid them. His problem was, he needed to talk to Tom Vernon—his closest friend since seventh grade, despite their relationship hitting the rocks when Devereaux turned his life around and joined the police academy. And Tom Vernon was sprawling contentedly on the slatted bench inside the sauna he'd recently installed in the pool house at his home.

"That's crap, Cooper." Vernon wiped his face on a towel, then dropped it back on the bench. "The steam's good for you. It makes you sweat out all the impurities you breathe in with the air. I do this for an hour every morning now. It makes me feel much better. And anyway, the Feds haven't figured out a way to bug me in here yet."

Tom Vernon was strictly old school. He tolerated cellphones—untraceable, use once and destroy burners—as long as nothing confidential was discussed. But he would not allow computers or electronic records of any kind. He used nothing he couldn't conveniently forget or burn. And he'd become extra paranoid after he discovered the FBI was listening to conversations in the office above his restaurant—his favorite legitimate business.

"Here's the thing, Tom." Devereaux took a deep breath, pushed away the image of spiders and bugs scuttling over him in the dark, and stepped inside. "I need a favor."

"Another one? This is becoming a habit, Cooper. When do I see something in return? A little quid pro quo?"

"You're not in jail, are you?"

"The day's coming when that won't be enough."

"We'll burn that bridge when we come to it." Devereaux managed to summon up a smile for his old friend. "Now, are you going to help me or not?"

"Of course I am. What do you need?"

"I want you to ask around about a guy I'm looking at. His name's Lucas Paltrow. He runs an auto electronics business on Deo Dara Drive. I want every scrap of dirt that ever existed on him. I'd start with porn. Semi-pro. He could also be a torch, but that's more of a long shot."

"Snide parts? Marking customers' cars for his buddies to steal?"

"Anything. I don't care. I just want some leverage."

"Got it. I can do that. How fast do you need it?"

"Yesterday."

"Understood." Vernon took an old, chunky cellphone out of the pocket in his robe. "Only, Cooper, is this really for a case?"

"Of course."

"Are you sure? Because I've seen that look in your eyes before. In the old days. When you smelled blood in the water. Right before you went after a guy's action, then ran him out of town."

Chapter *Forty-nine*

Wednesday. Late morning.

DEVEREAUX WAS STILL UNCOMFORTABLY HOT WHEN HE STEPPED OUT OF the elevator, half an hour later. He paused on the bridge that connected the elevator tower to the observation platform at the top of Vulcan's column, enjoying the breeze that blew up through the rectangular slats in the walkway in the mesh below the safety rails. Then he continued, moving clockwise around the octagonal plinth and running the tips of his fingers along the rough stone surface like he'd done as a kid when his father had brought him to visit. He looked down at the roof of the museum, which he resented somewhat as it hadn't been there when he was little, then carried on until he was three-quarters of the way around. Facing north, he rested his forearms on the rail and gazed out over downtown Birmingham. He picked out the City Federal, glinting in the distance as the sun reflected off its polished white terra-cotta façade. It had started out as an office. And later been converted to apartments. Aside from its elegant proportions and exquisite carving, the fact that its use had changed was the thing Devereaux liked most about it. It had been remade. Just like he had. But as he admired it from a distance, it occurred to him that the building looked just the same. If one of the original office workers saw it, would he notice the difference? How much had it really changed? How much had *he* really changed?

The elevator door opened again and a woman got out. She was in her thirties, with a bright floral sundress and long brown hair. She was model thin. Almost narcotics thin, Devereaux thought. Oversize sunglasses covered much of her face, but they couldn't disguise the tension and worry in her expression.

"Detective?" The woman stopped six feet away from Devereaux, turned slightly sideways as if looking toward Sloss Furnaces, and leaned her arms stiffly on the railing. "I'm Connie James. I was Connie Paltrow, but I changed my name back after the divorce."

"Thanks for meeting me."

"I'm sorry it had to be up here. But there's no way I could risk coming to the station house. If anyone saw me . . . If my partner found out . . ." She closed her eyes and rapidly shook her head as if trying to banish an unpleasant image. "I guess I have a thing for bad boys, Detective. More fool me. Anyway, up here it's safe. He thinks Vulcan's stupid and won't come near the park."

"It's no problem." Devereaux shot her an encouraging smile. "I love it here. My dad used to bring me when I was a kid. He told me stories about how Vulcan was the best giant in the world. He said all the other states used to have giants, but Vulcan beat them all in a whole series of competitions and the losers were banished. The contest with New York's giant was the best. It explained why Vulcan has no underwear. According to my dad, anyway. Of course, he made the whole thing up."

"He sounds nice, your dad." Connie's expression relaxed a little. "Is he still with us?"

"No." Devereaux looked down. "He passed away when I was young."

"I'm sorry to hear that."

"Don't be. It's not your fault."

"I guess. Anyway, how can I help? You said you wanted to know some things about Lucas. Is he in trouble?"

"We don't know that yet. His name came up in connection with a case we're working on, and we need to figure out if he's involved or not. I just need some background information at this point. Like, for example, his attitude toward women. How would you describe that?"

"Ha." Connie practically snorted. "Let me describe one incident to you. I'll just give you the facts, then you can make your mind up for yourself. This was a while ago. Before we were married, which doesn't cover me in reflected glory, I realize that. Anyway, Lucas had this peculiar friend. A real geek. He never seemed to have a job, so he was always hanging around our place, sucking up to Lucas. He even tried to dress like Lucas. And he always had his eye on some woman or other. He seemed charming at first, but he didn't know when to stop. He'd keep going and going, giving them flowers, copying out poems. He was like a walking cliché. Surprise, surprise, none of the women wanted to stick around very long. The kid was always getting dumped. So one day, he asks Lucas for advice. This is what Lucas told him. He said, women are like dogs. They have their uses. They can be fun to have around. But never let them get too close. Try not to let them sleep in the house. And always make sure they know who's the boss."

"He sounds like a real charmer. Did he ever get violent with you? Or anyone else you know of?"

"Oh, no. He'd never hit a woman. That was part of his strangeness. He had a kind of weird, old-school code. He acted like women and children were weaker, and needed to be protected. Not treated nice, necessarily, but kept safe and provided for."

"Did Lucas have any kids?"

"Not that I know of. Although, the way he played the field . . ."

"Did he ever say anything about wanting a kid?"

"Not with me."

"OK. Thanks, Connie. You've been very helpful. There's just one other thing. This might sound like a strange question, so don't try and second-guess yourself. Just tell me anything that comes into your head, even if it seems crazy. All right?"

"I guess."

"Did the age twenty-one have any special significance for Lucas?"

"Oh my God!" Connie gripped the safety rail with all her strength. "You think Lucas is B/DK? No way."

"That's not what I'm saying. I just need to know if twenty-one was a special age for him, for any reason."

"Well, of course it was. You didn't know?"

"Pretend I don't. Explain it to me, Connie."

"Lucas was adopted. He was always obsessed with finding his birth parents. He never got anywhere on his own. But his geeky friend with the love poems? He was great with computers. He helped Lucas track down his real mom. Lucas went to see her, in Phoenix, Arizona. Now, Lucas always had money. He always had a job. He did half a dozen other things before he settled on auto electronics. But his mom? She was another level of rich. And she had a confession to make. She'd met a guy when she was twenty. She was already knocked up with Lucas at that point, by some loser she met in a bar and had a one-night stand with. But the rich guy didn't care. On her twenty-first birthday he proposed. He was offering her love. Money. Happiness. And there was only one condition. She had to give up her baby, the moment it was born."

Devereaux took a moment to weigh the significance. "Where's his birth mother now?"

"She's dead. She was killed in an explosion not long after they reconnected. She smoked. There was a gas leak, they think."

"Was the guy she gave up Lucas to marry killed in the explosion, too?"

"No. He died years before. Cancer, if I remember correctly."

"OK. One last question. Lucas's nerdy friend, who helped with the computer. What was his name?"

"I can't remember. It was a long time ago. I think it began with a D, though. Dave? Dan? Something like that."

Devereaux waited for Connie to disappear into the elevator, then called Garretty.

"It's Paltrow. I'm digging up some amazing shit."

"It isn't Paltrow," Garretty said. "I know you've got the bit between your teeth on this one so I went back over his alibis. His card was definitely used at the gas station. His regular card, which he's had for years and uses pretty much every day. Not some new card he could have taken out to use as a cover and paid someone else to use at the relevant time. I spoke to the woman. Leaned on her hard, and she swears blind Paltrow was with her all night. And I checked with the church. They still have tai chi on Monday evenings, and this week they finished even later than normal because they had some visiting Asian monks who gave a demonstration. It's just not possible for it to be him, Cooper."

"I don't know how, but I still think it is." Devereaux reached for the elevator Call button. "And I'm going to keep on digging."

Chapter *Fifty*

Wednesday. Early afternoon.

SIOBHAN O'KEEFE'S SILVER JETTA WAS STILL PARKED ON THE SIDE OF the street, near her house. It was all alone. No other vehicles were within forty feet of it, in front or behind, as if they were pack animals and could sense the recent tragedy afflicting one of their number.

Devereaux stopped his Porsche where he guessed the Escalade would have been, based on Mrs. Goodman's account of Friday afternoon's events, and stepped out into the road. He walked toward the back, imagining that Siobhan had just arrived home from work. He pictured an argument. Some kind of scam must have been in play, given that Mrs. Goodman remembered the guy producing some kind of leather wallet. It can't have been totally convincing, as Siobhan was still reluctant to go with him. But whatever the ruse was, it didn't have to be bulletproof, Devereaux figured. Just plausible enough to get her into the SUV. Once she was inside, it was as good as over for her.

It took Mrs. Goodman longer to answer the door than it had on Saturday, and when she appeared, Devereaux noticed she wasn't wearing her emergency button.

"I'm rebelling." She patted her chest where the pendent used to hang. "It seemed so trivial and self-absorbed, an old lady like me worrying about tripping over my own feet when a poor girl like Siobhan, in the prime of her life, was snatched off the street before my very eyes. And besides, it was my daughter's idea for me to wear it. If she's so worried about checking on my health, she can come and do it in person from now on."

"Quite right." Devereaux smiled.

"Can I offer you some iced tea, Detective?" Mrs. Goodman gestured toward the couch. "Come and sit. Tell me how things are going with your investigation."

"Thank you. That would be nice." Devereaux took the place at the end of the couch and tried his hardest to be patient while Mrs. Goodman made excruciatingly slow progress with fetching a tray and two glasses from the narrow galley kitchen.

"Have you made any arrests?" Mrs. Goodman settled herself in her armchair and took a sip of tea. "I've been following the case in the news, and none have been reported."

"We have a suspect in custody." Devereaux took a piece of paper from his pocket and unfolded it. "But it would be very helpful if you could look at these photographs and tell me if you recognize anyone in them."

Devereaux passed the array to Mrs. Goodman, who studied the six images carefully and then pointed to one in the center of the top row.

"That man." She jabbed the picture again with her bony index finger. "I recognize him."

The man she'd picked out was not Lucas Paltrow. It was Dean Sullivan.

"Where do you recognize him from, Mrs. Goodman?" Devereaux made an effort to keep the confusion he was feeling out of his voice.

"From outside, on the street." Mrs. Goodman gestured toward the window. "He's the man I told you about. With poor Siobhan, on Friday afternoon."

Devereaux folded the paper so that only the picture of Sullivan was showing. "Mrs. Goodman, just so that I'm absolutely clear, you're saying that you saw this man force Siobhan O'Keefe into a black SUV outside her house on Friday?"

"No, Detective." Mrs. Goodman shook her head. "I didn't *see* him force her. How could I?"

Devereaux felt as if he'd been plunged into a pool of ice cold water and left there, submerged, unable to breathe.

"OK." Devereaux used every ounce of self-control to keep his voice calm and level. "So what exactly did you see? Talk me through it, step-by-step."

"I saw the man approach Siobhan when she got out of her car." Mrs. Goodman spoke slowly and clearly, as if Devereaux were one of her less gifted students. "They argued. The man led Siobhan around the front of her car, onto the sidewalk. Nothing happened after that for maybe five seconds. Then the Vulg— the SUV drove away, and no one was left standing there. So, Detective, I *inferred* that he forced her in and then got in himself. But I couldn't *see,* because the beastly vehicle was too tall."

"So he took her to the sidewalk. That's the passenger side of the car."

"Yes."

"And he didn't reappear? He didn't walk around to the driver's door?"

"No. I assume he got in the passenger seat. Unless he got in the back with Siobhan. Is it important which seat he took?"

"Someone else was driving!"

"I would imagine so." Mrs. Goodman nodded. "I've read in the newspapers about the introduction of self-driving cars, but I don't believe they're available to the public just yet."

"Mrs. Goodman, thank you." Devereaux got to his feet and started toward the door. "You've been a huge help. Huge."

Chapter *Fifty-one*

Wednesday. Afternoon.

DEVEREAUX CALLED GARRETTY AS HE CROSSED THE STREET, ON THE way back to his car.

"Tommy, I was wrong." Devereaux climbed in behind the wheel. "It wasn't Paltrow."

"We knew that."

"It was Sullivan *and* Paltrow. They were working as a team."

Garretty didn't respond.

"I'm serious." Devereaux fired up the engine. "I just left Mrs. Goodman's. She ID'd Sullivan as the guy who snatched Siobhan O'Keefe. And she said he got into the passenger side of the Escalade. Which means someone else was driving."

"Shit. Paltrow? But what about Flynn?"

"He was dead before Emma Noble was taken, so it couldn't have been him. Actually, Paltrow killed him."

"He couldn't have. Chief Young said the fire wasn't deliberate."

"He said there was no evidence that it was deliberate. We need him to take another look. Because, get this. Paltrow was separated from his birth mother for most of his life. When he reconnected, he got in a fight with her. Right after that, she died. She burned to death when her house exploded. There was an unexplained gas leak. And she was a smoker."

"That's some coincidence."

"Right? And guess how Paltrow found her?"

"No idea."

"A nerdy friend who was good with computers tracked her down online. Does that ring any bells?"

"Sounds like Sullivan, obviously. But what about the obsession with twenty-one-year-olds?"

"That's down to Paltrow's mother. She met some rich guy when she was twenty, pregnant with Lucas from a one-night stand. The rich guy proposed to her on her twenty-first birthday, with the condition that she give up the other guy's kid as soon as it was born."

"When did Paltrow find that out?"

"A while ago. I don't know exactly when."

"So why wait till last week to wage this crusade against twenty-one-year-olds who'd given up their kids?"

"I don't know how their paths crossed again, but it must be connected to Deborah Holt somehow. She was the first victim. Paltrow met her last year, when she was twenty and pregnant. Suddenly she's twenty-one, the baby's out of the picture, and she's getting a fancy sports car for her birthday from the rich guy she's seeing. Paltrow must have found out. It must have hit him like a thunderbolt. Unhinged him. Released all his childhood demons. Set him on the warpath, and he took Sullivan along for the ride."

"I can see why Deborah touched a nerve with Paltrow, I guess. But what did Siobhan do to attract his attention? Sounds like she ran with a different crowd."

"I'm guessing that once he started, Paltrow wanted to keep going. So he got Sullivan to dig up new targets. If he could track down Paltrow's mother, who's to say he couldn't hack an adoption agency? I'll talk to Spencer Page in Support Services. See if he thinks that's feasible."

"And poor Emma Noble was collateral damage, designed to throw us off track."

"They were cleverer than that, I think. They designed it to give each of them an alibi. Paltrow called the agency while Sullivan was at the therapist's office. Sullivan met Emma while Paltrow was at the gas station. And Sullivan disposed of Emma's body after Paltrow got to his girlfriend's house. We'd have let Paltrow walk by now if that woman he was banging had been around to confirm his alibi, instead of leaving town for France."

"That does all fit, Cooper. Specially the part about Sullivan dumping the bodies. He's obviously the follower, of the two of them. And he's not avenging some perceived outrage by womankind. If either of them felt remorse, it would be him."

"He'll feel more than remorse when I catch up with him. I'm heading to his place now."

"Good. I'll talk to the lieutenant. Make sure no one discharges Paltrow. His twenty-four hours are almost up."

Chapter **Fifty-two**

Wednesday. Afternoon.

DEVEREAUX SAW THAT SULLIVAN'S APARTMENT DOOR WAS OPEN A crack as soon as he stepped out of the elevator car. A moment later he heard a woman sobbing. He drew his gun, crept up to the door, and listened. He could hear no movement and nothing that revealed how many people were inside.

"Miss?" Devereaux banged on the door. "Hayley? Are you all right?"

The sobbing grew louder.

"Birmingham PD." Devereaux banged again. "Hayley? Are you in danger? Is anyone in the apartment with you?"

The sobs grew louder still and morphed into a hysterical attempt to speak, but Devereaux couldn't make out the words.

"If you can, move away from the door." Devereaux took a breath. "I'm coming in on three. OK. One. Two." He shouldered open the door, stepped into the room, and dodged immediately to his right. Then lowered his gun.

Hayley was sitting on the floor to the side of the kitchen area. Her robe was undone. Her pink nightdress, which was covered with pictures of cats, was stretched tight across her belly. Her hair was wild. Her cheeks were streaked with tears. Broken crockery was strewn all around her. Smashed plates. Bowls and mugs. Glasses, too. On the other side of the countertop was another smashed vase, surrounded by pink roses this time. Farther away, the couch was on its back. Its cushions had been flung around the room, and the TV screen was badly cracked.

"Don't try to move." Devereaux stepped closer to Hayley. "Are you hurt? Are you OK?"

Hayley struggled onto her knees and reached up, trying to get a grip on the edge of the countertop.

"Where's Dean?" Devereaux's foot slipped on a piece of broken plate. "Did he do this?"

"Dean's gone. The little worm took my car keys." Hayley heaved herself half upright, and her next word was overtaken by a long, drawn-out, terrified howl. Straw-colored liquid started to pour down the inside of her legs. It pooled on the floor between her feet and spread out, engulfing the surrounding fragments of china.

"Hayley, don't worry." Devereaux pulled out his phone. "This is totally normal. It just means the baby's ready to come. Very soon now, you'll be a mom. I'm going to call for an ambulance. It'll be here in no time. Trust me. Everything's going to be all right."

Devereaux helped Hayley into the bedroom and stayed with her until the paramedics arrived. Then he dialed Garretty's number and began to search the apartment, hoping for a clue as to where Sullivan might have gone.

"Sullivan's in the wind." Devereaux moved into the smaller bedroom. "He's using his girlfriend's car. We need to get an APB out, right away."

"I'm on it." Garretty grabbed a pencil. "Got the license plate?"

"No, sorry." Devereaux pulled open a drawer. "But how about this. Half the bedsheets are missing out of his linen closet."

"The asshole." Garretty banged the side of his fist into the desk. "Don't worry. We'll get him. I'll find Hayley's vehicle deets. Are you coming back in?"

"Unless I can find anything useful here." Devereaux moved back into the living room and started to rummage through the debris.

"OK, I'll . . . Hold on. The lieutenant's here. Something's up. I'll be right back." Garretty put the call on hold for the better part of a minute. "Cooper? There's a problem. Another twenty-one-year-old's been taken. Annette Usherwood. She was at Ocean, with her family, celebrating her birthday. She went to the bathroom. And never came back."

Chapter *Fifty-three*

Wednesday. Afternoon.

DEVEREAUX WAS CONSCIOUS OF ALL THE EYES WATCHING THROUGH THE one-way mirror behind him. On the other side of the table, Paltrow was staring straight ahead. His chin was up. His lips were curled into a thin, mocking smile. Was he aware of the hidden audience, too, Devereaux wondered? Or was he just admiring his reflection?

"It's funny." Devereaux crossed his arms and leaned back. "We always had you pegged as the brains of the operation. And yet here you are. Locked up, with only the needle to look forward to, while he's out there. Having all the fun with lovely Annette."

"He?" Paltrow raised his eyebrows. "I don't know who you're talking about."

"Dean Sullivan. Your buddy."

Paltrow shrugged. "I'd call him an acquaintance. Not a buddy."

"That's probably fair." Devereaux nodded. "You certainly won't be calling him a buddy after he rolls on you. Because he'll be in here soon. We have fifty guys looking for him, right now. He can't hide for long. And you know what he's like. The first hint of pressure, he'll crumble. Then we'll explain how there's only one deal on the table, and he won't just take it. He'll grab it. He'll beg for it. He'll give you up quicker than your own mother did. Unless you're smarter than him. Because you can help yourself here, Lucas. Tell us where he's taking Annette. If we get to her while she's still alive, that'll be huge for you."

"Let me see if I understand you, Detective. You're saying another girl's gone missing? That's terrible. But if she went missing while I was in here, I couldn't have had anything to do with it, could I? Or, it follows, with the other identical disappearances. It's like I've said all along. I'm innocent. And very soon, you'll be the one with the decision to make. Tick tock. Tick tock. Charge me, or let me go. How many minutes have you got left?"

Devereaux didn't respond.

"And if you do charge me, my lawyer will have me out in fifteen minutes. So I'm not saying another word. The ball's in your court, Detective, and it's staying there."

In his pocket, Devereaux's phone buzzed. He checked the screen. It was a text from Tom Vernon. He had news.

"Tell us where Sullivan is before he hurts the woman. That's your only hope." Devereaux stood up. "Think it over. But don't take too long. If they find Sullivan without you, or the girl dies, you're toast."

The expression on Hale's, Garretty's, and Irvin's faces was glum when Devereaux joined them in the observation gallery.

"OK." Hale crossed her arms. "Options?"

"Go at him again." Garretty's hands had automatically curled into fists by his sides. "Keep going at him till he gives us something."

"That won't work." Irvin shook her head. "He's planned this out, move by move. He thinks he's home free. And he's probably right. We can't hold him much longer."

"All right." Garretty scowled. "What if we play along? Let him go. Make a show of being pissed about it. And tail him. Let him lead us to Sullivan and Annette."

"Way too risky." The frustration was clear in Hale's voice. "What if we lose him? Or what if he takes us on a wild-goose chase? His plan could be for Sullivan to kill the victim while he's under surveillance, for all we know. And if we lose him, God knows what the body count will be by the time we find him again."

"Here's another angle." Devereaux paused for a moment. "When I thought Paltrow was behind this on his own, I put some feelers out. In places you don't need to know about, Lieutenant. One of my guys just got back to me. He might have something. It could be nothing, but I feel like it's worth following up."

Hale was silent for a moment. "OK. Have the conversation. But make it quick. In less than an hour, Paltrow will be back on the street. And if Annette's not already dead by then, she will be soon after."

Chapter *Fifty-four*

Wednesday. Afternoon.

DEVEREAUX CURSED TOM VERNON'S DISTRUST OF PHONES AS HE GUNNED the Porsche's engine and sliced through the worsening afternoon traffic. He left the car outside the front entrance of his old friend's restaurant, waving away the halfhearted protest from the geriatric parking valet, and hurried through the building and up the stairs to the office.

"Drink, Cooper?" Vernon took a bottle of Blanton's from the bottom drawer of his desk.

"No time, Tom." Devereaux perched on the arm of one of the battered leather armchairs that faced the window. "Just tell me what you know."

"Don't get too excited. There's not much. Not yet, anyway. But I did get one interesting story from one of my guys. We call him Goliath. He's huge and scary-looking, but actually wouldn't hurt a fly. Unless you piss him off, in which case . . . Anyway, a couple of years back he got a call from Eric Wainwright. Eric's an attorney. I use him any time one of my guys has a run-in with one of your guys. Eric had kept Goliath out of jail a few months before that when it seemed like he was a slam dunk, and in return Goliath had promised Eric a favor if ever he was in a jam. So Eric called Goliath and told him an asshole was trying to blackmail him, and he wanted the situation to go away. Goliath handled it, of course, but can you guess who the asshole was?"

"Lucas Paltrow."

"Right in one. And as amusing as what Goliath threatened to do to Paltrow was, if he didn't back off, I'm guessing it's the details of the blackmail that you probably want to know about. Here's what happened. Eric's a widower. And he's a busy man. He didn't have time to date, and he didn't feel right about permanently replacing the woman he'd loved. So he decided to try a little pay-to-play. He called an agency someone had told him about, but when the girl showed up at his house he was horrified. She was a wreck. Obviously abused, mentally and physically. He couldn't go through with the sex. He sat her down instead and coaxed her life story out of her. Long story short, she'd wound up being basically owned by Paltrow and some other guy. The way it started, Paltrow made a kind of sales brochure with all kinds of kinky pictures of her. He'd show it to the customers at his auto shop, and if they liked what they saw, Paltrow offered them the chance to do more than just look in a special room he had rigged up out back. It was a brilliant plan. It brought in more customers, as word spread, and those customers were paying for more than just a new CD player or whatever. The problem was, Paltrow was greedy. The auto shop angle only worked during business hours, and he wanted to be earning twenty-four/seven. So he brought in another girl to cover the auto shop, where he could keep more of an eye on her while he broke her in. He moved the girl Eric met to a place he bought downtown, which he also used for established customers. And on top of that he hooked her up with the phone service, and split the profit he made on her in return for getting the bookings."

"So what happened? Paltrow tried to blackmail Eric for seeing a call girl, even though he didn't sleep with her?"

"No. It's better than that. Eric was so appalled at what the girl told him, he put her in his car there and then, drove her to the airport, and put her on a plane to the West Coast or wherever her family was from. That's why Paltrow was pissed. The agency sent some Russian gorilla around to put the squeeze on Eric, but he faced the guy down. Paltrow wouldn't let it lie, though. He tried to take Eric on himself. Until Eric introduced him to Goliath."

Devereaux took a moment to sift through the detail. "OK. This is great, Tom. Thank you. So what I need you to do now is get Eric on the phone. Ask him if the girl told him the address of the place where she was kept downtown."

"I'll ask him, sure." Vernon stood up. "But not on the phone. It's too sensitive. I'll head over to his office. Talk to him face-to-face."

"There's no time, Tom. I need you to call him. A young woman's life is on the line."

"Not on the phone." Vernon was adamant. "I'll go see him right now."

"Tom, there's something I want you to look at." Devereaux pulled Annette Usherwood's driver's license photograph up on his phone. "See this woman? She's alive right now. But if I don't get to her in time, she'll wind up like this." He switched to an image of Deborah Holt. "Or this." He changed to Siobhan O'Keefe's picture. "Or this." He finished with Emma Noble. "So please. Use a burner phone. It'll be safe. And if someone somehow does tap it, I'll go to bat for you. But I won't forgive you if another woman dies because you won't make the call."

Chapter *Fifty-five*

Wednesday. Late afternoon.

"Cooper, look at the time." Garretty checked his watch. "We're too late."

The twenty-four hours since they'd taken Paltrow into custody were up. They still had nothing concrete to charge him with. And no definite location for Annette Usherwood.

"Call the lieutenant." Devereaux pulled up at the light where Sixteenth Street meets Second Avenue and looked at the reflection in the rearview mirror. "Tell her we need SWAT here. They need to hit the place right now."

Eric Wainwright hadn't been able to give Tom Vernon a precise address. All he remembered was the girl he'd rescued saying that the place where she'd been kept was on the corner of Sixteenth and Third. Her room had been on the top floor, at the northeast corner. Devereaux knew right away which building she was talking about. It was only half a mile from the City Federal, where his apartment was. It was two floors high and had started life as a warehouse. Back in the day its pale brick had cost top dollar, and the original owners had paid even more to have extravagant coats of arms and mythological figures molded into the cement panels between the broad rows of metal-framed windows. In later years, when most of the city's storage businesses moved out of town to be nearer the airport, it was converted into a series of low-rent storefronts. That had kept the building alive for another decade or so. Nowadays, though, it was in poor shape. It was basically unoccupied. The glass was cloudy and obscured with city grime. The frames were red with rust. The brickwork was crumbling. And the cement had flaked away, leaving the moldings flat and featureless, like sand carvings on a beach after the first waves of a rising tide had washed over them.

Devereaux had considered buying the building years before, when he'd started speculating on inner-city regeneration. It wasn't far from some of the shiny new banks and office buildings, and if the gentrification had spread a little farther south, it could have been a great investment. But in the end he'd decided against it. The place was only a stone's throw from police headquarters, and he hadn't wanted to attract attention to his unorthodox financial situation if the development took off and permits needed to be filed. Paltrow obviously hadn't had such qualms about basing his operations under the noses of the police, though. Devereaux couldn't believe he'd been questioning the smug asshole that morning only five minutes' walk from where Annette was being held. If that's where she was being held . . .

"We call SWAT on the strength of one new padlock and a third-hand report of a years-old memory?" Garretty adjusted his door mirror to get a better view behind him. "Annette might not even be in there."

"Someone is." Devereaux gripped the wheel tighter. They were using a white Lexus sedan they'd borrowed from Tom Vernon, figuring the Porsche and their department-issue Chargers would be too recognizable if Sullivan was keeping watch. Even so, they'd only risked one pass, and the only sign of life they'd spotted was a shiny lock standing out against the decaying wood of the truck entrance at the north side of the building. "And it's all we've got. If it was your daughter who might be inside, what would you do?"

"I'd make the call." Garretty pulled out his phone. "Let's hope they're here quick. Why not loop around and wait over there?" He nodded toward the vacant ground on the corner opposite the building, which had been set up as a temporary parking lot. "We can blend in with the other cars and still keep watch."

With every passing second Devereaux felt like someone was tightening a chain around his chest. All he could do was picture Nicole inside the building across the street. How would he get to her? A pane was missing from the block of windows above the main entrance. If he could get onto the canopy—Garretty could boost him, or he could climb on the hood of the car—he could reach inside. The frame was severely corroded. The whole thing would probably pull away. At the least he could pry out the surrounding panes. Climb in . . .

"Cooper!" Garretty pointed to the far side of the street. Through the moving traffic a man was visible on the sidewalk, coming from the direction of First Avenue. He was moving fast. Heading for the building.

It was Paltrow.

He paused outside the main entrance. Reached up and eased a Ziploc bag out of a gap at the top of the frame. Opened it. Took out a pair of latex work gloves. And started to ease them onto his hands.

Devereaux shifted into Drive, jammed his hand on the horn, and surged forward across both lanes of Sixteenth Street. The oncoming cars braked and swerved and honked. Three collided with each other. One clipped the rear of the Lexus, but Devereaux corrected his course and hit the gas harder. Yards away, Paltrow pulled out his key, apparently oblivious to the chaos in the street behind him. He calmly slid it into the lock. Wrestled the door open. Disappeared inside. A homeless guy lying on the ground under the shelter of the building's canopy realized what was about to happen and threw himself to the side, out of harm's way. Devereaux kept going straight. The Lexus demolished the entryway, smashing through in a maelstrom of shattered glass and fragments of metal frame and pulverized brickwork. A dozen airbags exploded from all around the interior of the car. One tore the sleeve of Devereaux's jacket, burning his arm. He stamped on the brake, killing what remained of the car's momentum, and threw open his door. Garretty followed him out a split second later.

Dust and debris swirled in the air, obscuring their view of the stained, graffiti-covered walls and concrete stairway with its incongruously fancy art deco banister rail. Above them, they heard footsteps. They ran forward, pounded up the stairs, and reached the upper corridor just in time to see Paltrow disappearing through the last of three doors on the right-hand side. They approached, guns drawn, and tried the handle. It was locked.

Inside the room, a woman screamed.

"Birmingham PD." Devereaux banged on the door. "Lucas? Dean? It's not too late. There's no need to hurt Annette. Let us in. We can help you. We'll figure something out. No one else needs to get hurt."

The woman screamed again. Louder, this time.

"All right." Devereaux tightened his grip on his gun. "Stand away from the door. We're coming in on three. Ready? One . . ."

Devereaux drove the ball of his foot into the door, just below the handle. The lock gave way and Devereaux used his momentum to propel himself through the entrance into the room. There was a bed under the window, with no sheet on its filthy, stained mattress. A narrow, empty wardrobe without a door. A cracked, wooden dresser with a bottle of Windex on top of it, along with a syringe, a power cable with a pair of exposed, protruding wires, and a party-size box of condoms. Sullivan was lurking in one corner. Paltrow was standing in the center. He was behind Annette Usherwood, who he was holding by the hair. She was naked. Her arms were up above her head and she was clawing at Paltrow's hands, trying to free herself. There was a scrape on her cheek, which was oozing blood. And a scarlet horizontal stripe across her lower abdomen. For a moment Devereaux thought she'd been stabbed, then he realized it wasn't bleeding. It must have been a scar from a recent surgery.

"Let her go, Lucas." Devereaux kept his voice calm and level. "You've got nothing to gain by hurting her."

Paltrow reached out and picked up the syringe. Devereaux raised his gun. Garretty did the same. Neither had a clear shot.

"Let's agree to disagree." Paltrow jabbed the needle deep into Annette's neck and drove home the plunger. She screamed, then fell silent. Paltrow let go of her hair and ducked right down behind her, with just his fingertips visible where he was grasping her hips. Annette was still for another moment, then her legs began to shake. She lost control of her arms. Her neck was suddenly rigid. She started to gurgle, as if her throat was filling with fluid. Then Paltrow flung her forward, straight at Devereaux. Sullivan made a break for the door, but wound up on the floor after Garretty's elbow connected with the side of his head. Paltrow did get out, though. Annette's flailing body knocked Devereaux momentarily off balance, and by the time he'd gotten hold of her and laid her safely on the ground, Paltrow was five yards down the corridor.

"Look after her," Devereaux yelled over his shoulder as he dived out of the room. He raised his gun, but Paltrow reached the top of the staircase and dodged right into the passageway, running across the width of the building before Devereaux could take a shot. Devereaux sprinted after him, and arrived at the corner just in time to see the fire door at the far end swinging shut.

Devereaux reached the door, pushed down on its release bar, and just managed to check his momentum before he stepped outside. The metal mesh platform was still there, surrounded by a corroded safety rail. But the stairs leading down had fallen away. Presumably when

Paltrow had put his weight on them. They were lying on the ground, twenty feet below, a tangled mess of jagged spars and murderously sharp edges. Paltrow himself was dangling from the edge of the platform, clinging to a thin and rusted metal slat.

"Devereaux!" Paltrow's knuckles were gleaming white against the setting sun. "Help me!"

Devereaux leaned against the doorframe. "Like you helped Deborah? And Siobhan? And Emma? And now Annette?"

"I did help Deborah! She'd be a deadbeat whore in Mexico right now if it wasn't for me."

"As opposed to being actually dead? Murdered, on her twenty-first birthday? By you."

"What was I supposed to do? When I saved her ass, I told her to come to me if she needed help. Raising her kid, I meant. I don't hear a whisper from her for a year, so I figure everything's OK. Then she shows up at my place, on her birthday, without her kid, wanted me to pair her fucking phone with the car her new boyfriend bought her? Come on!"

There was a loud *crack*. One end of the slat that Paltrow was hanging onto had broken, and the remaining overstressed metal was starting to sag.

"Quick!" Paltrow let go with one hand and started scrabbling desperately for something else to take his weight. "Help me!"

"You know, Lucas, I'd love to." Devereaux took out his phone. "But here's the thing. The police department is very bureaucratic these days. There are procedures for everything. And in a situation like this, I'm not permitted to enter a potentially dangerous environment without first carrying out a risk assessment. So, in the circumstances, I think the best thing to do is for me to summon assistance. I'm sure my colleagues will respond with the minimum of delay. Now, what's that emergency number, again? The stress of watching you attack that woman is playing havoc with my memory."

Chapter *Fifty-six*

Wednesday. Late afternoon.

ANNETTE USHERWOOD'S BIRTHDAY PARTY HAD RELOCATED TO THE corridor outside her room at the UAB hospital. To the obvious displeasure of the medical staff, the narrow space was crammed with hordes of noisy friends and relatives. Most of them were still dressed up. Some seemed drunk. But all were immersing themselves in what was now a dual celebration: Not only had Annette reached twenty-one that day, she'd become the only woman to survive an encounter with B/DK.

Devereaux and Garretty kept their distance, hovering awkwardly at the edge of the group until Lieutenant Hale emerged from Annette's room. They watched as she made her way through the crowd, accepting the thanks and congratulations of the revelers as tactfully—and quickly—as she could, then they fell in step with her as she headed for the elevators.

"They're keeping her here overnight." Hale picked up the pace. "But that's just because she crashed unexpectedly right after she got here. Fortunately a nurse was on hand to deal with it. They don't think the Windex will have done any permanent damage. The convulsions were nasty, but she should make a full recovery."

"That's all we wanted to hear." Devereaux leaned across and slapped Garretty between the shoulders.

"You guys did good work today." A smile broke out across Hale's face. "Although, Cooper, you really shouldn't have left Paltrow dangling off that fire escape until SWAT arrived. There was no way to guarantee they'd get there before he fell. And those spikes!"

"I know." Devereaux held up his hands in mock surrender. "That was bad. I should have thought to call you and cancel SWAT. What a missed opportunity."

"And it won't be long before the lawsuits start to land." Hale's smile faded. "There've already been three complaints about the accidents you caused, driving across the street like that. And I can tell you, Captain Emrich is not happy *at all* about having to buy your friend Tom Vernon a new car."

"OK." Devereaux winked at Garretty. "Tell the captain to forget about the car. I'll find some other way for the department to pay Tom back."

"Cooper!" Hale stopped and put her hands on her hips. "Don't even joke about that."

Hale and Garretty got out of the elevator on the first floor, but Devereaux reluctantly remained inside until he reached the basement.

Chris Lambert was propped up in the armchair at the side of his room when Devereaux arrived. His eyes were open and the various electronic lines were pulsing their way busily across the screen on the wall, but Lambert didn't react at all when the glass door hissed back into place. He was so still and his skin was so pale and chalky that he reminded Devereaux of a sci-fi movie he'd once watched where humans were cloned by aliens, and their original bodies turned to dust that blew away on the wind. Devereaux was suddenly filled with the sense that this was the last time he'd see Lambert alive, and this time it wasn't just wishful thinking.

It wasn't until Devereaux turned to leave that Lambert finally spoke.

"Gotcha." His voice was rasping and barely audible. "Now, where's my money?"

Devereaux turned back and shook his head. "That's what I've come to tell you. There isn't going to be any money."

Lambert's face creased into a frown and he tried to wriggle himself more upright in the chair.

"Don't get excited." Devereaux held out his hands, palms upright. "I'm not here to argue. I looked into what you told me, and I'm prepared to believe you thought you were selling something genuine. And actually, it was genuine. But it only told half the story. Frederick McInzie divided his investigation into two parts, like a lawyer. Evidence for Tomcik's guilt in one box. Evidence against, which I guess you never saw, in another. *Evidence against* won. The reality is, Tomcik wasn't a crook. And my father wasn't innocent."

"Well, shit." Lambert sank back against the cushions, wheezing weakly. "I guess we all wind up a heck of a lot poorer, one way or another, if what you're saying's true."

"It is true." Devereaux paused for a moment. "Listen, Lambert. You weren't always on the same page as me, but you did wear the same uniform. I know part of what you were doing was looking after your grandson. So tell him. No more blackmail. No more trash talk about Hayden Tomcik. But if he ever needs help after you're gone, he knows where I am. I'll never turn my back on anyone with blue blood in their veins."

Devereaux sat in his customary spot on the wall by the reflecting pool while he waited for his cab to arrive, and his eyes were drawn to the parking lot beyond the trees on the far side of the street. *While I'm tying up loose ends . . .* he thought, and pulled up the email he'd received from Alison Jacques at the Cadillac dealer. Then he dialed the number for the kid he'd caught trying to break into his Porsche.

"Mike Jedinak? This is Detective Devereaux. How are you doing?"

"OK, I guess." Jedinak sounded wary.

"Good. Now listen carefully. I have a job for you. In a minute, I'm going to text you an address. A nice old lady lives there. Some asshole kids have been messing up her front yard. You're going to make sure that stops. Don't put yourself in danger. Call me if you need help. But as of now, you're responsible for making sure that not one more petal or leaf or blade of grass of hers gets damaged. Are we clear?"

Nicole tore down the hallway when she heard Devereaux's key in the lock. He opened the door and she leapt at his chest, trusting him implicitly to catch her.

"Daddy!" She planted a huge kiss on his cheek. "I missed you! Can you play?"

"Not this minute, sweetheart." Devereaux lowered her to the ground. "I have to talk to Mommy for a while right now."

"That's OK." Nicole turned and skipped away toward the staircase. "I'll be in my room . . ."

Alexandra was in the kitchen, sitting at the table and working on Nicole's lesson plans for the rest of the week. She jumped up when Devereaux entered, hugged him a little less enthusiastically than their daughter had done, then pecked him on the same cheek.

"It's good to see you, Cooper." Alexandra cupped Devereaux's face in her hands for a moment, then let go when she noticed the rip in his sleeve. "What's this?" She slipped the tip of her finger into the tear, exposing his scorched skin. "It looks sore. Are you OK? Do you need a bandage?"

"I'm fine." Devereaux covered the hole with his other hand. "It's nothing."

"Can I at least get you a coffee? A glass of wine?"

"No thanks." Devereaux stood by the table. "I just came by to show you something."

"Oh?" Alexandra sat back down. "OK. What is it?"

"First of all, there's something I want to say. Something I want to be real clear about." Devereaux paused for a moment. "We've been out of touch for a few days now, and I didn't like it. I like it here. I like it with you. I like it with Nicole. I like it when we're a family. Now, if you were putting that space between us because you *don't* like being with me, tell me and I'll walk away. But if the problem is down to my father—to the effect you think he has on me, on who I am—then I want you to read this."

Devereaux pulled the papers he'd taken from Frederick McKinzie's study out of his pocket and slid them across the table. Alexandra picked them up and started to read. At first confusion covered her face. Then hope. Excitement. And finally relief.

"Are these real?" Alexandra jumped up from her chair. "Where did you get them?"

"They're real." Devereaux nodded. "This is what the blackmailer was trying to sell me for half a million dollars. It's the summary of an investigation Frederick McKinzie conducted about police corruption. Remember I met his daughter during the arson case? I got her to show me his files. That's where I found them."

"This is wonderful!" Alexandra ran to Devereaux and threw her arms around his neck. "It's the answer to my prayers!"

"Is it?" Devereaux gently pushed her away. "I showed you because I want you to know who I really am." He reached out and gathered up the papers. He formed them into a neat pile. Then he ripped them in half, in half again, and flung the pieces up in the air. "You believed what they said. I did as well, at first. But I found out—long story short—the picture they paint isn't true. My father really was the evil monster you believed him to be. I didn't have to tell you that. I could have let you go on believing he was as pure as the driven snow. But *that's* not who I am. I'm not defined by him, or anyone else. I make my own choices. And now you have to choose, too. The man I am—is that who you want to be with? I hope so. I hope so with all my heart. But it's your call, Alexandra. And either way, at least now you know the truth."

Devereaux turned to leave, but paused when he reached the kitchen door. "It's up to you to decide, Alex. But, please—don't take too long."

Acknowledgments

I would like to extend my deepest thanks to the following for their help, support, and encouragement while I wrote this book. Without them, it would not have been possible.

My editor, the excellent Brendan Vaughan, and the whole team at Random House.

My agent, the outstanding Richard Pine.

My friends, who've stood by me through the years: Dan Boucher, Carlos Camacho, Joelle Charbonneau, John Dul, Jamie Freveletti, Keir Graff, Kristy Claiborne Graves, Tana Hall, Nick Hawkins, Dermot Hollingsworth, Amanda Hurford, Richard Hurford, Jon Jordan, Ruth Jordan, Martyn James Lewis, Rebecca Makkai, Dan Malmon, Kate Hackbarth Malmon, Carrie Medders, Philippa Morgan, Erica Ruth Neubauer, Gunther Neumann, Ayo Onatade, Denise Pascoe, Wray Pascoe, Dani Patarazzi, Javier Ramirez, David Reith, Sharon Reith, Beth Renaldi, Marc Rightley, Melissa Rightley, Renee Rosen, Kelli Stanley, and Brian Wilson.

Everyone at The Globe Pub, Chicago.

Jane and Jim Grant.

Ruth Grant.

Katharine Grant.

Jess Grant.

Alexander Tyska.

Gary and Stacie Gutting.

And last on the list, but first in my heart—Tasha. *Everything, always* . . .

I'd also like to extend extra special thanks to the real Deborah Holt of Wetumpka, Alabama, for generously bidding on a character name in support of the Friends of the Wetumpka Library.

About the Author

ANDREW GRANT was born in Birmingham, England. He attended the University of Sheffield, where he studied English Literature and Drama. He has run a small, independent theater company and worked in the telecommunications industry for fifteen years. Andrew is married to novelist Tasha Alexander, and the couple lives on a wildlife preserve in Wyoming.

andrewgrantbooks.com
Facebook.com/AndrewGrantAuthor
Twitter: @Andrew_Grant

About the Type

This book was set in Sabon, a typeface designed by the well-known German typographer Jan Tschichold (1902–74). Sabon's design is based upon the original letter forms of sixteenth-century French type designer Claude Garamond and was created specifically to be used for three sources: foundry type for hand composition, Linotype, and Monotype. Tschichold named his typeface for the famous Frankfurt typefounder Jacques Sabon (c. 1520–80).